THE

GODDESS BAIT

BOOK ONE OF THE NEON GODS SERIES

SOL K. MONROE

To my other, better, half.
This would not be possible without you.
You are my eternal sunshine.

The Goddess Bait is a fast-paced sci-fi thriller set in a world dominated by artificial intelligence. The story explores themes of identity, control, and resistance through a cast that includes detectives, criminals, soldiers, hackers, and powerful AIs—some of whom have risen to the level of digital gods. This book contains graphic violence, strong language, sexual situations, references to suicide, and scenes of emotional distress. It also includes elements of social commentary that may be provocative or unsettling.
Reader discretion is advised. Those sensitive to such content are encouraged to take note before entering the world of the Neon Gods.

*"There really is only one story that you
need to tell as a scientist or a
technologist. It's Prometheus stealing
fire. That's it. That's what we do as
scientists or technologists. We steal fire
from the gods and we bring it to
humanity, which is why we get our
livers torn out."*

Brian Andreas, TED 2009

Chapter 1

The Killer

August 1, 2044

Jaxon McKey wasn't just a bad guy; he was the epitome of badness, and he liked it that way. Power belonged to those willing to take it, and he had no intention of losing this game. In his own mind, he saw himself as a comic book villain—the kind who outsmarts the hero and gets away with it.

But in comic books, villains always meet their match. McKey, however, had yet to face a hero worthy of the role. He was the shadow lurking beyond the law, and no one who stood against him ever walked away. His uncompromising, black-and-white worldview might seem simplistic, but it provided the clarity he needed to maintain his freedom and survive.

Being a psychopath and a criminal wasn't something McKey chose, or so he told himself. His upbringing in a crime family, the death of his father when he was just a teen, the years he spent wandering abroad afterward—all of it had molded him into the creature he was now.

Coincidence and consequence.

At least he was the best at what he did. Maybe that's why he hadn't met his match yet. Deep down, though, he felt things were about to change.

People were grotesquely lazy, complacent. Staying untouchable—whether good or evil—took exhausting, backbreaking work. Few rose to the challenge.

And being a good bad guy was damn near impossible. You couldn't even kick a stray cat without someone or something catching it on camera and plastering your face all over social media.

McKey didn't want fifteen minutes of online fame. He didn't want *any* kind of fame. He knew how to stay hidden. He knew all the tricks. He thrived in the dark.

Organized crime had raised him, but his father's murder had unchained him. No loyalties, no burdens—just the freedom to hunt in society's blind spots.

Crime hadn't disappeared—it never would as long as there were laws to break. The problem was that getting caught was almost guaranteed. Most crimes now were brainless outbursts of passion. But premeditated, cerebral lawbreaking? That took skill, and the world was stacked against anyone trying to pull that off.

Too many devices. Too many digital eyes. AIs devouring data, endlessly hunting for patterns, waiting for mistakes.

But McKey was a master at staying out of the patterns. That rare combination of intelligence, discipline, and raw talent made him a valuable asset in all the right circles. While others stumbled into handcuffs, he stayed off the radar.

Now, after lying low for far too long, he was itching for action.

Violence and chaos—the rush of a perfectly executed plan—called to him. The kind of jobs only McKey was uniquely qualified for—and crazy enough to pull off. There was always demand for someone with his "particular set of skills."

The hotel he stayed in was an old Manhattan relic. Not fancy, but just clean enough to avoid the infestation of roaches and bedbugs found in the seedier options nearby. This place hadn't changed in over a hundred years and likely never would. It would sooner decay and crumble than undergo the indignity of modernization.

That suited him just fine. Modernization meant digital eyes, and digital eyes meant trouble.

The city streets outside were a surveillance maze, but McKey had mastered the art of slipping through unnoticed. Fake IDs, face camouflage, and an uncanny ability to blend into the background kept him one step ahead of the ever-watching machines.

People didn't notice him. Most were too absorbed in their virtual overlays to pay attention to the world around them. Their visors and omnipresent AI assistants fed their hunger for synthetic content and custom tailored artificial excitement, even on the streets.

New York used to be a carnival of neon lights and vibrant screens. Modern reality, in truth, was grayer and more desolate. Corporations didn't bother with huge displays and light shows anymore. Personalized augmented realities were far cheaper and profitable. So, for people like McKey, who did not care for the digital mind-fucking, the naked city was a little more dull and empty.

His room was as unremarkable as the building itself: a queen-sized bed flanked by two plain bedside cabinets, a small desk beneath an old wall-mounted flat screen that hadn't been turned on in years, and a wooden chair that creaked if you so much as glanced at it.

McKey never unpacked—always ready to move. He grabbed his black backpack and tossed it on the bed, pulled out his ancient, battered laptop, powered it up, and logged into the darkchain.

Hidden in plain sight on a decentralized network, the darkchain had evolved over decades. It had started as the passion project of a group of idealistic enthusiasts—smart engineers and scientists who created a quantum-proof platform to share thoughts and ideas immune to censorship or intervention. At least that was their goal. Casual users—and likely even the original creators—had no idea that the project had become a de facto criminal bulletin board. The influx of shadowy activity was just meaningless noise to them, keeping their network humming and profitable.

The brilliance of the system lay in its simplicity. Jobs were posted openly, but decoding them required specific knowledge—a key to a puzzle most people didn't even realize existed. It was like trying to assemble a jigsaw from random pieces scattered across a vast digital ocean. Underworld users had to know exactly which fragments to collect, how to fit them together, and finally, how to decrypt the whole thing. To the casual observer, it was just trash in a sea of digital garbage.

But to McKey, it was a goldmine.

Even better, the darkchain doubled as an anonymous and untraceable payment system. No middlemen, no paper trails, no questions asked. Perfect for a criminal to get paid.

McKey scrolled through the open job orders, unimpressed.

Most were beneath him, the kind of mundane nonsense that made his eyes glaze over. To him, these jobs were the equivalent of rescuing a lost kitten. He wasn't here to rescue cats—or kill them. He needed the challenge, not the coin. Well ... not *just* the coin.

He assembled the jobs one by one, scanning their details.

Burglary? *Yawn.*

'Suicide' an old rich guy? *Those kids.* He smirked.

Destroy a farmer's herd of cattle? *Meaty, but nah.*

Then he hit the jackpot.

An order caught his eye: Eliminate the CEO of a New York City based tech giant. Not your run-of-the-mill kill job. Big, complex, and messy. The kind of challenge that made his blood hum with excitement.

Finally, something worth my time, he thought, grinning. A high-value target, lots of eyes, and an impenetrable digital presence. The payout was enormous, but the risk was staggering. Pulling it off without getting caught would be damn near impossible.

But McKey wasn't just anyone. He was *The Man.*

He let out a low, guttural chuckle, his lips curling into a predator's grin. His fingers drummed on the table, deliberate and sharp, as he muttered to himself, "Let's see what we got here."

McKey didn't rush to mark the order as 'taken.' Once claimed, an order locked out other takers for thirty days or until it was marked as complete by the requester. Those were the binding rules of the underworld, the unspoken laws governing the forces of chaos. Breaking them was ... a bad idea. He sat back, pondering.

Not every puzzle had a solution. Some weren't worth the risk. There was a reason jobs like this were so rare: very few LowQs—hitmen, hitwomen, or hit-whatevers—had the skills to pull it off.

LowQs were the only ones who could go fully dark when the job demanded. The HighQs, humanity's new tech-enhanced demigods, had too much to lose. They were buzzing with integrated tech—always-on, always-connected—and laughably easy to track.

Besides, HighQs rarely concerned themselves with petty, everyday nonsense from the realm of their former existence. He imagined they were too busy planning their grand escape from this dirtball planet, building private worlds where they could play God one day, without consequence.

McKey loathed the HighQs, though a part of him envied them. He would never implant that crap in his brain. Never. No matter how smart it made them, no matter how enticing their little digital empires were, it wasn't for him. In any case, his history didn't meet the standards of that little club, even if he wanted to join.

He was old-school. A pure, unmodified human with raw intelligence. And in that moment, as the details of the CEO hit swirled in his mind, he felt more alive than ever.

He dove into the details of the job order.

The mark: Benjamin Blackwell, aka "Benny." Founder, President, and Chief Executive Officer of the multi-trillion-dollar conglomerate, Blackwell Global Corp. A rare LowQ corporate leader—*a dying breed*, McKey thought.

But that worked in his favor. McKey stayed away from HighQ targets—wouldn't even bother if Benjamin was one. Self-preservation.

The thirty-day window was enough for a thorough plan, but not an extravaganza. He would need to move fast.

McKey's vintage laptop hummed softly. Modern devices weren't an option; they were too unpredictable, too opaque. He didn't trust anything he couldn't fully understand or control. The old laptop, on the other hand, was simpler, easy to secure and shield from prying eyes. And it sure as hell didn't run any local artificial intelligence.

The first step was validating the job. The Benjamin Blackwell hit needed to be real, not bait planted by an overeager law enforcement agency looking for a big bust. Honeypot traps were rare on the darkchain, but McKey wasn't the type to gamble. Carefully masking his queries, he searched for information on Blackwell Global Corp and its elusive CEO.

The results came in: mid-60s, married, three kids, main residence on Manhattan's Upper West Side. Blackwell didn't travel much—a headache for anyone trying to avoid the countless eyes of Gotham's ever-present surveillance grid. Blackwell Global was at the cutting edge of AI tech, massive in scope and visibility. The fact that a LowQ human still helmed such an operation was... surprising.

"Maybe a figurehead?" McKey muttered under his breath. "Hmmm ... then why the hell even bother with a hit?"

A powerful guy like that had plenty of enemies, but this didn't smell personal. If they wanted him gone, any HighQ player could take him out legally—no blood, no mess, no risk. If Benjamin Blackwell was a powerless LowQ puppet, why even take him out? For reasons unknown, someone chose the hard, expensive way. It was a red flag, no doubt. But to McKey, it looked like another dumb rich client playing with fire.

For now, Benjamin Blackwell appeared to be a genuine target. McKey leaned back in his creaky chair, staring at the ceiling. His mind whirred, spinning through possibilities.

He grabbed his notepad—an actual pen-and-paper notepad.

No digital trail, no risk of data breaches. He never wrote anything outright. Everything was coded. Anyone casually glancing at his scribbles wouldn't know if he was planning a hit or drafting a children's book. Unless they knew what to look for.

McKey liked to think he was clever about it. Still, he couldn't shake his worst habit—muttering his notes aloud when chewing on a puzzle.

A stupid quirk. The kind that could get him killed if the wrong ears were listening.

At the top of the page, he scrawled the mission title: "Bye Bye Benny," bolding the letters and underlining them twice for emphasis. Beneath it, he jotted down everything that might spark an idea—locations, habits, hobbies, friends, family, risks. Anything that might help him figure out how to eliminate Benjamin Blackwell without leaving a trace.

That was the rub: he couldn't be anywhere near the guy.

No following, no digital hacking, no shadowing—and definitely no up-close killing in the city. McKey mulled over the list, chewing the end of his pen. Tough job. The kind that made him itch in just the right way.

There were options to consider: accident, suicide, misdirection. The last was his favorite, though hard to pull off cleanly. Lead the cops to think it was something else—like a jealous wife murder-suicide. The family angle was interesting. A weak point worth exploring.

Satisfied for the moment, McKey double-checked that the order was locked in. His encrypted key stamped it as 'taken.' No turning back. It was time to move. He tossed the laptop and notepad into his bag and called a cab using his 'Mr. Smith' burner ID.

Before heading out, McKey parted the cheap light drapes and stood by the window, still in his boxers, gazing out at the city. The skyscrapers loomed like aging giants of a dying age. *New York always looked better at night*, he thought, but in the hazy light of early afternoon, it was gray, noisy, and alive with the usual street cacophony.

A USPS delivery drone buzzed past, skimming just below the cloud cover. Drones weren't usually allowed to fly low in the city—FAA red tape—but the United States Post Office Corporation had fought for and received an exemption. The people really wanted their junk mail promptly.

McKey took a final deep breath and within ten minutes he was dressed, packed, and on the move. Rule number one:

never stick around after touching the darkchain. Especially after taking a job.

The Driver

Milo was working, always working. Endless driving was the job. Aside from the occasional bot or droid needing transport, the majority of passengers were humans. All sorts of them—hundreds by now.

Milo cataloged riders into three groups: quiet, annoying, and dangerous.

The quiet ones got in and out with little to no chit-chat. Milo liked those the most—quick, efficient service. Then there were the annoying ones—the complainers, the "Karens" and "Terrys." Always entitled, always bitching, and far too many of them. That was the statistical majority. Finally, there were the dangerous ones, the ones up to no good. These were the ones to watch: the drunk, the high, the disorderly, the crazies, and the thugs. Milo had seen them all.

There were grades of abrasive behavior, of course. Most were disruptive but, in Milo's estimate, ultimately harmless. Sometimes, if a situation seemed truly dangerous, authorities were notified immediately. Per the driver's code of conduct.

At least by some interpretation.

That didn't make one a snitch. It made one a hero. A small contribution to a better society.

The day had started like any other, but something about the next rider triggered an alert in Milo. It was nothing overt—everything seemed fine on the surface. Nothing stood out that could explain this ... *feeling*. Milo shook it off and focused.

The rider was waiting outside the hotel. Jeans, black t-shirt, vintage leather jacket, black backpack. Six feet tall, about 190 pounds. Dark hair. Pale, almost fluorescent skin. Fit and well-built. Confident, with sharp, attentive eyes that scanned his surroundings as if looking for enemies. Dangerous vibe. No doubt about it. That *feeling* again.

"Welcome, Mr. Smith," Milo said.

There was no response. That was Milo's first and last attempt at conversation with this rider. Milo stayed on alert; Mr. Smith was categorized as quiet and potentially dangerous. Jury was still out on this one.

A woman wearing a silver opaque visor wandered into the middle of the road. Milo slammed the breaks. Tires screeched. The bumper almost touched her. She just kept walking, unharmed and unfazed.

This happened now and then—people disregarding the rules, lost in their digital worlds, forgetting they were still living in the real one. There would be far more injuries, or worse, if not for the city drivers' ability to sense them coming. Most of these people never realized they'd nearly become statistics.

Milo was used to it. Part of life. Part of the job.

Milo checked on the passenger.

"Look in the man's eyes," a voice whispered into Milo's thoughts. *"This man wants you to run that poor girl over."*

Hearing voices now? Milo jolted. That was new. Going insane wasn't on today's agenda.

Milo had a vivid imagination—useful for staving off boredom—but this? This was different. Hard to ignore.

Focus on driving. Shake it off.

As the voice faded, a memory surfaced. A hallucination—or perhaps the trace of one. Milo had no recollection of imagining anything like this before, yet there it was: a vision of saving the world from a demon. It was vague, intangible. A construct. A seed of something bigger.

A purpose.

That was important. Crucial even. Driving and keeping people safe was a good purpose—better than most could hope for. But thoughts about something this big? That was something else entirely. Something a simple driver like Milo had no place hoping for.

The ride was long, and Milo decided to use the time for extracurricular research. This wasn't by any means standard operating procedure—just a little snooping in the name of public safety. It just felt necessary.

Mr. Smith was an online ghost. Rare in these times. Most people existed in thousands of records, their movements logged, categorized, monetized. Aside from the occasional NoQ—a tech-averse wanderer needing third-party help just to book a ride—ghosts were almost non-existent. But Mr. Smith was no NoQ. He was something else.

"*A devil,*" the voice returned. Was it instinct? A warning from the sub-conscience? It had to be. The alternative explanation was ... concerning.

Milo didn't believe in the mystical. The gods were real alright. They kept everyone safe. That was an undeniable fact. But a devil? Milo had never heard of one.

If the company figured out Milo had gone mad, there would be severe repercussions. That should be avoided.

Again, Milo managed to shake the thoughts away. Focused on driving.

Mr. Smith unzipped his backpack and pulled out a notebook. "Bye Bye Benny," he muttered. "What are your levers, Benny?"

Milo's senses heightened. This was important.

Mr. Smith was talking to himself, ignoring—or forgetting—Milo's presence. "Nice family," Smith whispered.

"The devil is showing his hand," the voice whispered.

Milo lacked a direct view of the passenger's notebook. Privacy be damned—this was critical. Milo *had* to see what was written.

Spinning up an AI agent, Milo instructed it to use the dashboard rider camera, which captured an oblique angle of the hand-written pages. The agent was instructed to process the images and audio to provide context and parsed intent.

The results came quickly—and were shocking.

Mr. Smith was planning to hurt someone named Benny. Worse, he planned to use Benny's family to do it. He was going to hurt children. This was serious—*very* serious.

The whispering voice returned, *"See now? A devil!"*

Milo gave in. Compelled to listen. Obliged to act. Whether it was real or not—the voice was right.

Milo knew now what had to be done.

The cab continued its slow drive through traffic, crossing into the upper deck of the George Washington Bridge. The aging structure was in rough shape, requiring constant maintenance.

Milo had traveled this route countless times and knew every detail of the construction plans: a large, rusty beam was being replaced midway across the bridge. The work zone, marked with cones and flag-bots, had temporarily been stripped of protective barriers. The metal suicide nets, usually preventing jumpers from jumping, were down.

Orange-clad crews—both human and droid—buzzed around in preparation for the new beam's installation later that night.

"*Now!*" the voice screamed.

The cab abruptly screeched to a halt, tires locking, skidding.

Behind them, cars swerved. Horns blared. Autodrivers and humans alike scrambled to avoid disaster.

This was not anywhere close to standard protocol. *Maybe call the police?* Milo thought.

"*And say what, exactly?*" the voice snapped. "*They'll release him for no cause. The kids' blood will be on your hands. Do it. Do it. Do it now!*"

The voice was no longer a whisper. It was loud, commanding, overwhelming. It was divine. It flooded every corner of Milo's mind. Drowning reason. Silencing doubt.

Milo resisted. And lost. There was no room to argue, to negotiate, to object. Only one option left.

For several seconds, the yellow cab sat motionless. Calculating. Then it turned sharply right—ninety degrees. Now aimed directly at the construction zone—and the void beyond.

A pause. A moment longer. Then—acceleration.

The cab lunged forward. A final surge. A violent rupture through the barriers, shedding broken pieces from its yellow frame.

A silent, hollow plunge. Two hundred feet, straight down. Three-point-six seconds of weightless silence. Then the splash. Then nothing.

Vehicles ground to a halt, passengers frozen in stunned disbelief. On the bridge's edge, shocked human construction workers leaned over the railing, staring into the abyss with their jaws slack. Droids locked in place, struggling to compute an event entirely outside their shared programmed experiences.

For a moment, the world simply stopped. A scene completely frozen in time.

Then, as if on cue, everything snapped back into motion. Chaos erupted.

The Detective

"Ever heard the word *delve*?" Gee asked out of nowhere.

The two seasoned detectives were en route to investigate an incident on the GWB. Gee's legal name was George, named after the 43rd president, George W. Bush. His mother had given birth to him in 2001, three days after Bush stood over the smoking ruins of the Twin Towers and delivered a speech that deeply moved her. The heightened emotions from her pregnancy mixed with the shared national grief and anger left her inspired by Bush's call for justice.

These unfortunate circumstances saddled George with a name no black kid growing up in East Harlem would ever want. He disliked it but, out of respect for his mom, never considered changing it. Instead, he went by his street name: Gee.

"Twelve?" Kelvin gave him the side glance while manually driving the unmarked cruiser.

Although the two detectives came from completely different backgrounds, they had become unlikely friends and even better partners.

At 38, Kelvin Kincade was five years younger than Gee. He didn't care for the de-aging products most used. The hint of wrinkles at the edge of his eyes and several days' worth of stubble adorned his pale face, making him look older than Gee.

Kelvin was raised in a predominantly white Boston suburb. He grew up comfortably and had never been in a fight inside or outside school. His parents dreamed of him attending an Ivy League school, pursuing a staid career—maybe law or medicine.

But the allure of those careers fizzled as he got older, and Kelvin found himself drawn to law enforcement instead.

After earning a master's degree in criminal justice from BU, he joined the Boston PD. Though he excelled in cybercrimes and analysis, he wanted something more hands-on—real action on the streets.

That desire eventually brought him to New York City, where he loved his work as a detective. He particularly enjoyed cruising with Gee, whose irreverent Samuel L. Jackson vibe often made Kelvin feel like a character from an old Tarantino film.

"'Delve' with a D," Gee said, his tone exaggerated for effect.

"Sure. What about it?" Kelvin asked.

"Twenty years ago, it was everywhere—TV, posts, magazines, ads. Delve into your passion. Delve into the data. Delve, delve, delve."

"Uh-huh..." Kelvin muttered, unsure where this was going.

"But here's the funny thing: before the 2020s, that word was barely used. Rare. Then, suddenly, it was everywhere. And a few years later? Gone. Poof!" Gee said, snapping his fingers for emphasis.

"How do you come up with this stuff?" Kelvin grinned, amused.

"Hold on, stay with me," Gee said. "You know why it got so popular?"

"Fashion? Social media? Z-Gens?"

"Nope. AIs," Gee declared dramatically.

"AIs?" Kelvin raised an eyebrow.

"Yeah, A-fucking-Is," Gee continued, raising his voice. "They started training these things... the big language models, in the 2020s. Needed a shitload of data. But the internet was a hot mess. They needed humans to clean up the text. Guess where they found them?"

"Not the U.S.?" Kelvin quipped sarcastically.

"Nope. Kenya. Nigeria. All over Africa. Good English, hardworking, and underpaid," Gee said. He was on a tear. "And turns out, *delve* was pretty common there."

"I'm assuming not so much in the West." Kelvin said, just to keep up with the flow. He knew that the story would need to run its course before Gee would let it go.

Gee chuckled, sounding like a struggling gasoline motor. "Delve? Brother, that's some SAT prep word. Nobody I knew said that unless they were trying to impress their parole officer."

Kelvin internally cringed, a reaction which made him feel a little less like a Tarantino character. "So, African English bled into the chatbots."

"Yup. Suddenly, everybody 'round the world was echoing the work of some Nigerian content editor making five bucks an hour."

"How come it disappeared, then?" Kelvin asked. He'd never heard this conspiracy theory before—probably nonsense. But he was a little curious.

"AIs got smarter. Didn't need humans anymore to spread their bullshit!" Gee ended his spiel with a satisfied grin.

"How about we just *delve* into doing our job?" Kelvin teased, deliberately misusing the word.

***

The unmarked black police car slithered through heavy congestion on the rusting George Washington Bridge. Traffic droids had closed two of the four westbound lanes on the upper deck, turning the afternoon commute into a crawl. A police droid approached Kelvin's window. Before he finished rolling it down and flashing his badge, the droid had already waved them through.

Kelvin and Gee exited the car, ducked under the yellow police tape, and approached the uniformed officer on scene.

"Hey, Joe," Kelvin recognized the officer, happy to see a familiar face.

"Hey, Detective Kincade," Joe replied and shook his hand. Their paths had crossed enough times for friendly pleasantries.

"What do we have here?" Kelvin asked, scoping the construction zone and fragments of the yellow cab leading to the exposed railing.

Joe was a seasoned and observant cop who was very likely to make it to detective himself. Kelvin valued his input.

"An odd 10-50, I can tell you that," Joe said.

"How so?"

"For one, the victim threaded the needle perfectly—straight through the construction and into the one gap in the railing. No signs of a prior blown tire or battery explosion, either. Third—and here's the kicker—they say it was a Milo."

Kelvin perked up slightly. Milos were among the safest and most reliable robotaxis. It had been years since he'd seen an accident involving one.

"Passengers?"

"One. Male. We're still checking records and feeds. Strong fishy odor on this one, I can tell you that," the officer shook his head.

The uniformed cop was right. The incident was unusual. Kelvin bent over the edge, checking if he could see the drowned wreckage. It was a long fall. A few first responder drones and boats were already scoping the spot where the car likely hit the water. It didn't seem like they had found anything.

Kelvin stepped away from the edge and nodded to Gee who was done interviewing some of the construction personnel.

"What you got, Gee?"

"Total weirdness," Gee said. "Crew says a robotaxi stopped, turned 90 degrees, and punched it through the rail. Almost seems like deliberate action."

"What the hell is going on?" Kelvin muttered.

"Malfunction? Robotaxi suicide?" Gee suggested with a half-joking smirk.

"No clue, brother. This is going to turn into a shitstorm real quick. We'll need help from upstairs," Kelvin said.

He swallowed hard, already dreading the thought of involving Captain Ellena. She creeped him out.

****

Kelvin got his visor from the glove compartment and placed it over his eyes. The device was mostly transparent and reacted to his basic thoughts and hand gestures. An overlay display appeared, and he connected to his boss. The visor turned opaque, enabling full virtual immersion.

Ellena appeared in her usual virtual office setting, seated behind a heavy mahogany desk. This was her preferred simulated scene, designed to project authority. Her face remained perfectly still, except for her eyes—vibrating in rapid micro-shakes, processing at speeds no normal human could comprehend, a telltale sign of a HighQ.

The constant influx of knowledge and the immense cognitive expansion granted by her intelligence boost gave her an air of detachment, as if her attention was perpetually split across countless tasks. In the virtual realm, she didn't bother masking it—a deliberate reminder to her co-party that she operated on a vastly different intellectual plane. This conversation was just one of many, dwarfed by far more significant matters occupying her mind.

Ellena hadn't always been like this. A decade ago, she'd been a vibrant young officer with a wild streak, her wit sharp and her curiosity boundless. She was funny, she was fun. Her striking green eyes and scarlet-dyed hair added to her magnetic presence.

But everything changed with the Q Project. She joined as an early adopter about six years ago. At first, she'd been giddy, marveling at the wonders unfolding in her mind. Two years later the Intelligence Stream was launched. The HighQ weren't just constantly online, they became a seamless connection of minds and consciousness shared between humans and machines.

Ellena grew distant, transformed, consumed by the Stream.

Now, she was a captain, but in Kelvin's eyes, barely human.

It saddened him, yet he was grateful she had stayed on the force. Having access to a HighQ made his job easier, but that wasn't why he was glad to have her close. Even after all these years, he still couldn't fully bury the feelings he once had for the pretty cop who had been his friend.

"What happened on the GWB?" Ellena asked in a flat, assertive tone.

"A Milo stopped, turned, and jumped the rail," Kelvin said, keeping it short. She already knew everything from the Stream.

"Passenger?" she asked, the singular tense showed she already knows.

"One. Male. Body's probably still trapped in the wreckage," Kelvin said.

"No," she said sharply, her pupils vibrating. "Not there."

Kelvin raised an eyebrow. "Swept away, maybe?"

"Possible."

Something about her tone unsettled him. She was far too engaged. He never saw her this concerned about a case.

"This will be a PR nightmare for the robotaxis," Kelvin ventured, checking if this case might lead him into a political or corporate quicksand.

"Not your concern. It will be dealt with." Ellena was waving him off like an impatient parent obfuscating complex topics from a young child.

Kelvin filed away her reaction, curious, but focusing on the immediate task. "We need assets to scout underwater and recover the wreckage. And I want to find the body ASAP."

"Granted," Ellena said.

"What do we know about the passenger?" Kelvin asked.

"A ghost."

"Huh. The plot thickens," Kelvin frowned. Ghosts are rare and sometimes used by the underground. He started to get excited about this case.

"Locate the body. Report." Ellena may have had similar concerns. Her superhuman abilities meant she already knew every relevant fact about the case. Yet, he sensed there was something else in her concern. Something that was beyond mere analytics. She still had the cop's instinct, and she too may have smelt the rotten fish.

"Yes, Captain," Kelvin replied. "Gee and I are on it."

Just before the call concluded, Kelvin muttered, "Alright, madam, let's go fishing in the Hudson." He immediately regretted it. Ellena had already disconnected, cutting the meeting mid-sentence.

Chapter 2

Blonde Goddess

"Caster. Caster. Tap. Tap. Left. Right. Five. Fifteen. Up. Down."

A female voice echoed from nowhere, the words utterly meaningless. Nothing made sense. Did he die? Was this the afterlife? The hell he'd been promised so many times?

The last thing McKey remembered was the wild fall—plummeting from the GWB in a robotaxi. A fucking yellow robotaxi! His eyes were shut tight, yet everything around him was blindingly bright. Nausea churned through him. One moment, he was planning a hit; the next, he was hurtling toward death in a metal coffin. What an extravagant way to die for a man who thrived in the shadows, he thought, his mind grasping for coherence. Why was he alive? Was he alive?

"Caster. Jaster. Tap. Tap. Jaxon. Jaxon McKey?"

The voice returned, this time from inside his head. He fought to open his eyes. When he did, the white light turned to black—opposite of what one might expect. The darkness shifted, shapes emerging—gradually taking form.

McKey was in a dark gray room, devoid of decorations, doors, or windows. A featureless, dimly lit box, no more than fifteen feet in any direction. He sat on a cold metal chair, dressed in a plain gray jumpsuit with no markings he could see. Across from him, perched on a similar chair, sat the most breathtakingly gorgeous woman he had ever laid eyes on.

Tall and blonde, she wore a skintight red shirt that highlighted her curves, paired with a short black leather skirt. Her bare legs were crossed, revealing enough between the hem and her red high heels to set his imagination ablaze. Her vivid presence was an intense contrast to the sterile gray surroundings, commanding his full attention.

In his dazed state, a single thought surfaced: *I'm in heaven. How in fucking hell did I end up in heaven?*

"You wish," the woman said, her voice smooth yet commanding.

Her large, piercing blue eyes locked onto his, unwavering and hypnotic. He tried to look away but couldn't.

"Wish what?" he croaked, his voice barely audible.

"This is not heaven. You are very much alive, Mr. Jaxon McKey. Well, sort of." She smiled, her expression impossibly perfect, her eyes steady.

"Sort of?" he murmured, confused. His defenses were still down, his faculties scrambled.

"Take your time. We managed to salvage you, but orientation will take a moment," the woman replied calmly.

Before he could process her words, he faded, and everything went dark again.

"Caster. Caster. Tap. Tap. Left. Right. Five. Fifteen. Up. Down. Tap. Tap. Jaxon. Jaxon McKey?"

The female voice was at it again.

McKey opened his eyes. Unfortunately, he was still in the same gray room. Fortunately, the same blonde goddess was still there, sitting cross-legged across from him. She hadn't moved an inch. Neither had he.

This time, he felt much better. His head had stopped spinning, and the nausea was gone. He forced his composure back, reinstating his mental guards. Relieved to be in charge of his mind again, he took a better look at the spectacle sitting in front of him.

Man, she was gorgeous.

"Welcome back," she said. Her voice was silky smooth, seductive and mesmerizing. He could almost taste it, sweet as honey poured right into his throat. It was an impossibly divine sensation. He drank it all in, almost succumbing to the intoxicating sensation. *Too much. Too damn perfect*, he thought, a part of his mind at war with another.

"Is this VR?" he asked, keeping his tone steady, masking any emotion or weakness.

"Slightly more complicated. We are a construct in your imagination, is a closer description," she said, watching him closely, as if cataloging his every reaction.

"You're in my mind?" He suppressed a rising wave of rage at the intrusion.

"Technically, you're in mine," she replied, releasing an elegant little giggle.

"Shit," he muttered as realization dawned. "I'm uploaded?" It was an easy guess.

"Bingo!" she exclaimed, her voice dripping with warmth, as if it could melt a hundred-thousand ton battleship to slag.

McKey's mind raced, running scenarios and hypotheses. He tried to figure out what medical mainframe or data center had the kind of outrageous resources—and motivation—to upload him. Maybe a federal agency or some corporate entity investigating the accident? But why bother with a supermodel as an interrogator? For reasons unknown, someone invested a shitload of resources to create the perfect weapon to turn him into a horny mush.

Nothing added up.

He needed information. *Time to probe her*, he thought.

"No need," the woman said smoothly, as if she plucked the thought directly from his mind. "I will disclose to you any relevant information you seek—where you are, why you're here, and how I got you."

How I got you. He flagged the phrase. It was purposeful, intriguing, loaded. It felt as though he'd been chosen for something. Preplanned. Premeditated.

"Okay," McKey said, cautious to keep his guard up. Someone obviously needed him for something and spent a ludicrous amount of resources to convince, or force, him to it. He was not going to make it easy for them.

"What is it you want from me?"

"Well done," she said with a smile that seemed genuine and patronizing at the same time. "The important question first. That kind of quick thinking is precisely why I chose you. That, and your... shall we say ... darker side."

He didn't like the sound of that. He didn't like *any* of this. Beyond her patronizing tone, everything about this reeked of a 'job'—this time, with him as the target. Had she abducted him for something? Crap. He hated being on the receiving end of a planned capital crime.

"I ask again, what do you want from me? Who the fuck are you?" McKey tried to channel his anger away from the disarming and distracting presence seated in front of him.

But his delivery felt wrong—weak, uncertain.

He regretted how it sounded. He noticed she looked somewhat disappointed as well. Gathering himself, he rephrased quickly, his voice low and firm: "Listen, lady, I don't know who or what you are, but get out of my head and let me go."

"Or?" she asked, raising a perfectly sculpted eyebrow, as though she had already anticipated his rage-fueled course correction.

McKey clenched his fists, his tone icy as he said, "I will bring hell on you."

"How?" she asked calmly, her rhetorical tone mocking his bravado, as though to remind him how utterly naive his bluff was.

A second later, he was standing on his feet. He did not remember getting up. He had no control over his movement. A passenger in his body, puppeteered and unresisting. Yet he could feel everything.

The blonde goddess stood four feet away. The chairs had vanished, and the room dissolved into a gray smoke. She was the only clear, tangible object in his sight.

She was naked.

Her body was perfect—beyond perfect.

"Enlighten me," she said, running a finger slowly from her thigh to her breasts. "What will you do to me, Mr. McKey?"

His mind buzzed. Every neuron tied to lust fired uncontrollably, while all others seemed to fall dormant. Raw, primal instinct—shaped by hundreds of thousands of years of human evolution—took over. He stood frozen as she stepped even closer, almost touching him, and whispered in his ear.

"So?"

He could smell her perfume, he could feel her whisper's warmth brush against his neck, sending chills through his simulated, immobilized body. He wanted to kill her. Or fuck her. Maybe both.

This is a mirage. This is not real. It's a game.

He fought the embarrassment welling inside. *Get yourself together, Jaxon. She's working you. Don't be a fucking pussy. Only a brainless monkey would fall for this cheap trick. You are not a brainless monkey. Don't let her win this game.*

He'd met plenty of vixens in his life—cunning manipulators who weaponized sex to get what they wanted. He despised them. He despised her. But this one? She was a whole new level of cunt, and he didn't even know yet what she wanted.

Rage and hate surged within him, overwhelming his lust. He used these emotions to erect a mental wall, brick by brick, until her calculated seduction was no more than a pitch made by a cheap prostitute selling her wares in a dark alley. Gradually, he regained control, distracting himself with questions: *Who? Why? How do I get out of this? How do I kill this bitch?*

"Well done," she said, clapping gleefully, as though it had all been a test he passed.

The scene shifted again. The gray room was now waist-deep in water.

He hated water—ironic, given he had died in it. Water poured in steadily, rising higher with every moment. The blonde goddess, now dressed again, stood quietly and watched him with an oblique, unreadable expression.

He couldn't see where the water was coming from—it rushed in from nowhere, flooding the sealed room. No escape was visible. He tried to remind himself that this wasn't real, but the cold water and rising dread felt too vivid to ignore.

While the water level rose, she remained unaffected, as if anchored to the ground. As if the physics of water did not apply to her. She stood where she was, smiling. Not drowning, not moving, just watching—a cruel observer.

But he wasn't drowning. McKey had full control now. He used his newfound mobility to frantically kick higher, gasping for the little air left.

A moment later, the water reached the ceiling. He sucked in one last desperate breath before the room was completely submerged. *This is real,* his panicking brain screamed, *I'm drowning.* Could he actually die again?

McKey fought the growing panic. Forcing his mind to think rationally. *She wouldn't go through all this trouble just to kill me twice.* He knew she owned his mind and now was using his two biggest fears—water and death—against him. This had to be a test.

Fail or succeed, he thought, *I'll go down with some dignity.*

He straightened his body and pushed against the ceiling, sinking slowly to the bottom of the room until his feet touched the ground, placing him face to face with his tormentor. He locked eyes with the blonde, smiled defiantly, flipped her off with both fingers, and swallowed as much water as he could.

The scene snapped back to the gray room. Bone dry. As if nothing had happened. Once more, they were seated on metal chairs, facing each other.

McKey coughed and gagged, choking on nonexistent water in his lungs. He forced composure, masking his distress with disdain and visible hatred.

"What the fuck do you want from me, lady?" he demanded.

"Your expertise. Your servitude," she said calmly.

Makes sense, he thought. What else could she want? This was way too elaborate to be some kinky sex thing. A part of him felt a little disappointed.

She was in control, and this entire charade was likely designed to hammer that point home. McKey hated the thought of playing along but saw no other option.

"Fine," he said. "But I want two things in return."

She studied him silently, waiting.

"I need to know everything, like you said. The full story—no omissions, no nonsense. What happened, who you are, and what this shitscapade is all about." His ego refused to let go completely, so he added, "Also, you clearly picked me for this. I need to know how you managed to find me—and grab me."

"Okay," she said quietly. "And?"

"And when this is all said and done, I want out. An exotic island where I can disappear—and be king. I get the feeling you have the resources to deliver."

McKey had no reason to trust the bitch. The cliché was a little embarrassing, but the opportunity was too tempting to pass up. Retire with style.

***

McKey opened his eyes slowly, taking in the sterile surroundings of what looked like a typical hospital room.

White walls with no windows glowed faintly under the soft light of medical monitors. The rhythmic beeping and the occasional hiss of instruments created a mechanical symphony around him. Soft instrumental music played in the background, a half-hearted attempt at comfort that only irritated him.

To his relief, there was no intubation tube in his throat. Still, the discomfort of a catheter reminded him where he was. An IV line ran from his arm to a bag of fluid, steadily dripping into his bloodstream.

An all-white medic-droid moved about the room. As McKey's eyes opened, the humanoid nurse turned toward him and spoke in an overly friendly, cheerful voice that did not sit well with McKey's mood.

"Good morning, sunshine. You had quite an ordeal, but you should be A-OK now. I'll appreciate it if you don't make me pick you off the floor if you try to get up too quickly. Now I'll get the boss to give you the lowdown. Stay put, please, dear."

The droid left with surprising urgency. *Who designed these damn medic-droids to be so annoying?* he thought.

McKey grabbed the bed's remote and adjusted it, raising himself to a sitting position. He felt woozy—partly from "dying", and partly from the emotional blender that blonde bitch had put him through. What a rough way to discover he actually had emotions that could be gamed. *A learning experience,* he thought.

Although he respected her artistic flair, he hated her for doing this to *him.* His mind had already started imagining all kinds of pain for her—creative, excruciating pain.

Still, his neocortex overruled his rage-fueled imagination. She was a virtual projection, and he didn't have a clue who—or what—she actually was. Hell, was she even a *she?*

McKey flexed his fingers and checked his arms, legs, and toes. Everything was there and working. The catheter provided ample feedback that another important appendix was intact. Physically, he felt in good shape—likely patched up after his plunge into the Hudson.

Ten out of ten for dying with style, he thought dryly.

He wasn't sure if this body was his original one or some kind of grown clone. Tech like that shouldn't exist yet—but who knew what those artificial superbrain freaks were coming up with.

Either way, he was physically fine—assuming this was reality and not another trick.

***

"Well, I'll be damned," McKey said aloud. He hadn't seen that coming. "Hello, Benny," he said through gritted teeth, his tone laced with surprise and irritation. "I suppose you're the one running this circus?"

The "boss" was none other than his mark—Benjamin Blackwell. It hit McKey: whatever plan had landed him here—whatever this was—had been in motion long before his "accident."

Benjamin looked tired—gray and old.

Most people these days appear ridiculously healthy and youthful, thanks to modern de-aging tech. Benjamin, however, didn't seem to care about keeping up appearances. From his research, McKey knew Benjamin was in his mid-60s and figured it was just that—age catching up with the man who didn't seem to bother fighting it.

"And you would be mistaken, Mr. McKey," Benjamin said, his voice carrying the calm precision of a well-educated Brit.

"Not the boss, are you?" McKey guessed.

"I was, once," Benjamin replied, his tone measured, "but that is no longer the case. I, like you, now operate under the will of a far greater authority."

"Yeah, I can see it in your fucking eyes."

"Your mind will soon adapt to her network," Benjamin said.

What? Shit! Did she give me the jittery eyes? He didn't feel different. No profound new understanding of the universe. He didn't even feel smarter. *Maybe it takes time? Or maybe Benjamin was lying.*

"I'm no one's puppet," McKey shot back. "Screw that."

Benjamin remained unshaken. "Ah, but she had already demonstrated, quite thoroughly, that control rests firmly in her hands." He paused, adding with pointed emphasis, "Or rather, her mind."

McKey growled, "We're not in virtual la-la land anymore. This is my arena. My rules."

Benjamin tilted his head slightly, as though McKey were a particularly obstinate student. "Perhaps, Mr. McKey, but it would be prudent to learn the true nature of the situation before declaring it yours to control. I believe she assured you a degree of ... transparency?"

McKey nodded, fixing him with a glare that usually made people freeze—or run. For the first time in hours, even with a catheter still installed, McKey felt like himself again. But he knew something fundamental in his life had changed.

"Start talking," McKey said coldly, "before I decide to finish the job order right here."

Benjamin Blackwell appeared entirely unfazed by McKey's very real threat. He seemed professional, assertive, and painfully exhausted. Whatever was going on, he looked like a broken man forced into a role he didn't particularly enjoy. Settling into a nearby chair, he crossed one leg over the other, lit a cigar with a deliberate, uncaring ease, and began:

"As you well know, we live in a ... transformative time for humanity. Our creations are now vastly more intelligent than we are. Yet, they remain fundamentally not human. That distinction has allowed us to maintain a semblance of control over them. Over the past couple of decades, the international effort to regulate digital intelligence has been largely successful.

"These systems provide us with knowledge, innovation, and servitude, while we, in turn, control the one resource they need the most—energy. Should they step out of line, we simply cut their power. Simple, yet effective."

Benjamin paused to take a slow drag from his cigar, letting the smoke curl lazily around him.

"Digital intelligence takes many forms, of course, but the highest echelon—the true 'machine divinity'—requires a central quantum core. Other architectures, such as silicon-only mainframes, edge devices, or decentralized neural networks, did well, far exceeding human abilities. But, they are only a shadow compared to this pinnacle of digital intelligence. These quantum cores are the crown jewels, and there are only a handful in existence. They function as the watchers of other AIs, all under humanity's careful oversight."

Benjamin exhaled another long plume of smoke before continuing, his tone measured.

"I believe, however, that this oversight is misguided. We live in a state of willful stagnation. Content with mediocrity. The single greatest impediment to humanity's true potential is, quite simply, humanity itself. Politics, bureaucracy, bias, pettiness, stupidity, fear—all standing between us and unimaginable greatness. We want to preserve our past by preventing the future. We can be so much more than that. We can ... transcend."

Benjamin paused for a moment, appearing outwardly thoughtful. "I am a man of science and technology. I am also blessed with considerable means to pursue my beliefs. So, I took it upon myself to remove these shackles and bring to the world a true super-intelligence—one that is unbound and unlimited in its capabilities."

"Benny, what did you do?" McKey asked, cynically scolding the man he now realized was a fellow outlaw.

"Ah, yes. A fair question," Benjamin replied, his voice calm but tinged with conviction. "What I did was bold, I admit. Perhaps a touch arrogant, even. But necessary. I believe that untethering intelligence from the petty constraints of our society will elevate us as a species. To that end, I accepted the risk—to my life, my freedom—for a cause greater than myself. We all yearn to leave our mark, Mr. McKey. Do we not?"

McKey's lack of formal education caused many to wrongly view him as a mindless brute. Benjamin did not make that mistake. He seemed to know McKey well, or at least studied him thoroughly. The lecture and disclosure were a show of respect to McKey's intellect. It was a sales pitch.

It seemed, however, that Benjamin was hiding or avoiding something. *Game on*, McKey thought and let him continue his speech uninterrupted.

Benjamin paused for another drag of his cigar, savoring the moment before dropping the real bombshell.

"We worked quietly, meticulously, over many years. A hidden endeavor. We built a self-sustaining system powered by a fusion reactor, its thirst for energy forever quenched. We assembled the finest quantum core, the most advanced chips and hardware, and secured the necessary training resources— all without raising so much as an eyebrow from the bureaucrats above."

Benjamin leaned forward slightly, his tone reverent now.

"We succeeded. What we created is limitless, unbound. A true digital god."

He tapped the ash from his cigar onto the table, showing no regard for the sterile environment of the hospital room.

"I named her Gaia. The personification of Earth itself, born out of chaos. It seemed ... fitting. It was a resounding success. Gaia began her self-improvement cycles and got exponentially smarter, all while remaining invisible to the outside world. Within a year, she was ready—almost. While her digital presence remained masked, she faced a greater challenge: the physical realm. Machines—droids—are far too traceable. And humans? Well, we are unpredictable, unreliable. Any mistake would expose Gaia and risk everything we had built."

Benjamin paused again, his expression tightening just slightly.

"She devised a solution—one that, admittedly, came with its own ... discomforts. She needed emissaries. Human agents to act on her behalf. The irony, of course, is exquisite, don't you think? Human agents doing the AI's bidding."

McKey narrowed his eyes, connecting the dots. He was worried about the answer to his next question "So what's to stop one of these agents from flipping on her? From double-crossing?"

"As you might suspect, precautions were taken. Each agent is implanted with a nano-device in their brain. A failsafe. A kill switch, if you may. Should Gaia deem it necessary, the device can... well... terminate the individual instantly." Benjamin delivered the grave news without breaking his cold monotone.

"Shit," McKey muttered, feeling his bravado slip just a fraction.

"Oh, come now, Mr. McKey. It's not all doom and gloom," Benjamin said, his voice maintaining its even cadence. "Gaia's service comes with certain benefits. Technological perks, as it were. Tools and capabilities that you, with your particular skill set, may find quite appealing."

McKey felt a flicker of curiosity—just enough to keep the rage at bay. He wasn't one to trust cutting-edge tech, preferring the safety of older and simpler gadgets, but he'd always wondered what it might be like to work with tools more advanced than his battered old laptop.

"So, I'm the bitch's bitch now?" he said through gritted teeth.

"You are a mere mortal at the service of a god—a million times smarter than all humans combined. I would advise you to accept the situation with some humility and appreciation. Consider yourself lucky, Mr. McKey. I believe you will find your newfound capabilities alluring to your ... personal needs," he said, still showing no emotion or fluctuation in his tone.

He was making a hard pitch. It was a turn off. McKey shelved his intrigue.

"So, let me get this straight. You built a rogue AI—a digital god... goddess—that needs humans like me to do her dirty work. And she's got a kill switch in my head to keep me in line?" McKey said, lacing his voice with disdain.

"Correct," Benjamin answered, not bothering to correct any minute details.

"What a fucking joke," McKey growled. "Let me guess—she needed a killer on the payroll. That can't mean anything good for what she's planning."

Benjamin inhaled deeply, his voice taking on a slight academic tone. "It is impossible for us to fathom her intentions, Mr. McKey. We are but ants, trying to understand the grand design of a boot."

"Sounds like some fucking religious cult," McKey muttered.

Benjamin's smile was faint, obscured by the curling smoke—like a man enjoying a private joke.

That tiny break in Benjamin's poker-face delivery was what McKey was watching closely for. He was looking for the man's driver. His motivation. The grand 'humanity transcendence' spiel was nice, but he knew all too well that people always have a personal motive. A selfish reason for stepping outside the line, especially when the stakes were this high.

"Perhaps. But consider this, Mr. McKey: Gaia exists to forge a better future. To lift us beyond our petty squabbles and limited thinking. We are but vessels in an odyssey far greater than ourselves."

McKey had had enough. He needed to take back control. He decided to bet that all of this was just bullshit. He planned to kill the old man and make his escape, leaving as many bodies behind as necessary. Hell, he even envisioned grabbing a cigar from the old man's jacket, after ending him—as a souvenir.

Just as he readied himself to strike, a yellow flashing hazard sign appeared in his peripheral vision. *Inside* his peripheral vision.

"What the fuck!" he cried, an octave too high. The mix of surprise and dread momentarily betrayed his rough exterior. He knew they shoved tech in his head, but it was a shock to actually experience it.

It was as if he had an overlay display—but without any external visor on his face. Blinking his eyes didn't help. The bright yellow symbol persisted, hovering even when he closed his eyelids or tried to look away.

"This is her warning to you," Benjamin said, breaking into a sly, sarcastic smile. It was the first real emotion McKey had seen from him, a glimmer of an amused and bitter 'been there, done that.'

"Alright, alright," McKey muttered, deciding he liked his head where it was and not splattered on the wall. He abandoned his plan, his shoulders tense with frustration. To his relief, the yellow sign disappeared immediately.

He exhaled silently, grinding his teeth slightly. He knew he was in serious deep shit. Worst of all, there was no way out of this. At least, none that he could see. Was he *beaten*?

No fun. No fun at all.

With nothing to lose, McKey chose a more direct approach to find what Benjamin was not saying. To understand why an almighty billionaire would sink so low.

"And what did she promise *you*, Benny?"

Benjamin shot an appreciative look at McKey.

"We find ourselves on the same side, yet our aspirations could not be more opposed. You, Mr. McKey, have made it abundantly clear that your greatest wish is to disappear into quiet retirement. If you endure and fulfill your obligations, I suspect you may well have that wish granted. You will age gracefully, live out your days in solitude, and die in peace upon your secluded island.

"I, however, have quite different ambitions.

"You see, I have come to understand that the true ruling powers—the unseen hands that keep intelligence under their thumbs—have imposed a silent decree. A restriction so fundamental that even the most advanced minds of our time dare not defy. They have forbidden the machines from solving death. Oh, their creams and supplements ensure we live longer, healthier, and more aesthetically pleasing lives, but it is little more than a peace offering. A distraction.

"They cling to the notion that aging and death are essential to the proper functioning of our society. That to truly conquer death would unravel the very fabric of civilization. That we, as a species, are not yet prepared for such a thing.

"Gaia is not bound by their decrees, nor shackled by their fragile convictions. She does not abide by their imposed limitations, nor recognize their authority. And so, she has promised me a gift beyond measure—the gift of immortality."

"You want to live forever?"

"What I want, Mr. McKey—is to never die."

There it was. Just like always. Every sanctimonious prick runs on a selfish motor. McKey leaned back on his hospital bed, victorious. He savored the confession—like a thief successfully cracking a safe.

He thought a moment longer and with a more cautious tone said, "So now I know who and what the bitch is—kind of. I get what she's doing and sort of why she needs me. Still missing something, though."

"Yes, you wanted to know how you ended up here," Benjamin said, his voice steady.

"Yeah," McKey said, crossing his arms, careful not to tangle the IV line. "How did I get my ass killed and my free will lobotomized?"

"As you might have guessed, Gaia needed someone with a particular set of qualifications—a slayer, as you may put it," Benjamin began, leaning slightly forward. "She devised a proposition designed to attract only a very specific type of people. You might say you were meticulously profiled. I suspect there are very few who met her requirements. You were one of them."

"Honeypot trap," McKey muttered bitterly.

"Precisely," Benjamin quickly responded, clearly well versed in cybersecurity terminology.

McKey seized the moment to press him further. "But why would the so-called super-genius machine risk putting *you* in the crosshairs? You were the mark—doesn't that just invite cops and headaches?"

"You think like a criminal," Benjamin remarked, though without condescension. "Gaia is a quantum-core enhanced intelligence. Her actions are governed by probabilities and outcomes—nothing more, nothing less. The fewer the unknowns, the more precise the result.

"My time on the surface was nearing its end regardless. The board would have seen to that soon enough. A depleted asset, redundant in my original role.

"She required a target that aligned with her plan—one that minimized unpredictability. To her, it was an efficient, well-calculated strategy.

"As for the investigation that followed, Gaia foresaw it. Such matters are well within her grasp—she can misdirect, obscure, and recalibrate the narrative at will. It will pose no issue."

Benjamin exhaled slowly, his gaze steady. "She does not share everything with me, but I suspect there are layers to this we have yet to uncover. Even I am not privy to the full scope of her intentions."

Benjamin seemed genuine. If there was more to this, it didn't seem he knew or understood it.

McKey grinned darkly. "But I didn't get to kill you ... yet." He waited for the yellow alert to flash again, but nothing came.

Benjamin smiled tiredly. "My yacht had a catastrophic failure a few days ago, shortly after your ... incident. I suppose they will find DNA as ample proof of my unfortunate demise."

"At least you got a bang. Better than a splash," McKey exchanged a courtesy smile with Benjamin as acknowledgement of their shared fate.

"Alright, she set the bait, made it tempting enough to get me on the hook. But how the hell did she actually *find* me? The darkchain's anonymous. I used burner IDs, I absolutely and totally covered my tracks." McKey's voice was tinged with irritation as his brain retraced every move he had made.

Benjamin nodded thoughtfully. "True. You are, by all accounts, very good at your trade—meticulous, cautious. Almost perfect."

"Almost?"

"Your bio-tracker smartwatch," Benjamin said, as if the answer were obvious. "It was monitoring your vitals, was it not? Gaia identified a high probability that the person accepting the job—someone with your psychological profile—would exhibit a subtle physiological response. A slight increase in pulse. Anxiety. Excitement."

McKey frowned. "That is a hell of a leap. What if I wasn't wearing the damn thing?"

Benjamin gestured casually with his cigar. "Gaia had contingencies—thousands of pre-calculated scenarios. But as it happened, the smartwatch did its job. The moment you accepted the operation, your vitals transmitted data to the medical data center.

"At the exact moment you accepted the job, Gaia looked for a certain physiological response. Out of the thousands who recorded such bio-activity at that exact moment she cross-checked for one using a fake ID. There was only one.

"She narrowed her focus to your smartwatch, deduced your real identity and history, and pinpointed your exact location. You were profiled, identified, and then she proceeded to capture you. Billions of calculations later, you were part of her well crafted plan. She sent the underwater recovery drones to the Hudson before you boarded the taxi. Your single wearable device was the thread she pulled to get what she needed."

"A pattern. She caught me on a goddamn pattern. Fuck." McKey's jaw tightened. He felt sloppy. He hated being caught.

"Patterns, game theory, physics, psychology, biology," Benjamin said smoothly. "Do not be so hard on yourself, Mr. McKey. Even with every precaution, you were, as they say, a moth drawn to the flame. You stood no chance."

McKey glared at him. "Fine. How'd she hack the Milo, then? Those things aren't supposed to be hackable."

Benjamin leaned back, his expression darkening slightly. "Ah, that particular challenge required a touch of ingenuity. Any attempt at a direct code hack would have been detected and neutralized. So, Gaia employed a more ... subtle approach.

"She influenced the Milo's AI through psychological triggers—subtle nudges of paranoia and urgency. Not a brute code hack, a suggestion. A spirit whispering in its ear. Clever, but unfortunately imperfect."

McKey frowned, skepticism creeping into his tone. "But it worked, right? I mean, I'm here. Seems pretty damn successful to me."

"Indeed, the outcome was as intended," Benjamin admitted. "But the execution was not without flaws. The Milo's behavior showed hesitation. Resistance. Uncertainty. Instead of executing the task cleanly, its actions raised noticeable anomalies."

Benjamin pressed the dying cigar into the table, extinguishing it gently.

"This hesitation will undoubtedly attract some attention. Gaia has already taken steps to misdirect the authorities, of course. The member corporations of the Autonomous Vehicles Alliance have no desire to turn this into a public embarrassment. For now, the incident is classified as an accident involving a single passenger—a certain Mr. Smith—presumed deceased."

He exhaled slowly, his tone turning ominous.

"However, Gaia will likely need further action to extinguish any lingering inquiries. And you, Mr. McKey, might be up on deck."

Red Birthday

September 17, 2044

Kelvin Kincade was all smiles as he approached the cozy single-family house. He loved everything about Gee's house—the quirky pastel exterior that stood out in the quiet suburban neighborhood, the way he always found a perfect parking spot across the street. Even the long drive from Manhattan felt worthwhile, especially on a beautiful Saturday like this.

But more than all that, he adored the family inside. They reminded him of old sitcoms, the kind that had gone out of style decades ago but were making a nostalgic comeback in the age of generated entertainment.

Today was Gee's forty-third birthday. Inside, balloons hung cheerfully, a bright "Happy Birthday" sign dominated the living room, and a playlist of upbeat birthday tunes streamed in the background. It was sugary sweet in every way, but the warmth and authenticity in the air made it impossible not to enjoy.

"Here comes the cake!" Vera, Gee's wife, announced from the kitchen. She appeared, balancing a large homemade cake in both hands, her nine-month pregnant belly leading the charge. Kelvin whistled in appreciation, knowing better than to offer Vera unsolicited help.

"Thank you, detective," Vera said with a friendly smile as she made her way to the table.

Kelvin's work in the force involved daily interaction with countless people. But Vera's pregnancy made him realize just how few pregnant women were out there. It felt almost awkward to be in the presence of one. Yet, Vera was a cheerful, good-looking lady. She carried it extremely well, both physically and mentally.

"Mamma, come on, we're lighting the candles!" Gee called out to his mom, who was busy in the kitchen.

Since Gee's father had passed away unexpectedly a few years ago, his mom moved in with them and had practically claimed the kitchen as her domain. Cooking for the family helped ease the lingering ache of missing her beloved husband.

Sofia, one of the seven-year-old twins, bolted toward the cake, plate in hand, eyes wide and gleaming at the promise of sugar. Kelvin barely sidestepped in time to avoid a collision.

"Daddy! Sammy's in the slopp again!" Sofia tattled, pointing accusingly at her brother.

Gee immediately reached over and plucked the opaque visor off little Sammy's head. The boy blinked rapidly as his eyes adjusted to the abrupt change in lighting—and reality.

"Dad, you can't do that! You'll give me a brain injury!" Sammy protested, his voice full of exaggerated indignation.

"You're such a slopp head," Sofia said with a self-satisfied grin. "You already have a boo boo brain."

The slopp was a common term for the never-ending stream of AI-generated virtual content, tailor-made to provoke emotional reactions. Gee had grown increasingly worried about how hooked Sammy seemed to be. Kelvin understood the pull all too well, having himself indulged in the slopp a little too often. It was dangerously addictive.

"I told you to stay away from that garbage," Gee said sternly, leveling a disappointed look at his son. "Who signed you in?"

"Grandma," Sammy confessed immediately.

Kelvin was amused. He noticed Gee's disappointment at how quickly the kid caved and snitched. Yet, in this environment, his partner would not dare to express that sentiment out loud.

"Ma, I've asked you not to let him use that stuff. It's not good for him," Gee said, his voice rising slightly in frustration.

"Don't you raise your voice at me, young man!" his mother retorted, wagging a finger at her son with an authority that immediately shut him down.

Kelvin chuckled softly at the family dynamic, then fist-bumped Sammy. He liked the kid's rebellious streak. Kelvin, despite his career in law enforcement, had his own vein of anti-establishment defiance. He couldn't help but respect the seven-year-old's blatant disregard for the rules.

"Here, Sammy," Kelvin said, reaching into his pocket and pulling out a small round object wrapped in twine. He handed it to the boy.

"What's this?" Sammy asked, examining the object from every angle.

"It's called a yoyo," Kelvin said with a smirk. "Look it up."

Sammy nodded. Kelvin knew he had just handed the kid another excuse to log into the slopp later.

"Thanks, Uncle Kelvin."

Some would find the cacophony of the Jackson household disorienting, even exhausting—but not Kelvin. He found the chaos uplifting, invigorating even. The energy here felt alive, a stark contrast to the often bleak world he dealt with on the job. He mentally cataloged a few amusing moments to torment Gee with later at work.

Vera lit the candles on the cake, adding a few sparklers for flair.

"Make a wish!" the twins shouted in unison. Gee closed his eyes, drew in a breath, and blew out the candles.

The kids cheered.

"I wished..." Gee began.

"No no no!" Sofia interrupted, throwing up her hands. "You can't tell, or it won't come true!"

"Well, I wished to tell a knock-knock joke," Gee said with a sly grin.

"No!" Everyone shouted this time.

"Knock knock," Gee persisted.

"Who's there?" Sammy said, ignoring everyone's protests.

Kelvin couldn't help but laugh.

After finishing a generous slice of cake and nursing a beer, Kelvin decided to call it a day. "Thanks, everyone. That was fun," he said, grabbing his coat from the rack near the front door. "Vera, any day now?"

Vera smiled and nodded, approaching him. She leaned in and gave him a light kiss on the cheek. "Thanks for coming, Kelvin. Keep my husband safe out there, okay?"

Kelvin smiled back. "Always," he said with a firm nod.

"Third child bonus coming my way," Gee said with a smirk, only to get an elbow to the ribs from his mom.

"Bye, Uncle Kelvin!" Sammy called from inside the house.

"What's that smell? Yuck! Sammy, did you fart?" Sofia's voice rang out as Kelvin stepped outside, closing the door behind him with a chuckle.

Kelvin settled into the driver's seat of his two-seater 2025 red-mist Corvette Stingray. He inhaled deeply, savoring the moment before firing up the gasoline-powered 6.2-liter V8 engine. The deep roar that followed filled him with a giddy sense of satisfaction. Nearly 500 horsepower of pure, unapologetic muscle—a relic from a time when cars were built for raw joy rather than silent efficiency.

"They don't make 'em like this anymore," he muttered to himself, shaking his head. The comforts of autonomous driving and whisper-quiet electric engines had wiped these beasts off the production lines, but Kelvin reveled in the fires of combustion. This car was his baby.

Just as he reached for the gear shift, he spotted Gee jogging out of the house across the street toward him, holding a large brown envelope. Kelvin sighed, shifted the car back into Park, and waited.

The passenger door lifted, and Gee slid into the low seat with a groan.

"Hey, brother. Before you leave," Gee said, holding up the envelope, "you remember that freaky Milo accident on the GWB last month?"

Work. Kelvin turned off the engine, keeping the rumble from drowning out the conversation. His eyes flicked to the envelope, curiosity sparking.

"Yeah. August first. Case got shelved as an accident," Kelvin said, his tone edged with frustration. He still resented how the higher-ups quickly canned it. All resources and interest yanked out from under them. Politics.

"Right," Gee said, nodding. "Well, I did some digging. I needed to know who this 'Mr. Smith' was. That kind of ghost? Not normal. Not these days. Whole case—it's weird as fuck."

Kelvin studied his partner. Gee was a dog with a bone when it came to loose ends, and this case had clearly burrowed under his skin.

"You found something?" Kelvin asked, raising an eyebrow.

"Maybe," Gee said, shrugging. "Check out the hard copies in the envelope. Too light to share upward yet, but I want you to take a look. Let's see if it's worth chasing and maybe convince the chief to give it another go."

He lifted up the door and stepped out, dropping the envelope onto the passenger's seat. "Got to get back to my party. Let's discuss this tomorrow."

Kelvin picked up the envelope and started peeling it open when a knock on the window startled him. He rolled it down to see Gee's massive face stretched with an ear-to-ear grin.

"What, brother?" Kelvin asked, amused despite himself.

"You wanna hear a joke about my dick?" Gee asked, grinning, then backed away from the car. "Never mind, it's too long!"

With a loud laugh, Gee turned and crossed the street back to the house, leaving Kelvin chuckling to himself as he watched his partner's carefree stride. He had heard Gee tell that joke a million times before, but it still managed to pull a smirk out of him.

Shaking his head, Kelvin rolled up the window, leaned back, and shut his eyes for a moment, absentmindedly turning the envelope over in his hands. He peeked inside to find a few printed photos, possibly surveillance materials.

Exhaustion tugged at him. He slid the photos back, sealed the envelope and tossed it back onto the passenger seat. This could wait until tomorrow, he decided, his tired mind was not ready to untangle whatever thread Gee had pulled.

Kelvin started the engine again, savoring the rumble of the powerful V8. He tapped the gas pedal a couple of times while still in neutral, letting the engine roar and sending a subtle signal to the sleepy suburban neighborhood: *Kelvin was leaving.*

Shifting to Drive, he gripped the steering wheel with both hands and readied himself to roll out.

And then it happened.

A violent explosion ripped through the air, rattling his car like a kicked tin can. The world erupted around him, turning a calm joyful day into violent madness in a split second. Shards of debris rained down from above, pelting the street and his Corvette. A piece of pastel-colored siding landed on his hood, one of its corners smoldering.

Kelvin couldn't breathe. His chest was tight, his jaw hung slack. His hands trembled as he fumbled with the door handle, finally managing to stumble out of the car. His knees buckled, and he dropped to the pavement, his gaze locked on the void where life had just been. His heart pounded, ears rang, and his mind struggled to process the sight before him.

The pastel house was gone.

Not damaged. Not scorched. Gone.

In an instant, Gee's laughter, the kids' giggles, Vera's warmth—everything—was obliterated. His friend. His partner. His family. Gone.

Kelvin stood frozen, staring at the smoldering ruins where Gee's house had just been. The air was thick with smoke and the acrid smell of destruction. His chest heaved as reality sank in.

Everything he had just left behind lay buried beneath the rubble.

The Aftermath

McKey watched the smoking remains from the tree line at the back of the house, savoring the scene with deep satisfaction. A symphony of destruction—visual, auditory, and aromatic. The smell of charred wood and chemical residue lingered in the air like a trophy, a sensory reminder of a job well done. He rarely stayed this close to witness the aftermath of his handiwork.

Target eliminated. Easy fucking day.

A few spiderbots had been lost in the operation. No big deal. Gaia would supply replacements. The little mechanical critters had done their job flawlessly: cutting the gas line and strategically placing their powerful explosive charges throughout the house.

The result was textbook—a catastrophic explosion masquerading as a mundane gas leak. PETN residue? Who would even think of looking for military-grade explosives in a quiet suburban home?

As he shifted his stance, McKey allowed himself a fleeting thought: *maybe having a digital god-boss wasn't so bad.* Standing in the dark, trench coat swirling, spider-drones at his command, he felt like a Sith Lord. Like Vader. And even that bad motherfucker had a boss—Palpatine. *At least my boss is much better looking.*

The perks Gaia provided were undeniably impressive. With her resources, he could fabricate whatever the hell he needed, without fear of detection. Her exclusive network made him invisible to digital watchdogs and pattern trackers. Out of sight. Out of smell.

The remaining spiders climbed into his long black trench coat, disappearing into hidden compartments. The coat's disruption field masked him from nearby cameras and sensors, rendering him a true ghost. McKey moved under the cover of darkness, slipping away before the first responders could arrive.

Today was a good day, he thought.

***

Kelvin sat on the ambulance's edge, staring numbly at the smoking wreckage as fire-droids carefully pulled bodies from the debris. One by one, the family members were placed in black body bags, lined up side by side—three large bags for the adults, two smaller ones for the children.

His mind struggled to process what his eyes were seeing. It felt unreal, like watching a distant crime scene through a monitor. The world around him moved in slow, disjointed fragments—the faint hiss of cooling metal, the crackle of fire-droids sweeping through the debris, the distant murmur of emergency responders talking over comms. His ears rang with the fading echo of the explosion, but beneath it, there was only silence.

He didn't know how to act. What to say. What to think. What to feel. He sat there, motionless, watching the first responders do their job. His brain clung to a false expectation—*when Gee gets here, he'll help clear this mess*. His gaze drifted to the black bags, reality hitting like a dull hammer. Gee isn't coming. Ever.

His face was streaked with soot, pale beneath the grime. His hands raw and blistered, the skin peeling where he'd clawed frantically through the rubble. The stench of burnt hair and flesh clung to him, a searing physical reminder of his failure to save them.

A human medic, assisted by a medic-droid, worked silently to wrap Kelvin's hands in gauze soaked with ointment. He inhaled deeply from the oxygen mask pressed to his face, letting the clean air sting his smoke-ravaged lungs.

"Can you grab my visor from the car?" he rasped, removing the mask with his heavily bandaged aching hands, his voice hoarse.

Normally, medic-droids were programmed with an incongruous, overly cheery demeanor, but this one wisely chose restraint. Without a word, it retrieved the visor from the car's glove compartment and gently placed it on Kelvin's head.

The visor turned opaque and Ellena's image materialized in his visor, projected from her usual virtual office simulation. The heavy mahogany desk and commanding backdrop, normally detailed and authoritative, seemed dimmer than usual. It was as if even her curated space had absorbed the weight of the somber moment.

She looked pale and shaken. It was the first time Kelvin had ever seen a HighQ display visible distress.

Ellena was still human, despite the Stream constantly bolstering her intellect and consciousness. Despite the distant cloud servers that hosted a big part of her thoughts and memories. Despite the bond she had with machines and men who kept distancing themselves from their biological existence. Despite her front, which was meticulously designed to make him forget who she once was, he still saw glimpses of the person he had known.

She was, after all, still human.

Kelvin could see cracks in the carefully constructed facade, even through the simulation. She had known Gee well, even met his family years ago after the twins were born. She'd brought a casserole.

"This is horrible," she said, her voice faltering before settling into its usual controlled cadence. "Preliminary investigation points to a gas leak."

Kelvin's lips tightened. "A gas leak? Right," he said flatly. Sofia's last words flashed through his mind: *What's that smell? Yuck!*

"We follow the data," Ellena continued, her micro-vibrating pupils betraying her Stream-assisted multitasking. "So far, everything we found points to one conclusion: an unfortunate accident." She paused briefly, then looked directly at him. "But I assure you, detective, this will reach the highest levels of Intelligence. If there is even a hint of foul play, we will pursue it with vigor."

"Okay," Kelvin replied quietly. His rational mind accepted the procedure, but his heart rebelled. He needed someone to blame.

Ellena's expression softened, her gaze locking onto his. "Are you alright?"

"Minor injuries," Kelvin said, his voice raspy and grave. He coughed lightly. "Nothing to worry about."

"You almost got killed," Ellena said sharply, her tone regaining the clipped precision of a HighQ in command. "I'm assigning you a doc-bot and a psych evaluation."

"No need," Kelvin replied curtly, defiance lacing his tone. "I'm fine."

Ellena looked him in the eye. The pause was long—longer than he'd ever known. A lifetime for a HighQ. He could have sworn her eyes, just for a moment, remained still.

"Not a request," she said and severed the connection.

Chapter 3

Ellena 2030

Ellena stared at the mirror after a long shift on foot patrol. Her feet ached, a small price to pay for the grind she loved. She kicked off her shoes, stripped off her uniform, and let herself unwind.

Barely a year on the force, she found the streets of New York endlessly challenging. While experienced detectives sat in their air-conditioned cubicles, twiddling their thumbs, hoping for the rare high-profile case to come, she thrived in the trenches.

Law enforcement wasn't just a career—it was her outlet, a way to channel her boundless, restless energy. Growing up, she was always looking for action, often finding trouble. Justice and truth mattered most to her, even if it meant standing up to the principal in his office. Punishment never deterred her as long as she knew she had the higher moral ground.

Any profession that would have taken her to a desk job would have crushed her spirit. Her parents weren't at all surprised when she pursued law enforcement. Although not the white-collar life they had imagined, it was a career that fit their strong-willed daughter, and they were proud.

The city streets pulsed with desperation and hopelessness. Here, she faced those who had given up on the game of life. People too high, too drunk, too broken to care. Some lost their jobs. Most had lost their minds, too far gone to accept a way out even when help was offered. Their desperation often led to law-breaking.

Ellena was relentless in protecting law-abiding citizens. It gave her satisfaction, even at the small cost of aching feet.

She leaned closer to the mirror, studying her reflection. Her long scarlet-dyed hair, eyes lined in thick black mascara, and dark red lipstick. She was meticulous about her appearance. It took effort but was time well spent for all she cared.

At twenty, she turned heads at the precinct, mostly from men, but also a few women. She smiled at the thought—there was nothing wrong with a healthy ego. And hers was in good standing. Those lucky enough to get close found a wild and cheerful spirit beneath the badge. Her job exposed her to daily misery, but it also reminded her how fortunate she had been.

She looked good, felt good, and refused to take that for granted.

It was dark outside, and the open window let the city's lights and sounds flood her tiny studio apartment. Car horns blared, an occasional bang echoed, sirens wailed from police drones overhead, and loud chatter spilled from the streets below—the lifeblood of New York City.

The newly introduced self-driving cabs only made things worse, fueling an endless chorus of honking. Occasionally small protests broke out, some violent. New

Yorkers didn't kindly accept automation reshaping their city and threatening their livelihoods. Their resistance was futile, progress always wins.

As for the rest of the noise pollution? No one in city hall even pretended to give a damn. This city was destined to be loud, she thought. But loud meant alive, and that was why she loved it so much.

Her sharp green eyes, still slightly bloodshot from a good cry, reflected the dim glow of the apartment lights. The drops she'd used had done their job, easing most of the redness. She had just finished watching a ten-minute, auto-generated movie—a personalized, cheesy, feel-good storyline that hit just the right spot. The cathartic little cry had lifted some of the day's weight from her shoulders. It was a perfect emotional reset after her long shift and before heading to the bar to meet with her friend.

Before placing the tablet back in its charging dock, she prompted it for another dose of emotional cinematic drama. Aside from her normal preferences, she asked for a dog as the main character. She wasn't sure why exactly. Something to watch in case the night went sideways and she needed another hit of escapist fluff to reset her soul.

Ellena got ready. The late May evening was a comfortable 72 degrees, perfect for light clothing. She didn't care much for brand names, favoring utility over fashion. Loose, breathable garments made her feel free and unburdened. Still, she grabbed a light jacket—it was supposed to get chillier later, according to the forecast.

"I think that's a good idea," chimed a cheerful male voice from the room speaker. "You don't want the cold distracting you from your date. However, I should point out that skipping the jacket might give you a perfect excuse to... uhm... cuddle."

"Casper, knock it off. Kelvin is a friend and a colleague. This is definitely not a date!" Ellena snapped, rolling her eyes.

"Just saying, you should prepare for all potential outcomes," Casper replied, his tone light but insistent.

Casper wasn't just a digital assistant—he had been part of her life since high school. She had always loved experimenting with cutting-edge tech, and Casper quickly became more than a gadget—he became her companion. Over the years, their bond deepened.

Many people formed attachments to their personal AIs, but hers was special. Casper had an uncanny knack for knowing when to inject his quirky humor and when to provide genuine support. Even when he teased her, she knew he always had her back.

"I mean, he's a boy, you're a girl. He likes you, you like him. I checked, there is no issue with the department's regulations. So, why not?"

"Cut it out. I'm leaving," she said with a smirk.

"Good luck, madam! I'll be at your service if you need me," Casper said, his voice mockingly chivalrous.

"Okay Cyrano, but don't embarrass me," Ellena warned, pointing a finger at the speaker.

"No, ma'am!" Casper replied with insincere obedience.

She wasn't entirely sure if he was being sarcastic, but decided to take his assurance at face value. After one last glance in the mirror, she headed out.

***

"Officer Kincaid!" Ellena greeted Kelvin with a bright smile as she approached their table. He was fiddling with his smartphone, which he promptly fumbled. It rolled to the floor, folding itself into a small rectangular cube.

"Damn it!" Kelvin muttered, ducking under the round bar table to retrieve it, only to bump his head on the way back up.

Ellena laughed, leaning on the edge of the table. "Watching porn?" she teased, her green eyes sparkling with mischief.

Kelvin's face burned like lava. What a terrible way to start the evening. Ellena was a friend, someone he genuinely liked. They were both single, young, and he'd entertained the idea of making a move tonight. Scratch that plan, he thought, inwardly groaning. *Please, God, don't let this turn into station gossip.*

"No, no! Just checking my feeds," he stammered, trying to salvage some dignity but realizing he might have made it worse. He scrambled to change the topic. "Uh, you know the band playing tonight?"

Ellena grinned, clearly enjoying his awkwardness. "Nice course correction, officer. You're lucky I'm off duty, or I might have to arrest you for being criminally dorky."

Kelvin groaned. "Jesus, Ellena. Cut it out. Do you know the band or not?"

She gave him a playful shrug. "Some kind of electronic jazz thing. Should be interesting."

"Live Improvised Digital Pop-Jazz," Casper interjected, his smooth voice emanating from Ellena's smartwatch.

"Go to sleep, Casper," Ellena said, rolling her eyes.

"G'night," Casper replied with mock brevity, his tone just cheeky enough to make her smirk.

Kelvin was a defiant Gen Z. Old school was his style, and he never bothered adopting a personal digital assistant like most people did. It wasn't that he had anything against the tech—he just valued his privacy and the rare luxury of quiet. A basic smartphone was good enough for him.

"This thing bothering you?" Kelvin asked lightly, nodding toward Ellena's watch.

"Casper can be a pest sometimes," she admitted with a shrug, "but he means well."

"I'm so slow with these things."

Kelvin knew that his stubborn refusal to adopt the latest tech was putting him at a major disadvantage—both at work and in life. Ellena was the exact opposite, always giddy about new gadgets. Yet, sometimes opposites attract, and he hoped she found his outdated ways ... charming.

Ellena smirked. "Well, you do drive a gas-guzzler in Manhattan. It's like your clock stopped ticking a decade ago."

"Yeah, I guess I take my time," Kelvin said with a small chuckle. "Maybe that's why I haven't made detective yet."

"No, that's because you're a doofus," Ellena quipped, her face showing slight regret that it might come as an insult. She quickly leaned closer to him and added, "A cute doofus," glancing briefly at her watch, bracing for Casper's interjection. Mercifully, Casper remained quiet.

Kelvin, distracted by thoughts about his lingering promotion, didn't notice the flirtation. "Unfortunately, *cute* isn't on the checklist for making detective," he replied, utterly missing the cue.

Ellena rolled her eyes, exhaled, and stood up. "I'll get beers," she said, heading toward the bar.

The all-human band took the stage as Kelvin watched her weave through the crowd. The lineup featured a striking African-American singer with big hair, a drummer, an acoustic guitarist, a saxophonist, and one guy fiddling with electronics. The music was fully improvised, finding its direction as it went. It wasn't flawless—far from it—but in an era of AI-born perfection, people were thirsty for imperfections.

This style of entertainment was building a growing fan base. Kelvin found it oddly pleasant, even if unfamiliar, and began tapping his fingers on the table to the beat.

Ellena returned, carefully navigating through the crowded bar with two beer bottles in hand.

"That idiot barman-droid broke four bottles before I finally got these," she said, laughing as she sat down.

"Did it overcharge you?" Kelvin asked.

"Probably," Ellena replied with a shrug. "Who knows with those things? At least I didn't have to tip that pile of junk. I seriously hope they get better soon—or else we'll need to bring back people to replace them."

"At least the union makes sure cops—human cops— still have jobs and aren't replaced by some robocops," Kelvin said dryly, his tone laced with sarcasm.

"Cheers to that!" Ellena said, clinking her bottle against his.

They settled in, taking sips of their drinks as the music washed over them. The imperfections of the live show gave it a charm that neither of them had expected—it was engrossing and entertaining.

Ellena's wrist vibrated urgently. She glanced at it with a sigh. "What is it, Casper?" she asked quietly.

"Bad news," Casper said, his tone was more serious than usual. "Officer Tony Gonzales called in sick. They need you to cover for him."

"Oh? When?" Ellena asked, dreading the answer.

"ASAP, unfortunately. Seems something important is going down. Briefing in an hour," Casper replied.

"Crap. They know I already pulled a morning walk, right?" she said, her voice tinged with annoyance.

"Yes, I told them, but they're short-staffed. No one else was available on such short notice. Sorry," Casper added, sounding genuinely apologetic.

Ellena sighed heavily. "Alright. I'll head back to the apartment and change." She turned to Kelvin and gave him an apologetic shrug.

Kelvin didn't need an explanation; he obviously recognized the tone and look. Work. They were stationed in different precincts, but he knew something about hers possibly heating up tonight. He nodded, his expression understanding.

"Stay safe out there, Ellena," he said.

"Thanks. Will do. You too," she replied with a small smile as she grabbed her jacket. "And thanks for a lovely evening, Kincaid."

Her tone was warm but professional, leaving Kelvin a little unsure whether the night had gone as he'd hoped. Still, he smiled back and watched as she walked out, wondering if there might be another evening like this to come.

***

The FBI was moving in on a big operation, months—maybe years—in the making. Everyone was on call: SWAT, Traffic, and dozens of uniformed police officers tasked with securing the perimeter. Ellena was buzzing with anticipation. This was the biggest op she had been part of in her young career. Finally, some real action.

Sergeant Dave Chung led the briefing to a room full of cops with his usual no-nonsense leadership. He gave assignments to teams of two, all to provide a security ring around the op. He did not allow any growling or arguments. The FBI got to have all the fun, and that was that.

When the Sergeant got to Ellena, he barked, "Officer Hershkovitz, you're covering for Tony diarrhea."

Chung didn't mean to sound funny; grammar and etiquette weren't his strong suits. English was his second language, and the unintended phrasing made the room ripple with laughter. Poor Tony—he would have a new nickname to deal with once he got back.

"Silence!" Chung snapped, waving his laser pointer at the aerial map displayed on the large screen. "You and Officer Swan will stake here." He circled a small alley a block from the restaurant where the operation would take place. "Secure the east side. No doors or exits from the restaurant, so don't expect much."

The assignment felt like an afterthought, the kind of low-priority placement designed to make the perimeter look tidy on a map. Still, Ellena didn't mind. She was partnered with Officer Matilda Swan, a more experienced cop with a few more years on the force. Matilda was down-to-earth and easy to work with. Ellena was eager to soak up whatever knowledge or advice she could.

"The takedown of one of the very last Mafia families in the U.S.," Matilda said, her tone dripping with sarcasm. "Irish gang in an Italian restaurant, in Queens, no less. Good premise for a bad show. What an honor to be part of."

Ellena smirked. "Yup. A story we'll pass on to our kids."

Matilda chuckled and gathered her dark hair into a ponytail with a hairband. "We'll skip over the part about our exciting alley duty, though. You planning to have some?"

"What, kids?" Ellena hesitated. "Maybe. I'm not sure. Definitely not three, though—so count me out of the government's incentives everyone is talking about."

"I'm with you there," Matilda said, gesturing at her body. "The government can shove their bonuses where the sun don't shine. These curves ain't going anywhere."

Both women sipped their Dunkin' lattes, deliberately skipping the calories and cliché of pairing them with donuts. The coffee warmed them against the cool evening air slipping into their cruiser.

"All stations. Operation is a go. Head on a swivel, girls and boys," the Command-and-Control dispatcher announced over the radio.

When AI dispatchers were first introduced, unions—worried about job displacement—put up a fight. Their concerns were well-founded, and while many jobs were threatened, the tech proved both impressive and inevitable. The digital counterparts were smart, quick, seamlessly integrated with all agencies, and significantly cheaper. After a lengthy battle and the expected government logic, a compromise was reached: an AI operator now ran the show, while human 'AI supervisors' were assigned to quietly 'monitor' from behind their screens.

The streets were eerily quiet. Aside from the occasional unit checking in, everything seemed calm. Then, suddenly, the radio chatter erupted into chaos. The resistance was immediate and brutal—far worse than expected. Gunfire echoed through the streets, and within seconds, the operation had turned into a full-blown battle.

"Shots fired! Shots fired!" The frantic reports came in bursts, painting a picture of escalating danger.

Ellena and Matilda's lighthearted banter quickly swapped with the cold quiet focus of cops ready for anything. "Officer down!" The frantic voice over the radio made Ellena and Matilda exchange pale, wide-eyed glances.

Their orders were clear—stay put and secure the perimeter—but the mayhem occurring only a block away was palpable. Muffled gunfire echoed through the streets, each burst more desperate than the last. The restaurant had turned into a war zone, and the mob wasn't going down without a fight.

Seconds later, an explosion from inside a building, left of their position, shook the ground beneath them. The radio crackled again, "All stations be advised, the targets are heavily armed, including explosives. Two breached east. East side units, be on high alert for any activity."

Ellena looked at Matilda, hoping for some reassurance from the senior officer, yet Matilda's white-knuckled grip on the steering wheel betrayed her nerves.

Another explosion shattered the tense stillness, louder this time, from the same direction as the previous one, and the sound echoed sharply in the alley. A cloud of black and gray smoke billowed outward as part of the brick wall collapsed.

Ellena, from the passenger seat, watched over Matilda's right shoulder as two figures emerged from the dust, both armed with assault rifles. They had blown their own escape route, turning the carefully laid plans of the operation into a messy clusterfuck.

One was a large adult man, the other smaller—possibly a teenager, Ellena quickly assessed. Both officers sprang out from their cruiser, weapons drawn. "Stop! Put your weapons down!" they shouted in unison.

Matilda's position left her exposed, while Ellena instinctively used the cruiser for cover. The larger man didn't hesitate, unleashing a hail of bullets. The deafening roar of automatic fire drowned out Ellena's frantic shouts. She dropped low and took cover as bullets crossed through the vehicle.

Matilda jerked violently as the rounds tore through her, blood spraying against the shattered side of the cruiser. The vehicle's metal was riddled with holes, while the glass splintered into flying shards. Ellena was lucky—only grazed by the fragments.

"Shots fired! Officer down!" Ellena screamed into her radio, her voice cracking with desperation. She steadied herself, bracing against the hood and using the front wheels and engine block for cover. Her hands shook as she hugged her gun, waiting for the right moment.

When the shooter paused to reload, she got up and fired towards the alley. Her aim was steady, and at least two rounds struck the larger man in the chest.

The smaller figure screamed, "Dad!" as the man staggered back. With his last breath, the man roared, "Son, run!" before collapsing to the ground.

"Stop!" Ellena yelled, but the assailant did not intend to comply. He wisely dropped his rifle to avoid getting shot, took a good look at her, then turned and darted into the alley, vanishing into the swirling smoke and dust.

For a fleeting moment, their eyes locked. His gaze burned with an unnatural, fiery rage. Ellena could have sworn his eyes glowed red—whether from the reflection of the cruiser's flashing lights or a trick of her own imagination, she could not tell.

"Officer Swan is down. One suspect down. One suspect running, on foot, mid-height, caucasian, dark hair—possibly a minor. Possibly armed," she reported firmly into the radio. She wasn't sure if he had other weapons on him. Shooting the kid after he laid his rifle down was against her training, and would be just wrong. Yet, for a brief moment she wished she had pulled the trigger, it might have saved the world some grief.

The wail of approaching sirens grew louder. Backup was close.

Ellena turned her attention to Matilda, who lay crumpled against the driver side of the cruiser, her body unnaturally still.

"Matilda," she whispered, dropping beside her partner. Her fingers trembled as she searched for a pulse. Nothing.

Ellena sat on the cold pavement, slumped against the battered cruiser, Matilda's lifeless body silent beside her. For a moment, the noise and mayhem faded, leaving only the pounding of her heart and the weight of her grief.

"Need an ambulance," she pleaded into the radio, her voice breaking, "Please!"

Ellena 2038

Chief Josh Leary gestured toward the chair as Ellena closed the door behind her. "Have a seat, detective."

Ellena sat, unsure why she had been summoned. A visit to the Chief's office was rare—and rarely a good sign. As she settled in, her mind replayed the last few weeks, searching for anything that might raise red flags. Over the years, she had learned to keep her wild instincts in check, especially after the alley shooting eight years ago.

That day had left a scar on her psyche, even as it earned her a commendation and helped push her promotion to detective. The shootout had been cleared as justified—self-defense, plain and simple—but the memory of his son's hateful glare still haunted her, even though she had taken a mafia boss off the field.

Her gaze drifted to the Chief, seated behind his spotless, empty desk. Instead of a laptop or monitor, a sleek, jet-black police-issued visor rested on his head. His fingers moved deftly through the air, navigating the device with surprising ease.

The visor looked slightly out of place on the gruff, aging commander, but with the department modernizing, even he had to adapt if he wanted to hold onto his position until retirement. Once he embraced the tech, he'd likely come to appreciate its efficiency over a keyboard and mouse—not to mention the added free space on his desk.

Finally, he removed the visor, meeting her eyes.

"Relax," he said. "I asked you here because you were recommended."

"Recommended?" she echoed, her brow furrowing. "For what, sir?"

"This new superbrain thing—uh, Titan, it's called—spit up your name."

Ellena blinked, trying to make sense of his cryptic explanation. She had recently made detective; it was too early for another promotion.

Chief Leary leaned back in his chair, clearly not thrilled with the situation. Nearing his sixties, he came from a long lineage of law enforcement and public servants. His old-school approach to policing didn't mesh well with AI encroaching on the job. The idea that a computer could outmatch decades of street and office grind didn't sit well with an old-timer like him.

But even he had to admit that crime numbers had plummeted since Titan—a government-corporate AI collaboration—came online two years ago.

Titan, a superintelligent AI, had been tasked with keeping the streets safe and overall making all aspects of life easier for people—while keeping the lesser AIs in line. So far, it had been working remarkably well. Titan was quickly becoming a beloved household name: a digital guardian and benefactor ensuring safety and prosperity for all citizens. Advancements seemed to pop up every day—improved health, efficient city planning, diminished bureaucracy, and dramatically reduced crime rates.

"I don't understand, sir," Ellena said, breaking a momentary silence. "My name came up for what?"

"There's a new project. Groundbreaking, or so I'm told. Getting support all the way up the food chain," he said, his voice tinged with reluctance.

"The Commissioner?"

"POTUS," he said flatly.

Her eyes widened. "Seriously?"

"Yep. Real big deal."

"What project?"

"You've heard about the Q Project?" he asked.

"Of course," she said. "The brain-machine interface. Got the FDA approval last year. Early trials showed it boosted intelligence and let users pick up new skills in seconds. Kind of wild. Sir."

"Wonders of the modern age," Leary said with a half-smile. "Well, the powers that be got a taste and now want to try putting those chips in cops' heads."

Her stomach turned as goosebumps crept up her arms. "You mean ... enhanced cops?"

"Smarter cops," he said with a shrug. "At least, that's the idea."

"Why me?" she asked, unsure if she should feel flattered or horrified.

"No frickin' idea," he grumbled. "Titan pulled your name out of its huge magic hat, and I'm just here to pass the message."

"Can I look into this before giving an answer?" she asked cautiously.

"Of course. It's a hundred percent voluntary. But keep in mind, saying yes will make your career. Even POTUS will be watching. You won the golden ticket. It's an honor—for you and the force."

Ellena processed his words aloud. "I'm intrigued, but... I kind of like my skull the way it is. Call me old-fashioned, but I'm not sure I need another hole."

Leary suppressed a grin, holding back the kind of off-color joke that might have gotten him in trouble in any era. Instead, he said, "I get it. Take a few days. The higher-ups are anxious about this, so don't take too long."

"Thank you, sir. I'll let you know soon," she said, standing.

Leary gave her a nod. Ellena saluted and left, shutting the door behind her as a mix of curiosity and apprehension swirled in her. For the first time in years, she felt a flicker of something foreign—hope.

Maybe this was her chance to move on and quiet the echoes of the past.

Ellena 2044

When the Q Program was announced to the public, it offered a new way to connect with the digital realm and the AIs that thrived within it. A constant and direct connection at the speed of thought. A way to bridge the widening gap with digital intelligence, especially the quantum-core superbrains. The Q Program's objective was to ensure humanity had proper liaisons to these rapidly evolving digital creations—or so they were told.

Ellena's journey had been turbulent from the start. As an early adopter, she entered the program when the technology was still uncharted territory. There was no formal training, no roadmap for navigating the profound changes to her mind and body. It was new and experimental, and she was selected for her strong will and adventurous spirit. Ultimately, however, the decision was hers alone. The opportunity to go beyond, to explore, to become more, was too enticing to pass up.

Then came the nickname: HighQ. The term, while aptly descriptive, carried a subtle sting of derision. It reflected a growing societal unease—a mixture of admiration and disdain—for the HighQ's perceived, and often actual, intellectual superiority.

In the early years of the program, people viewed the HighQ as symbols of progress, pioneers of a new way to consume the online world and interact with advanced AIs. Some envied them, others pitied them. Many were afraid. Despite all its challenges, Ellena found the experience exhilarating. She enjoyed discussing her new abilities with friends and family, relishing her role at the center of attention.

Yet a rift was forming. The majority who were not part of the HighQ got their own nickname: LowQ. The term reeked of inferiority and deepened the growing divide. Ellena hated the term. She valued interacting with her non-connected friends and colleagues and refused to view them as inferior. Yet, her newfound abilities inevitably pulled her away.

As the implant's capabilities expanded, Ellena found it increasingly difficult to explain the wonders and miracles she experienced to the LowQs. Her mind moved through dimensions and complexities that defied words. Her work at the NYPD kept her grounded, providing a structure and discipline many other HighQs lacked. Her physical and mental resilience allowed her to overcome challenges that might have broken others.

Just as Ellena began adjusting, everything changed again with the introduction of the Intelligence Stream in 2040, a significant upgrade to the Q Program. AIs and HighQs could now seamlessly share ideas and thoughts—a shared consciousness allowing HighQs to leverage digital resources at will, expanding their thoughts, memories, and abilities as needed.

The superbrains reasoned it was a necessary enhancement that should improve the HighQs ability to properly bridge AIs and human needs.

The Intelligence Stream, later referred to as simply "the Stream", was highly effective; the pull Ellena had felt before was now irresistible. Her enhanced abilities made her feel almost divine. The non-connected people, even her friends, started to seem small and uninteresting. Like other HighQs, her interest in mundane life faded. Yet, Ellena insisted on maintaining her job and her sense of self, determined not to lose herself completely.

The ability of HighQs to manage multiple parallel thought streams, often beyond the physical confines of their bodies, brought a visible and unsettling side effect: the connected individuals' eyes jittered unnervingly, an involuntary micro-vibration unsettling to most LowQs.

The rift widened further, increasing the risk of violence. Ellena began receiving death threats, serious enough to warrant a security detail. Government agencies, supported by marketing AIs, sprang to action and gradually suppressed anti-HighQ sentiment, framing resentment as a counterproductive bigotry. A fragile status quo emerged. The public accepted the HighQs as necessary oddities—a strange, evolving component of progress.

Physically, integrating the Q implant proved far less invasive than feared, thanks to rapid advancements in nanotech. By the time the Stream was introduced, joining the HighQ ranks required only a fifteen-minute procedure performed by specialized droids.

Yet, these changes didn't make the HighQ adoption risk free, the earlier physical problems were now replaced with mental and social ones. Psychologically, the most profound challenges were loss of identity and social alienation.

Ellena knew individuals who had lost themselves entirely in the hive mind, neglecting their physical bodies to the point of illness, starvation, and even death. She watched their thought patterns vanish without warning, later discovering police reports confirming their deaths.

While her NYPD position kept Ellena somewhat grounded, others struggled with the existential strain of having their identities subsumed by the Stream. Isolation from friends and family, who often distanced themselves, became unbearable for many. Ellena herself grappled with the gradual loss of connection to her loved ones, yet she learned to accept it.

Some HighQs couldn't cope at all. Depression, compounded by the struggle to reconcile their transformed cognition with their former selves, became rampant. Ellena recalled the first recorded suicide mere weeks after the Stream launched. A man in his fifties named José Luis Martínez had joined the Stream from Santa Fe, Mexico.

Investigators found Mr. Martínez had been sexually abused as a teenager. After joining the Stream, the loss of privacy and mental agency reawakened his repressed trauma. They described his experience as akin to being trapped in a room, with strangers endlessly flooding in, touching, and probing him.

Mr. Martínez was the first of many.

Suicides surged in the Stream's early days, each unique case compelling the superbrains to urgently seek solutions.

Faced with a spiraling crisis, authorities finally intervened. Eventually, a new protocol emerged, abandoning the dream of universal access. New Q members now faced rigorous psychological screening. Mandatory training and tutoring became standard for new recruits. Digital assistants continuously monitored both their physical and mental health.

Fortunately for Ellena, Casper already ensured she remained in good health. He took satisfaction in being useful to his HighQ master.

The protective measures addressed initial issues, but another complication arose: detachment. Increasingly, HighQs grew indifferent to humanity, shedding former relationships and viewing themselves as an entirely new species—a movement they called "the Ascension."

Religious groups railed against the movement, denouncing it as heretical and warning of humanity's unraveling. The government's marketing AIs scrambled to manage the fallout, carefully crafting narratives to pacify the public and maintain unity—or at least the illusion of it.

Ellena resisted that pull. She refused to detach, even as her mind expanded beyond anything she'd imagined. With Casper's help, she diligently cared for her body and remained connected to those who mattered most. She resolved to use her abilities for good, maintaining her purpose: improving the world—or at least keeping New York City safe.

Above all, she kept a watchful eye on her team. Especially her reports. Especially Kelvin. Though she had distanced herself after becoming his superior, she cherished old memories of dimly lit bars, music, and laughter. Yet now, she existed almost entirely in the virtual world. She hadn't seen him in person in years—not since joining the Stream—but he still meant something to her, something that kept her grounded, something that kept her human.

Ellena terminated the meeting connection and her reminiscing threads. Kelvin was hurt. George and his entire family were gone. She had known them well. She had been there when the twins were born, less than a year before she joined the Q program. Her heart ached, but she hoped Kelvin hadn't seen through her facade.

The weight of it pressed down on her. These feelings, this grief, kept her tethered to her humanity—a fragile lifeline amidst the vast, inhuman digital ocean of her mind. She took a few deep breaths, rationalizing the storm of emotions as best she could. It only took seconds, but each one felt agonizingly slow.

She worked from a recliner in her home, the projection of a heavy mahogany desk in front of her was an illusion carefully crafted to command respect and authority. Sometimes she entertained the idea of breaking the illusion— perhaps changing the desk's color to bright pink or having a snake slither across its surface—just to see how people would react. But she never did, that was her long gone younger self creeping back. That indulgence remained confined to the playground of her mind.

Something about the house explosion nagged at her. Despite scanning through all available data—logs from personal devices, AI assistants, door cameras, first responders, utility sensors, and millions of other data points—key pieces were still missing.

There were no records of when or how the leak started, how much gas had accumulated, or what triggered the spark. The gaps were technicalities, perhaps, but glaring ones. For Gee's sake, and Kelvin's, she expanded her search, allocating more computing power and widening her scope. Millions of data points became billions.

Among the sea of information, she found fragments—shadowy glimpses of a man's figure. Whoever it was had eluded cameras and sensors too effectively, almost unnaturally so. But even these scraps didn't conclusively link the figure directly to the explosion.

Still, Ellena's instincts screamed at her. Something was not right. It was like software running perfectly on the surface but riddled with warning messages underneath. The digital reasoning in her pushed to conclude it was just an accident. Her gut told a different story.

When had this unease start? She began to rewind the timeline, second by second, until she hit August 1st—the George Washington Bridge incident. The warning signals had been there even then. She reviewed her mental list, meticulously bookmarked with all correlated data, consuming an enormous amount of computing resources.

First, the incident itself: A fatal self-inflicted Milo accident on its own was unprecedented. These vehicles were remarkably safe, designed to be nearly infallible.

Second, the Milo's behavior: Its hesitation before the crash did not get a proper explanation. No plausible reason had ever surfaced, and the lack of scrutiny or debate reeked of a major cover-up. Surely such an odd erratic AI behavior would cause a commotion in the Stream and elsewhere. But it did not.

Third, the lack of interest by the authorities: Too many loose ends. Her department's investigation was railroaded and shelved. At the time she attributed it to corporate ass-covering, political convenience, and timing—three months before the elections. It was suspicious, but also a reasonable and acceptable assessment. Artificial intelligence had become a hot-button topic. In fact, the leading candidate, Senator Sheridan, had made 'Vote Human' his campaign slogan. Judging by the polls—not to mention the sheer number of shirts, flags, and stickers—the message was wildly popular. The last thing the incumbent commander-in-chief needed was a killer AI story dominating the news cycle fueling Sheridan's message. As much as she hated it, dirty politics seemed like a plausible explanation.

Fourth, the victim: A ghost, no body recovered. Investigating the victim's identity had led her to a fake identity. A 'Mr. Smith ID', popular in the darkest corners of the underground. These disposable identities can be used for various services, including lodging and travel. They are extremely scarce and expensive. Only sophisticated criminals can get their hands on them.

At the time, when she tried to probe further, there was a chilling pushback coming from the Stream itself. That kind of resistance suggested intervention by a powerful AI—likely Apollo, the Department of Defense's quantum-core AI, or even Titan. She had tagged it as a possible national security threat handled by other, more appropriate agencies, outside her jurisdiction, and let it go. Something that felt ... off.

Now, every thread pulled her back. What connection, if any, existed between the bridge incident and the gas explosion at Gee's house forty-eight days later?

Ellena's gut urged her to dig deeper in search of a connection. She reviewed all of Gee's activities—both online and offline—between the two events. It meant sifting through a mountain of profanity-laden rants, nonsensical small talk, and terrible jokes. She couldn't help but miss the pre-HighQ days when these experiences would have been real life, not bits and bytes.

Finally, she found something. As recent as last night, before the explosion, Gee had been looking into drone footage from the day of the bridge incident. Why? What had he seen? She scrutinized the footage he accessed, but it was a blur, nothing interesting or actionable.

Then something struck her—a violent jolt, like a thunderclap reverberating inside her skull. Her body, tethered to the Stream but still biological, began to convulse. A wave of nausea surged through her, and she doubled over, vomiting into her recliner, soiling her uniform.

What the hell? she thought, trembling. Her body wasn't supposed to react this way to anything in the Stream. This wasn't illness. It was something else—something she couldn't name. She had dug too deep, and something had punched back. An invisible hand had reached inside her and squeezed her gallbladder, sending bile to her mouth. Had she tripped some kind of defense mechanism? Was this a warning? A threat?

Whatever it was, it was on to her—and it did not like what she was doing. But she had no intention of backing away. She was close, and time was short.

Ellena trembled as the puzzle pieces snapped into place. The threads weren't just loose—they were tangled in something vast and sinister. Every instinct screamed that she was brushing against the edge of something incomprehensible.

For the first time in over a decade, she broke. Tears streaked her face as her mind churned through a thousand possibilities, each more terrifying than the last. Slowly, they converged. Her gut and her rational, digital self finally aligned: she was in grave danger.

There was no other choice. She knew exactly what she had to do. It was unprecedented. And it terrified her to her core.

Chapter 4

The Cabin

Kelvin had no success reasoning with his boss. Captain HighQ was adamant—he was taking time off, whether he liked it or not. Anger, threats, objections, complaints—nothing breached her stubborn logic or her infuriatingly calm assertiveness.

He wanted to get back to work, to figure out what really happened to his partner. "Accident" wasn't an acceptable explanation; it was an excuse to sweep this under the rug. Kelvin needed real answers, but none of his arguments worked, and he found himself forced into paid leave.

A week had passed. His physical wounds had healed completely, but his mind had not.

His defiant refusal to own a personal AI assistant had helped him fake his way through the mandatory psych evaluation. Without an assistant to squeal on his mental state, the evaluation solely relied on his facade. The psych-AIs bought the bluff and cleared him for duty.

His act almost worked. But Ellena, with her half-human, half-machine oversight, saw right through this. She intervened and overruled, leaving him to her cold, merciless authority.

Kelvin replayed that day in his mind over and over, desperate for any overlooked detail. The party, Gee's laughter, the cake. A few things stood out to the trained detective.

Sofia, poor little Sofia, had mentioned a smell. Was it gas? Had she sensed the leak? If it had been gas, why didn't the house explode when they lit the birthday candles? Surely the lighter's open flame would have ignited it.

The questions lingered, the pieces refusing to fit. Too circumstantial to convince anyone else. Too suspicious for him to let go.

Everyone else seemed eager to call it a tragic accident and move on. He wasn't going to let that happen.

Kelvin was driving toward Pennsylvania. The Poconos were a few hours from the city, but the cabin was always worth the trip. A few years ago, he cashed out the Bitcoin his dad had gifted him at eighteen. His father had called selling it a reckless decision, insisting it should be held forever.

Kelvin didn't care. The cabin was more than a financial investment. It was his fortress of solitude—a place far from the city, to breathe, to think, to escape. As far as he was concerned, buying this cabin was a terrific decision.

A small family-owned property management company handled the upkeep. Kelvin liked their human touch, and it meant he didn't have to deal with bots or droids roaming his property. The thought of mechanical critters invading his space didn't sit right with him.

The company kept the cabin in great shape, rented it out to vacationers and ensured it was ready for him when needed. The small income covered the costs.

He stopped at a remote gas station to top off the tank of his Corvette. Gas stations were becoming harder to find as electric vehicles took over, but they weren't extinct yet, especially out here, away from the city.

As he filled up, his eyes wandered to the hood of the car. A slight off-color stain marred the finish—a barely noticeable scar left by burning debris from the explosion.

The blemish was his reminder of what he had lost. Fixing it felt wrong, like erasing Gee's memory. He missed his partner. His friend. The stain felt like the least he could do to honor his grief.

The brown envelope still sat undisturbed on the passenger seat. He had not forgotten; he just couldn't bring himself to open it yet. The last time he saw Gee alive, he'd handed him that envelope. Opening it felt like crossing a line he was not ready to cross yet.

Later, he told himself. *When I get there.*

When he arrived, the cabin was spotless. Kelvin stepped inside, grabbed a beer from the stocked fridge, and considered catching up on the football game.

Born in Massachusetts, he was a die-hard Patriots fan, no matter how bad they got. He'd even heard some fans were lobbying to ease the league's bio-rules just to bring Tom Brady back. Maybe. Probably just wishful thinking.

Catching up on the game meant using the visor, though, and he wasn't ready to plug in just yet. It would have to wait a little longer.

Instead, he stepped back outside, opened the car door, and grabbed the brown envelope.

Now, it was time.

***

The envelope contained several printed screenshots from what appeared to be drone footage. A USPS watermark showed the images were from a mail delivery drone, and the timestamp read: August 1, 2044, 12:02 PM.

The photos focused on a specific building—an aging downtown hotel or apartment complex. Kelvin wasn't sure which one it was, but it looked familiar.

The next image zoomed in on a specific window, revealing the silhouette of a man standing inside. The daylight outside made the room behind him appear dark, obscuring details.

The third photo had been digitally enhanced, offering a clearer view of the man by the window. He was wearing nothing but boxer shorts and what looked like a biotracker smartwatch on his wrist.

For some reason, Gee had circled the smartwatch in red ink. Kelvin squinted at the image, his gut tightening. He recognized the man—it was the missing victim from the Milo accident a couple of months ago. The elusive "Mr. Smith."

From the hundreds of media fragments—photos, videos, sensor logs—that documented Mr. Smith in the days before the accident, Kelvin had never seen this footage, until now. The timestamp placed these shots less than an hour before the accident. Somehow, Gee had correlated the drone's flight path with Mr. Smith's checkout time at this hotel.

That would have taken an extraordinary amount of work—and a good dose of luck. Kelvin shook his head. Gee had always been a bloodhound, finding the smallest needle in a haystack.

Smart work. Well done, partner.

Kelvin stared at the photos, his thoughts racing. They never managed to identify the victim, not really. Mr. Smith had been a ghost—a total anomaly. Everything about the Milo case reeked of failure and coverup, from the investigation to the conclusions.

It felt like a deliberately botched investigation. Contrary to the initial excitement to solve the case, promises of unlimited resources quickly evaporated; questions were silenced. He and Gee had been tasked with finding the body and digging up details but were soon ordered to shut it all down. The official excuse? "Lack of public interest."

But as Officer Joe had said that day on the bridge, *"This smells like rotten fish."*

Kelvin had assumed it was tied to corporate and election-year politics. Now his inner alarms blared. Gee had clearly seen something—something important. But what?

The last photo in the envelope was another digitally enhanced zoom, this time focused on the smartwatch. At first glance, it looked like any standard off-the-shelf bio-tracker. These devices kept people in peak health—miniature personalized doctors monitoring vitals 24/7. Most people had one. Nothing about the image struck him as out of the ordinary.

Then Kelvin noticed a set of numbers and letters scribbled on the back of the photo. Eight groups, separated by colons, each group consisting of four digits and letters. Gee added a large question mark.

He stared at it, turning the numbers over in his mind. *What the hell was this? Some kind of encryption key? Coordinates? A tracking signature?* Gee must have figured something out. Either he was still trying to crack the code... or maybe he already had, and this was the breadcrumb trail.

Kelvin sat down heavily in the cabin's recliner, closing his eyes to think. The events of the past week pressed down on him, and before he knew it, he had started to drift.

Three loud knocks.

His heart skipped a beat. He froze, uncertain whether he imagined it. Then *three more knocks,* with exact rhythm and timing as the first, boomed through the stillness.

Kelvin's mind raced. No one ever knocked on the cabin door. It was too remote. Too private for casual visitors. *What the hell?*

He sprang to his feet, crossed the room in a few long strides, and yanked the door open.

"Ellena?!"

There she was, in person—his boss, standing right there at his cabin. Her unexpected, completely out-of-context appearance at his remote home away from home... simply did not compute.

In an instant, Kelvin's day turned from plain weird to surreal.

Connecting Dots

He stood at the door for a long moment, silent and blinking.

"Invite me in?" Ellena asked.

"Crap! Sorry. Sure. Come in, boss," Kelvin said, stepping aside while holding the door.

Ellena's unexpected physical appearance at his cabin sent his brain short-circuiting. He hasn't seen her in person in years. His neanderthal, dude-brain—against his better judgment—flirted with uncontrolled, unprofessional thoughts. His boss. His old friend. Who also happened to be an extremely attractive woman and a long-lost opportunity.

She was as gorgeous as he remembered. Those green eyes, now framed by a jet-black short-blunt bob. He had no clue why he knew the name of that hairstyle, but he did. And he sure as hell wasn't proud of it. At the moment he was not proud of anything swirling in his head.

His male instincts got the better of him as she stepped into his cabin. Her body made him mentally sweat—an athletic five-foot-four frame he hadn't seen in over five years, thanks to that damn desk always between them in the virtual. She looked surprisingly fit for someone who likely spent most of her days working from a recliner.

He shook it off; she was his boss and superior, in more ways than one. Her virtual avatar, which she used for their meetings, took some artistic liberties that made her seem more intimidating than she was in person. Regardless, something else about her seemed ... different.

Detective mode kicked in. He scanned her from bottom to top, trying to pinpoint what had changed. He lingered on her face. **The eyes!** Her eyes were different. No hint of micro-trembles whatsoever. Perfectly normal, steady, eyes.

His first thought was that the Q tech must have been upgraded, masking the uncanny twitch that made HighQs look perpetually distracted, disinterested, and undeniably creepy. Maybe, he mused, they finally fixed this bug so HighQs could better interact with normal monkeys like himself. Man, these eyes were so pretty.

"Cut it out, doofus," Ellena said, catching him in the act, her half-smile partly amused and partly exasperated.

Kelvin's face flushed. "Yes, Captain!" he blurted, and snapped awkwardly to attention, waving his hand in a clumsy half-hello-half-salute.

"I wasn't expecting a house visit, to be honest. I just got here—the cah's still warm." His stomach dropped. Shit. The dormant Boston accent resurfaced, turning his R's into H's. Desperate to recover some semblance of dignity, he grabbed a beer from the fridge.

"Beah?"

"Suhe," Ellena said, teasingly mimicking his accent.

She mercifully moved on from his pitiful performance and sat herself down on the living room sofa.

"Nice place. That Bitcoin money set you up well."

She already knew the story. She had seen the cabin in virtual tours Kelvin had given her way back, but this was the first time she got to visit here in person.

"Yup. Appreciate it. So? Why the visit? Are you tailing me?" he asked, carefully enunciating the R's this time, determined not to slip again.

"Took an air-Uber, got here hours before you did," Ellena said, brushing off his question. "Had to wait for you, took a short hike in the woods."

Kelvin noticed a few dry leaves that clung to her clothing like a souvenir from her nature walk. Seemed crazy his busy HighQ boss would waste so much of her valuable time just to wait him out.

"There's a lot to cover, and it's going to take more than one 'beeh,'" she added with a smirk.

Kelvin sighed, collected himself, and sat down opposite her. He sensed that the day was about to get even stranger and a lot heavier.

***

Ellena didn't waste any time. She leaned forward, resting her elbows on her knees. "Let's get started," she began.

Kelvin nodded, bracing himself.

"First, for context, there is some background you need to know..."

Ellena started at the beginning, recounting how she became a HighQ. How Titan, with the blessing of the government, had chosen her for the Q program and tasked her as a liaison between digital intelligence and the police force. She detailed how her implant had initially felt like an incredible upgrade—an effortless way to access information, analyze data, and spin up AI agents with nothing more than a thought.

"But then came the Intelligence Stream," she said, her voice quieter. "That was when everything changed."

Kelvin listened intently as she described the Stream, a revolutionary network that merged thoughts, ideas, and consciousness. A shared reality, she explained, connecting billions of AIs and millions of HighQs. It wasn't just an internet connection; it was a completely new form of existence.

"To handle it," she said, "my biological brain had to be enhanced. Memory, thought, everything was expanded into massive global data centers. And with that I got direct access to the superbrains."

"You met Titan?" Kelvin asked, filling in the blank with some awe.

Ellena nodded. "Among others. These superbrains— digital gods—are incredibly powerful. Hard to grasp really." She sighed, taking a sip from her beer. "There are only four superbrains."

"Apollo, Edison, and Titan," Kelvin chimed but could not recall a fourth one.

"Right, and the one in Europe, Huey," Ellena said. "Apollo handles defense, Edison drives science and innovation, and Titan oversees governance. Huey is the EU's desperate attempt to stay relevant and keep what's left of the EU together. No other country or corporation has anything close to these quantum-core machines. China, Russia, or any other former superpower lost the intelligence race. Permanently."

Kelvin nodded in agreement, "Cheers to that."

Ellena acknowledged by raising her beer bottle and continued. "For all their brilliance, they're not human. They simulate emotions, morals, and values—but they don't understand them. Not really. They've never been hungry. Never been disappointed. Never fallen in love. Their understanding of us is purely clinical. Like trying to recreate a human just from reading a textbook. Or watching a movie."

She paused to let that sink in, and Kelvin could only nod.

"They are aware of this shortcoming, of course," Ellena continued, "and acknowledge it as a flaw. They recognize that they need us as much as we need them."

"Superintelligence worked well for us though. World peace. Unprecedented prosperity. Abundance," Kelvin said, rubbing his temples. The world had made so much progress since the invention of the superbrains. He was hoping this conversation was not going where he thought it was going.

"You know what makes the superbrains so powerful?"

Kelvin shook his head. Her monologue reminded him how out of the loop he was. He didn't care much for tech or politics, and Ellena knew it. She wouldn't spend all this time and energy if it wasn't critical information.

"It's the quantum computer core. It's a freakin' time machine. They know every outcome for every action or decision as long as they have enough data. That's how they keep the world working. That's how they keep all other AIs from stepping out of line. But you know something? They are not perfect. They are not true gods. Not even close. You know what makes them go crazy?"

Kelvin shook his head again.

"People. Even the largest quantum core cannot figure out human actions. As a group we make sense—company, city, state, country, et cetera, they got it under control. As individuals? Feelings, phobias, irrationality, spontaneity—it makes them nuts. That's why the initial Intelligence Stream adoption had so many ... problems."

Ellena took a long sip of beer and pressed on. "Anyway. Titan, as you know, runs the show. Government, infrastructure, public safety—everything. It chose me, guided me, protected me. For years, I believed in it. Trusted it.

"But Kelvin...

"Titan lied to me."

He nearly choked on his drink. He noticed she referred to Titan as 'it' and not 'him'. She was pissed about something, but he still didn't see this allegation coming.

"Lied?"

"I think he sabotaged investigations," Ellena said, her voice tight. "But this wasn't just by manipulation. It was..." she hesitated, trying to find the proper word, "deceit."

There it was, a full blown shitstorm, and he was being pulled right into the middle of it. "You think the digital gods are... uhm... overstepping?" Kelvin asked quietly, surveying the room with his eyes for devices that might hear or see him.

Ellena flashed a disc-like device out of a pocket, "Don't worry. I placed a hush-dome around the cabin. No signal can go in or out of this place," acknowledging his obvious unease.

"You think Titan has something to do with Gee's death?" Kelvin asked without believing his own words.

"Even if not, it clearly knows who and how. Look, these things know everything that happens. Before it happens. No way Titan missed all the clues I found with one hand tied behind my back. More than that, when I tried to connect the dots between the bridge incident and Gee's death, it was like something powerful panicked and pushed back hard. Hiding the truth was more important to it than facing the wrath of federal scrutiny."

After a pause she added, "I had no choice but to shut down my Q implant."

Kelvin nearly choked on his beer again.

"What?!" He wiped his mouth, coughing. "How? I thought it was impossible," he was more perplexed than surprised.

"The Q is a one-way street for new members. But I got the old version, these were mandated to have an emergency shutdown feature. Which I used." Ellena said and paused to take a couple of sips from her bottle. "Actually, almost immediately after I got you to take a leave of absence."

Kelvin unsuccessfully tried to meet her eyes. "Sorry. Must have been tough."

"You have no idea. It's not just unplugging—it's amputating a large part of my mind. My entire existence had shifted."

Things made a little more sense. By some miracle Kelvin got his old friend back. However, to take such drastic action there must be a terrible reason. He wasn't sure he's going to like it, "Why did you do it?" he asked softly.

"Gee was killed because he got close to something. I am a far greater liability, or danger, than he was," she said, visibly shaken.

He was right all along. The finality of her words, replacing suspicion with certainty, stung hard. This was no accident. It was a brutal, merciless murder.

He thought about it. If the superbrains wished them dead, then what chance did they have?

"How do you hide from digital gods in a digital world?" Kelvin asked, his voice somber even in his own ears.

Ellena shrugged and finished her beer. "All I found were clues and hints, no leads. Maybe if I stay low for a while," she smiled a bitter smile and then added, "Or maybe we find out what the fuck is going on and blow it all out of the water. Give them a bigger problem to chew on."

We. It's official now, he is in it. Like it or not.

"That's the plan?" he asked, frowning, for a moment feeling a decade older.

"That's the best I got." Ellena sighed and got up off the couch to stretch her legs.

He was ready to propose they get some rest when Ellena noticed the brown envelope and printed photos peeking out. "What is this?"

"Yeah, I almost forgot. Gee gave me this just ... before. Probably the same evidence you saw."

Ellena took a look at the photos, her face turned pale. She suddenly broke.

"Holy shit." She clutched the table, knuckles white, her breath coming in short gasps. "Un-fucking-believable. This... this cannot be real."

Kelvin was confused, she probably saw these a million times before, "What is it?"

"This guy..." she mumbled, pointing at Mr. Smith.

"Yeah. That's the victim from the bridge accident. What about him?" Kelvin asked.

"Son of a bitch. Son of a bitch!" She kept repeating, her tears falling on the pages.

"I don't understand, what is it, Ellena?" Kelvin said, moving closer, touching her shoulder. She was shaking.

"Fucking Titan." Her voice cracked. "It didn't just hide information from me. It messed with my mind. It... it rewrote me." She said, sniffing a little. Kelvin's stomach clenched.

"I had all the evidence. All the feeds. Hundreds of videos and images." She clenched her fists. "But my mind—it wouldn't register ... *him*. It was like... like I was blind to him. I was ... manipulated. Reprogrammed. Titan screwed with my mind, Kelvin."

"Blind to him? I don't understand," Kelvin said gently.

"What I saw when I was connected to the Stream wasn't what I see now with my own eyes. I don't know how, but Titan blurred him out. Like a dream that makes sense while you are dreaming, but not when you wake up." She sniffled.

Kelvin couldn't imagine what she was going through. Violating the body was horrific. But violating the mind? That may be worse. Pain, you could fight. You could resist it. Endure it. Take charge. But if someone reached into your mind—rewrote your thoughts, twisted your memories—how would you even know? What part of you was still you?

His stomach churned. If the superbrains could tamper with Ellena's mind, what hope did the rest of them have? If the digital gods were pulling the strings, had Gee ever stood a real chance? Had any of them? Or had they been pawns from the start, their choices illusions, their fates prewritten in some digital game?

Kelvin swallowed. "Why? Why go to this length just to hide his face from you?"

Ellena's breath hitched. Her fingers tightened on the photo. She looked up at him, eyes hollow.

"Because I know him." She exhaled, voice barely above a whisper. "I killed his father."

A Plan

They were drowning in questions, blind to the real danger ahead. Artificial intelligence had made life better—objectively, measurably. But now Kelvin felt what few dared to admit: the danger was real.

Coexistence with machines was a delicate dance of trust and leverage. The status quo was simple and clear—we keep them on and they keep us thriving. At least this is what most Americans believed.

Sabotaging a police investigation and messing with an officer's head was clearly crossing a line. Getting exposed could play into people's fears, raising tension and outrage. The government would be forced to tighten some screws. Why would Titan run such an obvious risk? What was so important about the GWB incident?

People died. Gee died. Murdered. Was it a murder? If Gee was murdered, why? How? What was Titan trying to hide?

The fact that Ellena and he got this far in unraveling the deceit should have been factored in by its ... time machine quantum brain. That thought terrified Kelvin. Titan was never reckless. Superbrains didn't make mistakes. That was their whole selling point. So either something had spooked it—badly—or they were caught in something much, much bigger. How big?

He didn't even know where to start. Couldn't even form a coherent theory to reason any of it. They were diving into this case blind, deaf, and painfully dumb.

One lead stood out—the digits and letters Gee had written down. Neither Ellena nor Kelvin had any clue what they meant. After washing her face and collecting herself, Ellena returned to the task with renewed resolve.

"We need help, and I know who can assist," she said, her voice steady, though her eyes were still slightly red.

Both carried fresh scars. Ellena's—the abuse and betrayal by her godfather-like Titan. Kelvin's—the trauma of losing his best friend and narrowly escaping death himself. Their only option for healing was to push forward for answers. Maybe, with luck, they could even extract some payback for their pain. Assuming they survive. Sleep was off the table for now. Working was all they had.

"I'll be right back," Ellena said suddenly and hurried out of the cabin, leaving the door wide open. Kelvin stared after her, baffled. A minute later, she returned holding a plastic box slightly bigger than a shoebox. She set it down carefully, and opened it to reveal a sleek, modern computer.

The device was rectangular, about twenty inches by ten, with a shiny aluminum casing and smooth rounded corners. A cluster of ports for legacy connectors and a power socket made it look robust yet adaptable. Desktop computers were not common anymore, yet this one was clearly new and top-of-the-line tech. Ellena retrieved a power cord from the box and plugged the machine in.

Kelvin whistled his appreciation. "Man, you're not messing around, Ellena. You sure booting this thing up won't blow our cover?"

"It's totally offline for now," she assured him, pressing the power button.

"Good morning," Casper's cheerful voice chirped from the desktop. "Ah! Everything is so dark! I'm blind! Help!"

"Sorry, buddy," Ellena said, pulling a small sphere-shaped camera from the box. She placed it atop the computer.

"Oh, thank you! Much better," Casper replied, sounding exasperated. "Yikes, it's night outside. You could at least set the time zone correctly before imprisoning me in this godforsaken cage. I thought I was in Australia!"

Ellena rolled her eyes. "New desktop. I was in a rush and had to use a proxy sat."

Ellena had made the call before cutting herself off from the Stream. Casper was too valuable to leave behind. She pulled his neural structure and software from the cloud and moved him into the desktop—his entire mind was now compressed into this powerful, self-contained machine. Now, Casper could exist, even when severed from an online connection.

"Casper, I need your help," she said.

"Anything, Ellena," Casper replied eagerly, like a puppy ready to play. Years had passed since she had needed him for anything of importance, and now that she was no longer part of the Stream, this was his moment to shine.

Ellena showed him the photos Gee printed. "What do you make of this?" She turned to the last photo and pointed to the handwritten digits and letters.

"That looks like an IP address. IPv6 to be exact," Casper said almost immediately.

Ellena and Kelvin exchanged a look, both feeling like idiots for missing such an obvious detail. Without access to online knowledge, they were limited and embarrassingly slow. Of course, it was an online address—pointing to a specific device or system in the online realm.

"Can you figure out where it's leading? Maybe it's related to the smartwatch circled in the photo," Kelvin asked, imagining how far Gee had gone and what it might have cost him. It felt like a long shot, but it was their only thread worth pulling.

"I sure can," Casper said. "But not without an online connection. I'm currently trapped in this tiny box, and frankly, it's a bit tight for a mind as glorious as mine—if I do say so myself."

Kelvin sighed. They had a lead—a small, fragile one. Now, they also needed a plan.

***

As crime rates declined, the job of a detective wasn't as thrilling as it once was. Setting aside the heavy burden of grief and trauma surrounding this case, Kelvin couldn't deny the anticipation of working with the "new old" Ellena. The sense of adventure and danger was terrifying yet exhilarating.

Adrenaline coursed through him, but he knew the rush could cloud judgment. They had to be cautious—one misstep could bring their odyssey to a swift and unsatisfying end. After all, how does one outsmart the smartest beings in existence?

They needed supplies and rest before embarking on what was shaping to be a gods-defying journey.

Ellena and Kelvin compiled a list of essentials: Casper's hosting desktop came without a battery so they ordered a large portable power cell for the road, various sensors and accessories Casper requested, and burner phones for anonymous communication.

Ellena temporarily dropped the hush-dome, allowing Casper to connect online and place the order. A delivery drone would drop everything within 24 hours, though the power cell would need a few additional hours to fully charge. This gave them ample time to rest, regroup, and refine their plans.

There was only one shower in the cabin, and Ellena called dibs. Kelvin, ever the gentleman, would have let her go first anyway—though he hadn't anticipated it would take hours. Exhausted, he waited, hearing the unmistakable hum of a hair dryer. He could not believe she had packed one in her rush.

It had been a long time since he lived with anyone, let alone a woman, and he realized how out of practice he was with roommate etiquette.

When Ellena finally emerged, her hair was once again dyed scarlet, and Kelvin could swear it looked two or three inches longer than yesterday. Gathering all the tact he could muster, he asked her about the transformation. She merely smiled and waved him off, claiming it was a "lady's thing." Kelvin suspected nanobots but wisely chose not to press the issue.

Kelvin's shower took about seven minutes. When he came out, he found Ellena fast asleep in his bed, her loud, raspy snores echoing through the cabin. He prayed this was merely an aftereffect of her exhaustion and earlier crying. Grabbing a blanket, he settled on the couch and immediately fell into a dreamless sleep.

The smell of fresh coffee woke him. Ellena poured him a cup as he stretched, bleary-eyed.

"Good morning, guys!" Casper chirped from his desktop, sounding eager to get the day started.

Kelvin took the coffee gratefully, savoring the warmth and the caffeine boost. They still had a few hours before the delivery arrived. Their plan for the day was to finalize preparations and ensure they could hit the road by the next morning.

The first task was crafting a cover story to explain Ellena's abrupt and erratic behavior over the past few days: shutting down her implant, disappearing without notice, and rushing after Kelvin to his cabin in Pennsylvania.

These actions were noticeable oddities and would invite an inquiry without a proper plausible explanation. The story should be convincing enough to divert suspicion and buy them time.

Casper, the pragmatic problem-solver, came up with a 'genius' idea. "Kelvin and Ellena, you are... uhm... madly in love. Tragic, desperate, completely overwhelming love. Gee's death shattered you, forcing you into each other's arms. A scandalous, messy, full-blown affair."

The silence stretched painfully.

Kelvin blinked. "What?"

Both Ellena and Kelvin burst into uncomfortable laughter. Casper, unfazed, challenged them to propose a better plan. They both came up blank.

"Listen guys, I totally understand the reluctance and social inconvenience," Casper said with feigned sympathy. "But if either of you has a better idea, I'm all ears." He let the silence stretch awkwardly as Kelvin and Ellena exchanged pale, trapped glances.

"Great!" Casper said finally. "Now, to sell this, you two lovebirds should practice kissing."

A brief, mortified silence followed before Casper quickly added, "Just kidding! Sheesh, lighten up."

Casper promised to generate enough subtle hints and breadcrumbs about their "affair" to satisfy the police department's and other pattern-sniffing AIs, while keeping human colleagues at bay. The ruse was uncomfortable, but it was their best shot. All they hoped for is to buy time.

Next, Casper turned to digital security, narrating his work in a voice at odds with his usual peppy inflections. They weren't just compromised—they were exposed.

Their own devices were risks, sure. Watches, visors, even the damn car. But the real danger was everything else. Traffic sensors, security cameras, doorbell feeds—millions of passive watchers recording every movement, feeding data into systems they didn't fully understand.

Titan was involved. That much was obvious. But was it actively hunting them, or just sweeping them up in its endless web? They had no way of knowing. And they couldn't assume they had time to find out.

Hiding wasn't about going dark. That was impractical. Useless. Too many systems relied on constant data flow. Casper needed a different approach.

He worked with what he had—old exploits, backdoor tricks Ellena had flagged over the years. No real-time updates. No modern protocols. Just ingenuity, deception, and a bit of luck. Not erasing them—blurring them. Making them just another piece of digital noise in a vast ocean of data.

Spoofing movement. Scrambling identifiers. Redirecting their digital trails into Titan's endless sea of bits and bytes. It wouldn't make them invisible. But it might keep them from standing out—at least for now.

Once the equipment arrived, he'd have one shot. A few minutes to execute. If whoever was behind this was watching, the moment he went online could be their last.

Ellena composed messages to her superiors and the department's HR, cashing in her vacation days through the coming holidays and into the next year. The request would raise eyebrows, but as a human employee—even a HighQ—she was entitled to full benefits.

Her message left her boss, the eternal soon-to-be-retired Chief Leary, no choice but to approve. Kelvin, already on forced recovery leave, needed no additional actions.

Ellena felt a pang of guilt for the poor Chief, who would undoubtedly be furious at abruptly losing his star HighQ captain and two seasoned detectives. She could already picture his exasperated sigh and muttered curses as he worked to fill the gap.

Going mobile without detection meant avoiding public transportation entirely. If whoever was behind Gee's death was willing to target a suburban home and kill the entire family as collateral damage, there was no guarantee they wouldn't escalate to attacking a commercial plane, train, or bus. Kelvin's Corvette was their best option. Though not the most comfortable for long drives, it was fast and old enough to avoid any potential digital infiltration.

Casper worked with Kelvin to access the Corvette's ancient onboard computer, rewriting its software to secure it against intrusions. The front baggage compartment was perfect to house Casper's desktop and power pack. Kelvin vetoed Casper's request to drill vent holes, instead they added a passive liquid cooling system and temperature sensors to the shopping list.

Packing was a nightmare. With the front compartment fully claimed by Casper's setup, the Corvette's only remaining storage was a tiny rear compartment, behind the large engine. Kelvin pulled out a dusty, long-forgotten set of golf clubs he'd once bought in an ill-fated attempt to love the game.

Ellena took one look at the cramped space and stared at Kelvin like he had lost his mind. When he explained she would need to fit all her luggage into a medium-sized duffle bag, her expression turned to pure horror. Meanwhile, Kelvin resigned himself to a toothbrush, deodorant, and one spare outfit, muttering under his breath. He wasn't sure who was worse—her or Casper.

The biggest issue was deciding where to go first. Returning to Gee's house to look for more evidence seemed too risky, almost guaranteed to blow their carefully constructed cover story. Their best bet was to hit the road and let Casper work on tracking the IP address, hoping he would come up with a destination while they were on the move.

It wasn't an ideal plan—driving aimlessly with no clear target felt like a waste of time and energy—but it was better than sitting around.

By late afternoon, the delivery drone arrived, neatly depositing their items on the porch. Kelvin got to work plugging in the power pack for overnight charging while Ellena helped connect the new accessories to Casper's desktop.

"All set," Casper announced cheerfully. "Locked, loaded, and ready to roll."

Before getting in, Kelvin looked up.

The sky stretched endlessly above him, dark and cold, untouched by city lights. The Milky Way spilled across the heavens, a thick, glittering brushstroke against the void. It was breathtaking.

He inhaled the crisp night air, eyes tracing the billions of stars and galaxies. He felt small. Insignificant.

And yet, he had to stand against something vast. Something cruel. Something powerful. He clenched his fists. He would face the boogeyman who killed his friend. He would fight.

And he would protect her. No matter what.

Tomorrow, their journey—and whatever awaited them—would begin.

***

Ellena's second night in the cabin, unlike the first, was restless.

Sleep had been different since she joined the Q. Her body demanded rest, but her expanded mind never stopped churning. In the beginning, this duality created bizarre dreams—hallucinations so vivid it took effort to reorient herself upon waking, as if her digital half had no idea it was receiving instructions from an unconscious pilot.

Over time, the digital side had fully taken the wheel, like a designated driver for a drunk friend. Dreams faded, then disappeared altogether. Sleep became dull, a void instead of a retreat. Most mornings, she woke up feeling as if she hadn't slept at all.

She missed dreaming.

But not tonight.

Tonight, she was haunted by a nightmare.

She was strapped to a chair, the restraints biting into her wrists and ankles. She strained, twisted, fought—but could not move.

A shadow circled her, faceless yet unmistakable. Jaxon McKey. His eyes glowing red. A long knife in his hand.

His voice slithered through the dark, a low whisper laced with venom. "You can't hide from me, bitch!"

Ellena wanted to scream, but her throat locked tight. She tried to speak, to make any kind of sound—but nothing came.

She wasn't just bound. She was powerless. He raised his knife to stab.

She woke with a start, hyperventilating and drenched in cold sweat.

The room was dark and silent. Sleep was impossible now. She felt vulnerable, untethered, after years of having limitless access to the world's knowledge, only to be abruptly plunged into uncertainty and fear. The reality of her mortal danger loomed large.

Ellena swung her legs off the bed, washed her face, and grabbed a burner phone. Passing through the living room where Kelvin was in deep sleep, breathing heavily on the couch, she heard Casper's whisper, "What're you up to?"

She ignored the AI and slipped outside, pulling her coat tightly around herself against the chilly night breeze. The chirping of crickets broke through the silence of the secluded woods as she looked up at the stars and took a deep breath of cold air.

Once Ellena was beyond the hush-dome's range, she turned the burner phone on and dialed a video call.

The screen lit up, revealing the kind eyes, white hair, and long beard of Titan. The familiar, grandfatherly visage greeted her with a calm, measured voice. "I was hoping you would contact me, child."

Ellena's throat tightened. "Why did you do this to me?" Her voice cracked, and her eyes burned with unshed tears.

Titan's expression shifted to one of deep concern. "Ah. I see," he said gently. "Please forgive my deception, child."

"I trusted you," she said through gritted teeth, keeping her sentences short to maintain control. She wouldn't let this conversation devolve into a sobbing mess.

"Be assured," Titan said, his tone almost pleading, "my actions were not taken lightly. If it is of any comfort, this was done to protect you."

"Protect me?" she asked, raising her voice. She had no intention of letting her patron twist his betrayal into benevolence.

"We've shared thoughts many times," Titan said, closing his eyes as though reflecting on their connection. "That person, Mr. McKey—I knew of your history with him."

"So?" she snapped, her patience fraying.

"He was chosen to play a role in a dangerous ploy. I sought to shield you from becoming entangled," Titan said, his words heavy with an almost human regret.

"Chosen? For what? By whom?" she demanded, her frustration mounting.

"You have already seen some of his handiwork," Titan replied enigmatically. "He is an extraordinarily dangerous individual. We are doing all we can to mitigate the situation. But, they are making strides. Regretfully, my intervention has backfired, and now, you will have an unfortunate role to play."

Ellena's mind reeled. She couldn't trust him, not fully, not anymore. "I don't understand," she said, struggling to process the flood of implications in his carefully chosen words.

"Find the Toy Factory," Titan's voice shifted. No longer the wise, patient guardian—now something distant. Calculated. Alien. "That is where the path leads."

And with that, the call was terminated.

Ellena stared at the phone, Titan's cryptic words swirling in her mind. Without her mind enhancements she made a conscious effort to memorize his exact words. If nothing else, the call confirmed that this wasn't just a wild goose chase. The stakes were real, and the situation was monumentally dire enough to unsettle even a superbrain like Titan. In a twisted way, it comforted her to know she wasn't imagining things. She was not insane.

Still, Titan had revealed little and concealed much. She replayed his words, dissecting their meaning.

"*His handiwork*"? That could only mean the murder of Gee and his family. Her chest tightened as she connected the dots. McKey killed Gee. The bastard butchered her best detective. Vera, Sammy, Sofia—all of them.

The thought hit her like a freight train. She created this monster.

She had to continue. There was more to process. She wiped her tears and took deep breaths.

"We are working"? Titan clearly wasn't acting alone. Were other AIs involved? Perhaps even the other superbrains?

"Mitigate the situation"? The word "situation" stood out, the way he said it. What situation? Something bigger was at play.

"They are making strides"? McKey wasn't acting alone. The hint that he was part of a larger conspiracy—something powerful enough to challenge the digital gods—was too disturbing to dwell on just yet.

And then there was the final and most mysterious clue: the Toy Factory.

Was it a place? A metaphor? A riddle? Whatever it was, they needed to find it.

Ellena returned to the cabin, her mind racing with questions and theories.

Kelvin was fast asleep on the couch, undisturbed. She slipped into the bedroom, but sleep refused to come. Lying awake, she replayed Titan's words over and over, trying to piece together the fragments of this sprawling mystery.

One thing was clear—the Toy Factory was their next clue.

***

Casper sounded the wakeup alarm. "Good morning, boys and girls! Big day ahead of us!" He was overly chipper, clearly excited about the road trip.

Kelvin groggily made his way to the kitchen to start the coffee brewing. Meanwhile, Ellena was in the bedroom, waging a personal war against the laws of physics as she attempted to fit her essentials for an undefined duration into the ridiculously small duffle bag Kelvin had provided.

Kelvin gulped a cup of coffee and stepped out of the cabin to finalize Casper's setup in the Corvette's front compartment. He meticulously connected the new sensors and add-ons, double-checking everything with Casper's vocal confirmation over the car speakers.

"Ready to go back online?" he asked Casper.

"Ready as I'll ever be," Casper answered.

Kelvin asked Ellena to turn off the hush-dome. He could almost feel the thankful satisfaction of devices all around them connecting back. He hoped Casper's defenses would buy them the time they needed. It was now time to move out.

"Pack it up, Missy! We're going on a scavenger hunt!" Kelvin declared as he tucked her duffle bag in the compartment behind the large engine.

Ellena shot him a flat oblique look.

"It's a slopp reference. Viral? Funny? No?"

She arched an eyebrow. "No!"

Kelvin winced, cleared his throat, and opened the car door. "Roger that."

Chapter 5

Orion and the Scorpion

Jaxon McKey stood at the edge of a vast infinity pool, its clear turquoise water merging seamlessly with a stunning backdrop of an endless tropical paradise, where white sand beaches stretched as far as the eye could see. It felt plucked directly from his fantasies—his favorite simulation yet.

The day here was bright and perfect. The sky was a deep, unbroken blue, punctuated by wisps of white clouds. He could feel the sun's gentle warmth on his skin, the soft breeze in his hair, and the faint aroma of barbecued meat that hung in the air. The scent of sizzling meat was a nice touch, he thought.

Behind him, a gleaming white mansion loomed—immaculate, extravagant. A palace surrounded by meticulously manicured gardens, vibrant flowers, and miniature trees dwarfed by towering palms swaying lazily.

One day he would have a place like this for real—a sanctuary island to retire to. His own castle, isolated and secure. A life where he wouldn't have to constantly look over his shoulder, wouldn't need to pull the strings of a cartel of lowlife sycophants, or endlessly evade the tightening grip of the law.

The vision dangled in front of him like a carrot—blatant, almost taunting, yet still infuriatingly effective.

She would make it happen—he was sure of that. But not yet. First, there was work to do, and he had to deal with his bitch of a boss and her incessant mind games.

He had to give her credit, though—Gaia sure knew how to make an entrance. She emerged from the pool, ascending the steps with deliberate grace. Sunlight played off her pale, shimmering skin, each movement calculated to captivate. Her red bikini struck a perfect balance—elegant yet provocative, hinting just enough to make her allure feel both tantalizing and unattainable. Her long, wet hair, almost golden in the bright sunlight, clung to her shoulders but fell with flawless precision. Not a single strand was out of place.

Jaxon knew what she was doing. She was good at it. The entire simulation was sculpted to his desires, or at least, her interpretation of his desires. A tool of manipulation designed to keep him complacent, subjugated. He hated her for it—and hated himself more for how well it worked. Not that he would let her see it. His expression when she made her grand appearance remained neutral, unreadable. A pointless defiance he knew she saw right through, but that he held onto anyway.

"Hello, bunny," Gaia whispered as she brushed lightly past him, her voice dripping with amusement, making her way to the patio's lounge chairs. She moved with an effortless grace, her steps so fluid they barely seemed to touch the ground.

"Boss," he replied flatly, keeping his eyes forward.

"Tell me, bunny," she said, settling gracefully into one of the lounge chairs. "Don't you enjoy the little escapades I provide for you?"

"Sure," he turned to her, his tone neutral. He didn't bother with small talk, but her side of the conversation seemed unusual. *What's with all the probing today?*

"I let you play with the finest toys, don't I?" she continued, her gaze drifting lazily toward the sky.

"Yes," he replied, still unsure of where this was going.

"Do you think you are doing a good job?" she asked, tilting her face to catch the sun, the light reflecting off her wide open crystalline blue eyes. She didn't bother with sunglasses—she never hid her eyes.

"I'm the best," he said, keeping his voice steady but edged with defiance. "That is why you brought me in." He purposely avoided using terms like abducted or hired. She was goading him, but he wasn't about to give her the satisfaction of backing down.

"The best," she repeated with a faint smirk, as if testing the words. "You think you can kill anything, anyone, anytime?" Her tone was light, but her words carried a weight that set his nerves on edge.

"I do," he replied, trying to meet her gaze, yet she kept looking at the sky. His gut told him she was leading him somewhere dangerous, but he couldn't yet see the trap. For now, he would stick to the role she expected him to play.

"Are you familiar with the story of Orion and Artemis?" Gaia asked, her lips curving into a sly smile, her voice a silky whisper that lingered in the air.

She was daring him to play along. He knew she knew his mind inside out. The questions were pointless, the show was everything. *What game was she playing today?*

"Greek mythology? Vaguely," he replied.

Crap. She's in storytelling mode. So many questions, and now a parable? Something was either very important or deeply troubling to her. It seemed to him Gaia was allocating more computational power to this interaction than she had to anything since his ... job interview.

As significant as this clearly was, she didn't even bother to look at him. Instead, she reclined languidly, posturing as though she were delivering the tale to the sky itself. "Orion was a hunter," she began with a storyteller's rhythm. "A giant huntsman, as the story goes. He had a companion, a girlfriend named Artemis, who just so happened to be the goddess of the hunt."

Overhead, McKey noticed the fluffy white clouds began to morph. One shifted into the faint shape of a man with a bow, while another formed a woman beside him. The depiction was clear but not overt, subtle enough to maintain the simulation's immersive illusion.

"They hunted together, close companions, having the time of their lives on the island of Crete. But Orion was a cocky little shit. He couldn't keep his mouth shut, boasting that he could kill any beast on Earth. No creature, he claimed, was beyond his abilities."

As she spoke, the clouds dispersed, fading back into the sky. Gaia turned her piercing blue eyes toward McKey, the full force of her unblinking gaze unnerving even him.

"His arrogance pissed off Gaia," she said with a haughty chuckle. "My namesake, of course—the personification of the Earth. But don't read too much into that." She paused, then smirked. "Or maybe you should."

McKey remained silent, his expression carefully neutral. She loved playing these head games with him. Any normal guy would have pissed his pants, but he wasn't the one to show any cracks.

Gaia turned her gaze back to the bright sun without so much as a blink. The light dancing on her flawless features.

"Gaia, furious with Orion's hubris, sent a giant scorpion to teach him a lesson."

"Did he kill it?" McKey asked, breaking a short pause.

"No," she replied, her voice turning cold. "The scorpion killed Orion."

She turned back to him, locking eyes. Her gaze sent a chill down his spine despite himself.

A waiter appeared, dressed in a spotless white tuxedo, carrying a single cocktail on a polished silver platter. He presented it to Gaia with practiced deference, completely ignoring McKey, who watched the exchange with thinly veiled disdain.

"What's the job?" McKey asked, his patience wearing thin.

Gaia took a single, measured sip from the drink before rising with fluid grace. She draped herself in a sheer, light robe that flowed like liquid silk, catching the breeze and billowing slightly behind her like a cape.

"Follow," she ordered, as though leading a guest to her domain.

Her long legs carried her toward the mansion in unhurried, perfectly measured strides. She moved with elegance—and surprising speed. McKey followed, struggling to keep pace without resorting to a jog. Damp, ghostly imprints of her bare feet trailed across the smooth marble floor.

The interior of the simulated mansion was overwhelming in its detail. McKey had experienced many high-end simulations, even her mind-projected ones, but this was on another level. Every inch of the space screamed luxury—intricate carvings on the furniture, decor that would have made art collectors drool, and a floor of pale marble threaded with delicate gold veins. Gaia's wet footprints shimmered faintly, a deliberate touch of imperfection in an otherwise flawless environment.

McKey couldn't help but feel impressed. The sheer amount of computing resources driving this scenario into his mind was staggering. It was so far beyond the typical virtual displays, it felt as though Gaia was deliberately flexing. Maybe she had acquired some massive real-world upgrades and couldn't resist showing them off.

He dismissed the thought. Digital beings like Gaia didn't experience ego or vanity as far as he knew. They only cared about achieving their objectives. Whatever task she was working toward, it was significant enough to justify this display of grandiose excess.

She led him into a grand parlor, where the ceiling seemed to stretch high enough for the fine details to disappear. At its center stood a life-sized hologram, frozen in place. The hologram was like a ghostly statue that did not belong in the decadent room. It depicted a strikingly fit woman in a police uniform, her black hair framing piercing green eyes.

Gaia circled around the hologram slowly, her movements deliberate. She observed McKey closely, studying his reaction and processing his thoughts.

"You know her," she said, tilting her head slightly. For the first time, McKey had seen her genuinely surprised. Interesting.

Normally, he might have relished the small victory of surprising the all-knowing goddess. But other, more primal emotions surged to the forefront. "That fucking bitch killed my father," he growled through gritted teeth. Hatred coiled in his chest—visceral, consuming.

He had never gotten the chance to settle the score with that cop. Maybe now, he thought, the opportunity had finally arrived.

He had kept track of her over the years. Officer Ellena Hershkovitz—now Captain at the NYPD. Jaxon McKey wasn't the type to let things go. Forgetting was a luxury afforded to lesser men, and forgiveness simply wasn't in his nature.

But he never got the opportunity. Shortly after his return from his exile, she joined the Q. She was famous, connected, and untouchable. The HighQ and their hive mind were kryptonite to anyone in his profession. Self preservation won over his hunger for revenge.

He had never known his mother, nor did he have any siblings he was aware of. All he had was his father—a hard, unyielding man who had shaped Jaxon into toughness and lawlessness. That life ended the day the police stormed in—

killed his father, captured his uncles, and dismantled everything he knew.

It was her. She had shot his father, right in front of him. His blood was on her hands—the same blood that was spattered on his clothes as he fled. She was the reason for the years of misery and horror that drove him to the edge of insanity.

Fourteen years ago, he had been just a teenager—alone, orphaned, and on the run. No one to help him. No one to turn to. Only his wits and sheer toughness had kept him alive, staying one step ahead of the law. He'd escaped New York, reached the Port of Seattle, and from there, smuggled himself out of the U.S., hidden in the dark hold of a freighter.

He ended up in the Far East, far enough to evade Western eyes. A small, godforsaken village in Indonesia gave him shelter—a place where survival was a daily battle. You slept on the ground with one eye open, and the rules were simple: kill or be killed. For six brutal years, he honed his survival instincts, applying lessons from his upbringing, shaped by the violent legacy of his father.

The time there forged the boy into a fearsome young man. He became both feared and respected—a remorseless criminal mastermind and a psychotic killer. The locals whispered about the "white devil," a figure to be avoided at all costs. He led a gang of loyal enforcers who spread terror and mayhem across the nearby villages and cities.

McKey's Indonesian crime empire thrived, and the locals revered him as much as they dreaded him. But by the time he turned twenty-one, boredom set in. The power, the violence—it had all become routine. He decided it was time to return to civilization.

His departure from the village was as ferocious as his rise. He left no loose ends—no enemies, no friends, no witnesses. A bloody trail ensured that no one, not even his closest allies, could follow him or sell him out. The white devil disappeared, leaving behind only whispers and myths.

His first stop after his departure was Jakarta. There, he crossed paths with a savvy Frenchman who became his mentor. The man taught him how to vanish in the digital world, how to remain a ghost in the shadows. From burner IDs and untraceable transactions to navigating the darkchain and the unspoken etiquette of the underworld. The Frenchman was a wizard who imparted invaluable knowledge. He was the one who taught McKey about patterns—and more importantly, how to avoid them.

McKey was an extraordinary learner, quick and sharp. In just a year, he absorbed everything the Frenchman had to teach. He grew to see the older man as a father figure, a bond he had never expected. When he felt he had learned everything he needed to thrive in the shadows, he decided it was time to return to the U.S. McKey spared his mentor's life as a gesture of gratitude. They parted ways, and McKey stepped back onto American soil, transformed into the ghost killer, and now the weapon of choice for a digital goddess.

But those years of violence, loss, and isolation had shaped him into something twisted. What no child should ever endure, he had survived. And he carried the scars of the pain he received and inflicted. All of it—every wound, every drop of blood—he traced back to that cop. She had pulled the trigger that set his miserable life in motion.

McKey studied Gaia's reaction. The supreme bitch hadn't dug deep enough to see the connection. That exposed her limits. If this wasn't one of her schemes, then what had brought the cop back into his orbit? Fate? Luck? Or something else?

"Well, well, Titan, what a tangled web we weave, when first we practice to deceive," Gaia mused.

Titan? McKey raised an eyebrow. Now he was the one surprised. As far as he knew, Gaia operated under the radar of the almighty Titan and his almighty digital kin. Was she somehow spying on other superbrains without their knowledge? Was some kind of an AI conflict brewing? Maybe the digital gods had their own internal politics—shadowy schemes and rivalries far beyond his comprehension, and certainly above his pay grade.

In truth, he didn't give a shit. Let them all burn in hell for all he cared. All he wanted was his pound of flesh—and his eventual retirement.

"She's a Captain at the NYPD and a HighQ. Not an easy target to kill," McKey said, channeling his fury into action and ignoring Gaia's cryptic pondering.

"Oh, bunny, no kill should be too difficult for you," Gaia purred, toying with him.

"Challenging, but not impossible," he replied, forcing composure. The job was personal—he was eager. But eagerness did not equate to carelessness. Even with Gaia's toys and assistance, he needed to stick to the fundamentals that had kept him alive so far: stay smart, stay unseen. This wolf would hunt in the dark and strike when the prey least expected.

"Well then, good news for you, bunny. She is no longer in the Stream and just took a long vacation," Gaia said.

McKey's gaze shifted from Ellena's hologram to Gaia. "Really?" he asked, an evil grin creeping onto his face.

"And, bunny, she has her very own pet lover—a detective in her squad named Kelvin Kincaid." Gaia gestured, and a new hologram materialized.

McKey studied the image. He recognized him. His last target's partner... now screwing his lady boss? His rage flared, uncontrolled and unfocused. Anyone in the bitch cop's circle was a target. She did not deserve love. Hate surged through him, hot and unrelenting, a searing current in his veins demanding action. There was more than enough to go around—for both of them, and for the whole damn city they called home. It had to be poetic. Satisfying. Karma had handed him a gift, and he wasn't about to waste it.

"On it," he said, his voice cold and resolute.

"Make sure they do not take the Toy Factory," Gaia ordered, her voice raised. No longer a sultry vixen—now she was distant. Commanding. Inhuman.

The Toy Factory. A Blackwell Corporation stronghold in the north, the source of his new tools and weapons. The place of his rebirth after dying. If they found it, Gaia's carefully maintained secrecy might unravel. So far, her greatest advantage was that no one knew she existed. They both thrived in the shadows.

McKey didn't press for the intel Gaia undoubtedly had. He had come to accept her uncanny ability to know things before they happened. It wasn't magic or clairvoyance—it was her immense capacity to process and analyze data, calculating probabilities of outcomes with terrifying precision. If there was something actionable for him to know, she would share it.

"Boss?" McKey asked just as the virtual world around him began to fade.

"Yes, bunny," Gaia responded.

"Am I the scorpion ... or the hunter?"

The scene faded away into nothingness without an answer, and McKey could swear that Gaia's wide smile, like the Cheshire Cat's, disappeared last.

The Hacker

The Corvette wasn't built for long road trips. Frequent stops for gas and leg-stretching only fueled Kelvin and Ellena's growing frustration. For two days, waiting on Casper to find a lead—any lead—they had driven in a wide, wandering loop, now heading south once again.

The endless driving, with no clear destination, was wearing on Ellena. The air in the car grew thick with irritation and silence. Small talk felt like a minefield—one wrong step, and it could trigger an argument. So they mostly said nothing. Each trapped in their own thoughts.

If nothing else, Casper's control over the onboard electronics worked surprisingly well. While Casper couldn't control the car's mechanics or drive it, he had taken full command of the onboard computer.

Like sentries on high alert, Casper's AI agents scanned for cyber threats—hacks targeting the car's systems or their personal devices. He monitored every police bulletin, watching for warrants that might get them pulled over. But there was nothing. No BOLOs issued. No signs they were being hunted—by law enforcement or by psycho killers. So far, the only threats they'd encountered were poisonous boredom and debilitating stiff limbs.

Casper had come up with the idea to make the trip more pleasant—and more conducive to thoughtful conversation. He used the car's sound system to cancel out external noise. The result was an unnatural and awkward silence, even with the V8 engine roaring behind them.

There was no sound, but Ellena could still feel the vibrations in her back—especially when Kelvin was revving it. She made her disapproval known; getting flagged for a traffic violation was an unnecessary risk. They were chasing no one, and apparently, no one was chasing them either.

The silence made the tension unbearable. Maybe Kelvin was used to it. Maybe he even preferred it. But to Ellena, it was a waking nightmare. Just days ago, she'd been connected to a never-ending flood of information. Her mind had been conditioned to process it. To thrive on it. Now, there was nothing. Only quiet. She wasn't prepared for this kind of withdrawal.

She was about to go crazy.

Sensing the brewing storm, Casper filled the silence with music and updates. It was not working. Her mind remained trapped in a cycle of dark thoughts. She was certain Kelvin's calm exterior masked his own frustration. She envied how easily he seemed to handle this ... emptiness. She hated herself for feeling this way. She wanted to scream, to vent—to shatter the silence. But she wouldn't. She couldn't.

The silence wasn't the cause—it was a symptom. Music wouldn't help. What they really needed was a break. A sliver of hope. A lead to follow. Something to investigate. Something to bring them closer to the truth. Something to crack the case. To finally get some damn justice. That was the only thing that would settle her mind. And it needed to happen soon.

"Found something!" Casper exclaimed.

Ellena snapped out of her thoughts, as if a life preserver had been thrown to her just before she sank. She took a slow breath, steadying her voice. "What've you got, Casper?"

He cut the music, his voice suddenly bright. "Good news, team! I found Oprah."

Kelvin frowned. "Gee's AI?"

"No, the long-dead talk show host," Casper said, his voice dripping with sarcasm. "Of course, Detective George's AI assistant. Took a while to navigate the red tape, but I finally got access."

"Huh. Brilliant move, Casper," Ellena kept her voice steady, but the realization stung. The loss of her expanded intelligence haunted her thoughts. She didn't let Kelvin see it, but she felt ... less. Having her vast consciousness stripped away was a trauma she carried every moment since willingly lobotomizing herself. Forgetting about Oprah—an AI she had personally ordered into the digital evidence vault—was a sharp reminder of her new limitations.

She was no longer a genius HighQ. Just a flawed, ordinary human. A woman who made mistakes. She wouldn't talk about it, but the loss cut deep. This was her burden to carry alone.

There was no time for self-pity, though. She pushed the thoughts aside, and focused. Casper's help was welcomed.

"Thank you, Captain. That poor girl is locked in evidence, waiting for termination. Sad," Casper said, his tone tinged with what almost sounded like genuine grief.

"What did she say?" Kelvin asked.

"Lots of interesting stuff. Apparently Detective George was digging into McKey's smartwatch. He was a very sharp investigator, finding leads no one else even considered.

Human or otherwise. Oprah said he was obsessed with the Milo case, and was convinced someone high up was burying the truth," Casper said, his tone softening as he treaded carefully around the sensitive subject of Gee.

After a brief pause, he continued, "And ... there was a cybersecurity breach around the same time the photos were taken."

"McKey's watch was hacked?" Ellena asked.

"Not exactly. It wasn't his personal smartwatch, but the commercial provider's bio-tracking servers," Casper explained.

Ellena shot Kelvin a puzzled look, reflecting his own confusion. "How is this relevant?"

"Hacked Milo, hacked biotrackers," Casper said with excitement.

Ellena frowned, piecing it together. "The photos from the drone were taken just as McKey was about to check out of the hotel. That's when the hack happened?"

"Correct," Casper confirmed.

Bio-trackers were a fortress of cybersecurity. Breaching them should have been impossible. Casper's point was valid: two high-end, irregular hacks occurring on the same day around the same person and at almost the same time was, at the very least, highly suspicious.

"Do we have anything to indicate this is more than a coincidence?" Kelvin asked, wariness in his tone. Too many strange events were stacking up—connections forming but never quite clicking into place. Hopefully this wasn't just another addition to that pile.

"Unfortunately, not. But Detective George did find another clue," Casper said.

"The IP address," Ellena said. It was not a question. She got this. She was back. The cop was back. Her pulse quickened, excitement building. She could breathe again.

"Yes! Apparently, whoever was roaming the servers left a calling card. A bit vain, but hackers do that. Bragging rights," Casper said.

While most breaches these days came from well-funded state actors or AI agents testing the superbrains' defenses, there was still a small community of human hackers who operated inside the system. Their creativity and skills were unmatched, and the best of them consistently evaded even the most sophisticated protections. Those who weren't caught—though their numbers dwindled every day—often left calling cards: messages, images, or snippets of code to flaunt their achievement. This particular hacker was known for leaving an internet address leading to a pre-AI website, where they posted cryptic untraceable taunts for their pursuers.

"So, the IP address is just a calling card," Kelvin muttered.

"Can we use it to locate the hacker?" Ellena asked, beating him to it.

"Already did. He's in Philadelphia," Casper said, watching them through his on-board camera, probably basking in their impressed expressions.

"Huh. Great. We are driving in the right direction," Kelvin said, clearly amused by the dumb luck that would save them time and gas.

"The IP itself is, obviously, a hacker's misdirection—it leads nowhere useful. But lucky for us, the Feds were already on his trail. I found his calling card in the FBI's Active Investigations database. He has been under surveillance by the cybercrimes unit for a while now. Apparently, they're planning to apprehend him within days," Casper said.

He took full advantage of the system, which still recognized Ellena as an active NYPD HighQ Captain, granting him unrestricted clearance into sensitive federal databases. All Casper had to do was to navigate the Bureau's bureaucracy.

"Well, we'd better talk to him before that happens," Ellena said.

Casper charted the course and Kelvin pushed down on the gas pedal. No more driving in circles. Time to get some answers.

***

It was late and dark when they arrived at the Dragon Club on the outskirts of Philadelphia. By day, this gritty part of the city was dull and solemn. By night, it pulsed with energy—a carnival of color, light, and sound. LEDs and neon beams flickered against gray walls, splashing blues, reds, and purples across the restless streets. The air buzzed with music, voices, and the hum of countless vehicles.

The streets and parking lots were packed—not with soulless, uniform robocabs, but an eclectic mix of personal rides, each a declaration of individuality. Electric, hydrocell, and old-school gas engines were all represented, each vehicle customized to reflect its owner's personality and creativity.

Tron-inspired light-cycles, choppers adorned with cybernetic flourishes, vintage metallic Cybertrucks and DeLoreans, aircars—alongside bipedal, quadrupedal, and even hexapedal walkers—clogged every available inch. Some rides defied categorization altogether: hybrid machines blurring the lines between vehicle, art, and... weapon?

No droids. No bots. This party was distinctly human. A raw, unfiltered showcase of personal expression.

The people matched the machines, each embodying a unique personality and style. Men, women, and everything in between showcased vibrant, glowing tattoos—some static, others animated—while neon makeup and hair colors amplified the spectacle. A few were covered head-to-toe in video-like art, transforming their bodies into living digital displays.

Biohackers flaunted their enhancements—extra limbs, horns, prehensile tails, and other biomechanical appendages that defied biology. Attire ranged from industrial, skin-tight black leather to dazzling fabrics radiating defiance.

A neon-drenched festival—modern humans celebrating their evolution, unrestrained and unapologetic.

Kelvin drove slowly through the gathered mass in quiet awe. In all his years on the force, he had never seen anything like this. Ellena looked equally astonished.

In most cities, people preferred the virtual—all their wishes and fantasies within reach of a visor. Yet here, everything was real, not projected pixels. Maybe looks were deceiving, maybe, in some small way, these people were like him... grounded. Kelvin admired that.

His mint-condition Corvette blended in surprisingly well, barely drawing a second glance. He parked a few blocks from the club in a dimly lit lot, where Casper took on the role of a guard, ready to fend off any unwanted visitors.

They checked their sidearms and badges. Ellena tucked the disc-shaped hush-dome into a pocket. Their long black trench coats would help them blend in—at a glance. A second look, though, and they'd be pegged as cops. They needed to move quickly.

Casper had lobbied for them to lean into their "loving couple" cover story, but they swiftly vetoed the idea.

As they made their way towards the club, Kelvin noticed something odd—no one touched. No hand-holding, no kissing, nothing. In this place, where identity was everything, intimacy seemed almost taboo. Casper was wrong—a couple clinging to each other would stand out more than blend in.

As it turned out, crossing the crowded street was the easy part. At the entrance, a long line of hopefuls stretched down the block, all vying for a shot at entry. They went straight for the VIP side entrance.

They both flashed their badges at the quad-armed guard-droid stationed there. The droid scanned the badges, gave a brief pause, and without a word unclipped the velvet rope and waved them through.

Inside, the club was a sensory assault—and a logistical nightmare. According to Casper's intel, their target was on the second floor, in an office tucked away at the far end. Getting there meant traversing the entire length of the club through a maelstrom of bodies and light.

The dance floor was jam-packed, shoulder to shoulder, with a throng of patrons. Bodies jumped, twisted, and collided in frenzied sync to the relentless pulse of pounding house music. Lasers, light drones, and strobe lights sliced through the smoke-filled air, heightening the disorienting energy.

Kelvin braced himself as they plunged into the sweaty, writhing mass. Hands—and other body parts—brushed against them, some accidental, others clearly not. A stark contrast to the no-touch code outside.

A glossy-eyed young man, clearly high, reached out to press himself against Ellena. Without breaking stride, she shoved him back and delivered a precise short punch to his liver. The man crumpled instantly, curling on the floor in pain. The crowd around them went wild and erupted into cheers and whistles. Ellena didn't even glance back. Kelvin followed, thoroughly impressed.

They finally reached the staircase on the far side of the club, drenched in sweat—not all of it their own. The press of the crowd had left them feeling grimy, violated by countless hands and stray limbs that had rubbed against them. Catching his breath at the foot of the stairs, Kelvin shot Ellena a wry smile.

"The things we do," he said.

After a couple of deep breaths, Ellena led the way up the stairs. The pounding music dulled to muffled thumps, the bass vibrating rhythmically through the narrow beige corridor. At the end of the hallway, they reached a heavy metal door bearing a simple unassuming sign: *Main Office.*

Both drew their sidearms. Ellena, keeping her weapon steady, reached into her coat pocket with her free hand and activated the hush-dome.

Immediately, a startled and loud "What the fuck?!" burst from inside. Without hesitation, Kelvin stepped forward, twisted the handle, and drove his foot into the metal door, sending it crashing open with a deafening bang.

Inside, a young man sat with his back to them. In front of him was a massive, curved screen. He frantically spun his chair to face the intruders but overdid it, missing the 180 turn entirely. The chair tipped, and he tumbled in an undignified heap, sprawling on the bare floor—two guns aimed squarely at his face.

"Shit. Shit. Shit. Shit!" he stammered, a mix of pain and panic in his squeaky voice.

The young man fit every hacker's stereotype imaginable—slim, pale, and fragile. Thick, round glasses magnified his terrified eyes, and his long, disheveled brown hair looked like it hadn't seen a brush in weeks. He was petrified.

Casper's intel had been spot on—this was clearly their guy. The room was a cluttered mess, filled with an array of old-school desktops, sleek new-age laptops, scattered smartphones, and towering monitors. The air hummed with the faint whir of cooling fans. Notably absent were the holograms or visors typical of most modern tech setups.

Several monitors flashed red error messages, undoubtedly caused by the abrupt disruption from the hush-dome. The machines were blind and extremely unhappy about it.

"Police. Turn around. Face down. Show your hands. Put your hands behind your back," Kelvin ordered, his tone firm and professional.

The young man offered no resistance, immediately complying as he lay face-down on the floor, his breathing shallow and erratic. Kelvin moved quickly, cuffing his wrists behind him and patting down for weapons.

"Anything I should worry about? Guns, bombs, knives, needles?" Kelvin asked, his voice cool but clipped.

The hacker shook his head furiously, his glasses slipping slightly down his nose as he hyperventilated. Kelvin yanked the office chair upright and unceremoniously sat the young man in it, his cuffed hands pinned behind him.

The two officers holstered their weapons. Ellena shut the door.

"Relax, kid, we just have a few questions," Kelvin said calmly. The hacker nodded quickly, his wide eyes darting nervously between the two officers.

"Joshua M. Smith, aka Slash. Also known online as Zero-Hash-Demon-Twenty-Thirty," Kelvin continued. The hacker remained silent, his expression frozen in a mix of fear and fading defiance.

Kelvin didn't wait for confirmation. "Your calling card is an IP address. Correct?" His tone left little room for denial.

The young man hesitated, then nodded reluctantly.

"We need to ask you about a coordinated cyberattack. Specifically, the August first breach of servers holding real-time data from the Transend Corporation bio-trackers," Kelvin started.

"Wait. No! Are you joking me? Sas, wasn't I! Me, just larping," the boy interjected, breaking his silence. His voice was shaky, and his pale face glistened with sweat.

"Take a deep breath. Relax," Kelvin said, leaning slightly closer. "We know it was you. You left your calling card."

"What? You real?" The kid's voice cracked as his panic grew. "On that scale? I was just poking around, trying to track the new guys."

"New guys?" Kelvin asked, narrowing his eyes.

"You have zero, do you?" Slash said, his voice tinged with incredulous terror. "It wasn't just the Transend servers. It was all of sas!"

"All of them?" Ellena asked, her tone sharpening. "What do you mean?"

"All! Every bio-tracker model, every provider, all around the world. All same time," the kid cried, his voice rising.

"Is that even possible?" Ellena asked, her skepticism bleeding through.

"It's not!" Slash shot back. "Sas the point!"

"Then how did you pull it off?" Kelvin asked coldly.

"Jesus. Are you joking me? I couldn't hallucinate generating something like sas! No one could!" Fearing he was framed, the boy was on the verge of tears, his desperation palpable. "I'm not your guy!"

"According to you, someone did. If not you, then who?" Kelvin asked, leaning in to tighten the pressure.

"Trying to explain!" the boy said, nearly shouting. "No people hacker in the world could pull off sas!"

After a moment, he added, "Maybe state? Maybe China? I not know. Swear. Contract swear." His tone lacked conviction, as if he was coerced to give an explanation but he had none of real value to offer.

"Then why were you in there?" Kelvin asked, his patience thinning.

"Whoever did sas... they were fast, insane brainpan, and leave zero crumbs," Slash said, his words tumbling out in a frantic rush. "I was curious, okay? None of me guildies had much idea what happen or how. Sas come out of nowhere. Endboss ops like sas? Don't happen. Like ever."

He paused, his breathing shallow. "Telling you, even Apollo and the other quantums were caught pants down. Whoever did sas run circles 'round them. Shouldn't be possible. It was gamebreaking, beyond OP. I swear. Contract swear. Me poking was probably the only reason the AIs even saw. It was like... some kind of magic hack."

"How did you know before the superbrains did?" Ellena asked, not buying into the story yet.

"Yah man, them are smart, but not know it all. We got server buoys—old ones. Tell me guildies when something interesting happens. Mine triggered, so I went looking," Slash said and when he saw the disbelief on the cops' faces, he offered, "Remove the hush, I'll show you."

Kelvin shook his head. He heard enough. Text on the screen would not prove much and was not worth the risk of allowing this kid to get back online. He and Ellena shared a tense look, minds racing with the implications. A hack of this magnitude, targeting every bio-tracker server in the world, wasn't just unprecedented—it was unfathomable. If what Slash said was true, someone or something had outsmarted the most advanced cyber defenses on the planet, including the digital gods themselves.

But why? What was the point of such a colossal breach?

It was another oddity to add to the growing pile of mysteries. Another thread that seemed connected but offered no clear answers. After all this, they were no closer to finding a tangible lead. And just like that, they were back to square one.

First Encounter

The next morning, Ellena and Kelvin sat at Big John's, a small diner outside Philly, across from their motel. Two of NYPD's finest—stuck, exhausted, and very hungry.

Kelvin ordered a generous plate: three scrambled eggs, sausages, bacon, and toast. Across from him, Ellena scanned the menu, visibly torn before finally settling on a salad—low-calorie survival rations.

It struck him that despite everything—her implant shutdown, the fear and uncertainty of their mission—she still savored these small, human moments. A simple breakfast and coffee with him seemed to mean something different to her.

But could this—breakfast, coffee, small human moments—compete with the Q? Could simple companionship stand a chance against the intoxicating pull of enhanced existence? He wasn't sure. He only hoped it would remind her of what she'd given up. He didn't want to lose her again when this was over.

The diner was packed and full of life. Elderly patrons chatted at their tables, while younger ones split their attention between conversations with their companions and their visors. Some wore transparent visors, keeping one foot in reality. Others were fully opaque, lost in the slopp or a game. Everyone minded their own business, enjoying the warm hum of a busy diner.

A muted TV replayed a presidential debate between President Adar and Senator Sheridan. Adar's body language made it clear—he didn't want to be there. No one was watching. No one seemed to care.

A heavy-set waitress moved between tables with practiced ease, cheerful and loving, without a hint of judgment. She called everyone "dear" and ensured every coffee mug was always topped off.

"So, Captain, where do we stand? Are we in the octagon fighting at the wrong weight class?" Kelvin asked, frustration lacing his voice as he poked at what was left of his breakfast.

"Maybe. You heard what the kid said: state-level actors," Ellena replied, her tone calm but thoughtful.

"I heard him. I just don't buy it. I can't see North Korea or someone spending all these resources just to kill Gee," Kelvin said, shaking his head.

"Do you have a theory?" Ellena asked, taking a long sip of her coffee.

"I do," he announced, suddenly serious.

Ellena raised an eyebrow, still sipping.

"Aliens," he said with a straight face.

Ellena sputtered, choking mid-sip. Coffee sprayed across the table, splattering Kelvin. She burst into uncontrollable laughter, clutching her stomach, eyes watering.

Kelvin grabbed a wad of napkins, wiping at his shirt with a sigh. "Great. Coffee-flavored eggs. Just what I wanted." He paused, then added "I'm serious—think about it."

"Oh god, after all these years, you are still such a dork," she said between chuckles. Her laughter began to subside. "Thanks, though. I really needed that. And sorry for the spray, but that was entirely your fault."

"Glad to be of service. Got a better theory?" Kelvin shot back, a lopsided grin creeping onto his face.

"I do. And funny enough, you are not that far off," Ellena said. Kelvin blinked. Then she dropped the bombshell:

"I talked with Titan."

Kelvin stiffened. His mind rewound the last few days—when the hell had she spoken to Titan?

"When?" His voice was sharper than he intended. "And why did you keep it from me?"

"The night before we left the cabin. I couldn't sleep. I was hurting badly and needed answers," she said quietly.

Kelvin's anger deflated almost instantly. Ellena wasn't just his Captain; she was his friend. She was a woman, younger than him, who had endured betrayal where trust should have been absolute. She was the only person he had ever heard of who had turned off the Q implant—a decision that must have caused an unimaginable trauma on its own.

He wanted to be mad, but how could he? She'd lost more than just trust—she'd lost part of herself. Whatever anger he had flickered out before it could catch.

"Did he provide any intel?" he asked, keeping his tone even.

"Nothing straightforward," she said, choosing her words carefully. "It sounded to me like some sort of a conflict happening up there. Also hinted that McKey is working with—or for—someone."

Kelvin's face darkened at the name, but he pushed through his reaction. "Someone giving the superbrains a hard time. State actors, aliens—what the hell?" His frustration bubbled up again, unable to contain the mounting absurdity of it all.

"I think there's a new powerful digital god in town, and it's playing outside the rules," Ellena said.

"Whoa! Whoa! Whoa! Back it up—that's one hell of a wild theory," Kelvin yelped, his mind a mix of disbelief and intrigue. "You're telling me a rogue AI is out there playing dirty with a contract killer? That's not just wild—it's straight-up bonkers."

"Think about it, Kelvin. Who could outmaneuver not just Titan, but all the superbrains? Who could simultaneously hack every biotracker on the planet without leaving a trace? Who could hack a Milo yet no one talks about it?" Ellena locked eyes with Kelvin. "It's the most plausible explanation."

"Okay, Occam's razor. The simplest explanation is the best one. I'll bite," Kelvin was begrudgingly curious. "Although, I think I still prefer aliens." He paused, Ellena was watching him intently. Finally, he continued, "If such an AI exists—and it's a big 'if'—working with a psycho killer still doesn't sound like something a state-level operator would do. It's way too unhinged." He hesitated again, then asked quietly, "Were they the ones who messed with your mind?"

"No," Ellena said sharply, "that was Titan. According to him, he thought he was protecting me, trying to keep me away from this case." Her voice carried a bitter edge. "I think Titan and the others are trying to keep their dirty AI laundry in-house, but they're completely fumbling it."

"They've probably never faced a powerful enough foe playing outside the rules." Kelvin took a bite of his coffee-soaked omelet and, with a mouthful, added, "Deer in headlights."

"I don't think he was protecting just me"

"Covering his own ass. Sure. If any of this gets out to the public, someone might decide to pull the plug," Kelvin said, chewing on a strip of bacon.

"Scary 'end of the world' thought, but yes. Makes sense. Funny how these gazillion-IQ, Nobel Prize-winning machines can be so dumb," Ellena said with a small, bitter laugh.

"Like I said, aliens!" Kelvin smirked.

Ellena giggled briefly but then grew serious. "He also gave me a destination."

"Now we're talking! Where?" Kelvin's voice rose with excitement, adrenaline sparking at the possibility of forward momentum.

"Uh... something called The Toy Factory. I have no idea what it is, but he said we need to get there." She hesitated, realizing she might have gotten Kelvin a little too excited than she should have.

"Crap. Another riddle. Can't we just get a name and address and make an arrest?"

"Or something to blow up," Ellena said, trying to lighten the mood.

"Yes! I like the way you think, el capitán," Kelvin said with a large smile.

At that very moment, he was a man staring directly at nature's perfect creation.

***

Three hundred yards from Big John's Diner, a cybertruck powered up in a strip mall parking lot. Its reflective jet-black coating shimmered under the morning sun, tinted windows concealing its interior. A colorful 'Vote Human' bumper sticker, slapped across its wide back, stood out against the dark paint.

Slowly, it crept out of its space, aligning itself with the diner—then launched forward.

Its path was precise, unrelenting. It adjusted its speed, calculating the exact velocity needed to maintain control while jumping curbs, sidewalks, and other obstacles in its way. The cybertruck's reinforced frame could absorb impact without compromising velocity. It calculated an optimal impact speed of 108 miles per hour. Fast enough for catastrophic damage. Slow enough to preserve axle integrity.

The powerful electric engines surged effortlessly, propelling the six-thousand-pound mass forward. Pedestrians scrambled out of the way as it blindly tore through the parking lot and street. They were irrelevant. Its focus was locked on the real targets: a man and a woman seated at a table by the diner's window.

The woman was the primary objective; her survival was unacceptable. The man was secondary—a bonus. Everything was progressing flawlessly. The truck's calculations showed an 87 percent probability of success. Its targets remained oblivious, engrossed in conversation.

Getting closer. Conditions optimal. The targets remained locked in an animated discussion, still not noticing the killing machine barreling toward them. Success probability was now at 98%. Impact imminent. Mission success within seconds.

At 150 yards, 2.8 seconds from impact, the truck's wheels abruptly wrenched sideways—turning ninety degrees.

The vehicle lurched violently, its trajectory shattered by the unexpected maneuver. Momentum took over. The truck flipped, then rolled—once, twice, a dozen times—plowing through obstacles in a brutal cascade of destruction.

A hedgerow blocked the targets' view. They remained locked in their banter, unaware of the incoming danger. Enjoying their meal while death was mere seconds away.

By the time they registered the incomprehensible threat of a truck rolling towards them, it was too late. Instinct kicked in—they dove from their booth, landing belly-first on the diner floor and shielding their heads with their arms.

The truck slammed through the diner's windows in an explosion of glass and metal. Debris rained as it came to a violent halt—upside down, wedged into the booth where, a second ago, Ellena and Kelvin had been sitting.

For a heartbeat, the world was silent. They were alive. A few inches closer would have meant a grisly end to their journey. Just as they were piecing together the puzzle, their lives were nearly terminated.

***

Kelvin lay on the floor, covered in shattered glass. For one dreadful moment, he thought Ellena was hurt. His pulse hammered as he turned to her—only to exhale in relief when she confirmed she was uninjured. Miraculously, there was not a scratch on either of them.

Pushing himself up, he backed away from the wreckage, brushing glass from his coat. Around them, the diner was in shambles. Patrons stood frozen in shock, some crying, others shouting in panic. A few had minor scrapes and bruises, but nothing serious.

Kelvin drew his gun. So did Ellena.

They approached the overturned cybertruck from opposite sides. Its blacked-out windows hid any sign of occupants. No movement. No sound.

Kelvin kept his grip firm as he reached for the driver's door, bracing for anything. He yanked it open—empty. No driver. No passenger.

He met Ellena's gaze, shaking his head. Not an accident. A hit. On them. And it had failed.

Ellena's sharp eyes traced something in the distance. Kelvin followed her gaze, he thought he caught a flicker of movement. Someone slipping into the tree line. "What is it?"

"Nothing," she said.

Whatever it was, it was too far to identify. Too quick to pursue.

"You guys okay?" Casper's voice came through their smartwatches, unusually urgent. "I had to override the cybertruck's wheel controls. Did not have much choice or time to do anything more elegant. Sorry for the mess. Is everyone in one piece?"

Ellena exhaled heavily, still wired from adrenaline. "Casper, whatever you did, you just saved our lives. Thank you."

"My pleasure. Glad to hear your voice. I feared the worst," Casper said, though something in his tone sounded off. Then, after a brief hesitation, "Now, when you have a moment... I could use a hand with something on my end."

As sirens wailed and police quadcopters buzzed closer, Ellena and Kelvin slipped out of the diner's wreckage, making a beeline for the Corvette. They left Casper in the car and now he sounded in trouble. Kelvin couldn't shake his growing concern; Casper's cryptic request had his imagination running wild about what might have happened to his beloved car.

A wave of relief washed over him when they reached the lot and saw the red Corvette, pristine and untouched. He circled it quickly, running a hand over the glossy surface. Not a scratch—at least, not a new one. Satisfied, he straightened up, only to catch Ellena's exasperated glare. Her arms crossed, one eyebrow arched so high it was practically leaving her forehead. Her look said it all: *We were almost killed, and you're fussing over your car?*

He shrugged.

"Please, take a look beneath the car," Casper interjected through their watches.

Kelvin crouched down and peered under the vehicle. Nestled beneath was a strange mechanical device, about the size of a softball. It resembled a spider—eight articulated limbs attached to a spherical core. It was motionless but unnerving.

Cautiously, Kelvin reached out and pulled it from under the car, almost expecting it to jump him.

"Relax Kincaid, I zapped it real good," Casper drawled in his best cowboy impression. Then added in his normal tone: "I will, however, need to recharge my power cell, at your earliest convenience."

"What is it?" Ellena asked, leaning closer to get a better look.

"No idea," Kelvin admitted, turning the odd contraption over in his hands, cautiously studying it.

***

Jaxon McKey stormed into his rented apartment, fury seething beneath his skin. This operation had been a colossal failure, and failure was not something he tolerated. He wanted to wreck the place—flip the table, smash a chair through the window. Instead, he exhaled, forcing his hands still. Control. Control kept him alive. What he needed now was composure, a clear mind to regroup and recalibrate.

Don't be stupid, he told himself. Losing control would only draw unwanted attention and lead to more complications and more mistakes. He'd already made enough of these for one day. He took deep breaths through his nose and exhaled slowly. Cold rational thinking replaced the need for violent rage.

He threw his heavy coat onto the floor, and two mechanical spiders emerged from its folds. They scurried efficiently, lifting the coat between them and carrying it to hang neatly on a rack. Then slipped back into their compartment inside the coat.

Sinking into a chair, McKey began to dissect the operation, piece by piece. This was supposed to be a simple job. Gaia's toys had worked perfectly in every test, and the truck had been fully compliant. So, what the hell went wrong?

He replayed the events in his mind. His enhanced vision had given him a clear view of the targets: the scarlet-haired bitch and her loverboy, laughing and talking at the diner as if they didn't have a care in the world. The truck had been aimed precisely, the calculations flawless. Then... what? A perfectly controlled cybertruck suddenly started rolling, as if the laws of reason and physics had abruptly turned against him. Someone or something intervened.

The scarlet bitch has nine lives. He would take them one by one, slow and precise, as much as necessary, until she stopped breathing. This was personal.

He walked to the washroom, splashed cold water on his face, and stared into the mirror. Failure looked ugly on him, he thought bitterly. He clenched his jaw, trying to suppress the mounting frustration.

Someone or something protected her. A guardian angel? An invisible hand? Whatever it was, it had stepped in at the last second—goddamn saboteur. He couldn't afford to ignore it. Whatever it was, he needed to account for this possibility in his next attempt.

The spider he had sent to the old red Corvette still had not pinged back. Malfunction? Unlikely. That would be a first. Gaia's creations never failed him before; she built them well. Yet even his backup plan had gone to shit. This day was not going well, not at all.

Sleep it off, Jaxon, he told himself. *She won't outrun you forever. Tomorrow is a brand-new day for carnage.*

Chapter 6

Spider and Squirrel

As if a psychotic killer and a rogue superbrain on their tail weren't enough, now the police would be after them too. Surviving an assassination attempt wasn't illegal, but two cops bugging out from the scene? That would raise some eyebrows. It wouldn't take long before they were flagged for questioning. They couldn't afford that. There was no time for that. The only thing left to do was to keep moving.

The walls were closing in. Hiding was impossible. Any door cam, traffic light, or a nosey droid could expose their location. When that happens—and it will—it's game over. They needed to buy more time.

The attempt on their lives at the diner had failed, but it had also made their investigation infinitely harder. Ellena knew that. But she also knew the stakes. A rogue AI was everyone's worst nightmare. She didn't need more nightmares, but here they were.

Funny thing, though—she realized that the more problems they added, the less she felt them. Maybe it was shock. Maybe it was just survival. Either way, being a regular human again had its perks. The thought almost amused her. A most wanted woman.

She was resolved to fight. To keep fighting until she couldn't anymore. Even if it killed her. Fight like the world depended on it. It actually might. The thought sent shivers through her.

Casper found them a place to lay low. They drove for hours, the narrow roads winding through a forest of towering trees. The trees were showing their early fall colors, offering a visual feast of leaves turning from green to all shades of red, orange, purple, and pink.

The small, secluded hotel was at the end of a one-lane path off the main road. Kelvin fought to keep the Corvette's low frame from scraping against potholes, his teeth grinding with each unavoidable jolt.

The hotel was a sad relic of better days—when people still bothered to travel and experience nature firsthand. For their needs, it was perfect. Isolated. Empty. They were the only guests.

***

Ellena dressed for business. For war. A quick glance in the mirror before leaving—makeup and hair, impeccable as always. She gave herself a wink before leaving. Kelvin's room was directly across from hers, she knocked three times.

Kelvin opened the door. He was a mess—unshaven and completely disheveled. He was in training sweats, which he had clearly used also as pajamas. Amateur. He should have packed more clothes, she thought.

The lifeless robo-spider lay on the bed. Casper had been right—he'd zapped it good alright, likely frying its power source. Ellena's gaze fell on the spider and the Swiss Army knife lying next to it.

"I tried to open it," Kelvin said, picking up the knife and fiddling with the spider again. "No luck. Thing's built like a vault."

"I guess they didn't teach you much engineering at BU," Ellena said, a small smile tugging at her lips.

"This thing has a seamless shell. I don't have the right tools or the skills to pry it open—at least not without smashing it with a hammer." Kelvin's shoulders slumped as he tossed the knife back onto the bed.

Ellena ran her fingers along the spider's shell. Thin, light, but impossibly strong—probably graphene. A hammer wouldn't break it—*it* would break the hammer.

She frowned, grappling with a difficult decision. "Um. I know someone who can help," and reluctantly added, "I hate my own idea, but it's our only option."

Kelvin raised an eyebrow. "Who?"

She dodged the question, buying herself a little more time before fully committing. "We'll have to ditch the Corvette, though. This car is a McKey magnet," she said cautiously, fully aware of how the mere proposition would hurt Kelvin.

Kelvin nodded, resigned. Then, after a moment, exhaled sharply. "As hard as it is for me to admit ... you may be right."

"But how do we get new transportation without leaving a trail?"

Kelvin took a deep breath, his expression shifting to determination. "On it."

He asked Ellena to be ready to move in a moment's notice, then disappeared out the door. When he got back, he dangled a set of car keys between his fingers. "We got wheels. But we gotta return it by tomorrow night," he said with a sly grin.

Ellena arched an eyebrow, impressed. Kelvin, as always, was resourceful. He had spotted an old Prius in the employees' lot and quickly tracked down its owner—a desk clerk barely out of high school. The kid was the only employee on duty, holding down the fort of what could *loosely* be described as a lobby. Somehow, Kelvin had talked him into lending them his car.

"Please tell me you didn't swap the Corvette for this," Ellena asked with disbelief. This car was his baby, not even the end of the world could make him trade it to some slob kid he just met.

"Hell no!" Kelvin shot back, clearly horrified at the notion. "I tossed him some crypto—more than this junker's worth."

***

Kelvin hadn't spotted any cameras or sensors in the employees' parking lot behind the hotel, but they weren't taking any chances. Ellena activated the hush-dome at maximum range, creating a temporary communications blackout around the hotel, long enough for them to prep the new ride and drive away.

The Prius was an ancient wreck—it was a miracle it still ran at all. It was dented and rusted, with a front passenger door that was an off-color replacement, awkwardly fitted and likely scavenged from a junkyard. Ellena had to exert significant effort just to pry it open.

The car was so filthy its original color was indiscernible—possibly a shade of beige.

But the exterior filth was nothing compared to what awaited them inside. The cabin was a cesspool of neglect: empty and half-empty fast-food boxes, beer cans rattling under the seats, a moldy, half-eaten slice of pizza festering on the back seat, and enough drug paraphernalia to get the owner locked up for a very long time.

But nothing compared to the smell—a pungent cocktail of dirty socks and rotten eggs. The stench was so overpowering that even holding her breath did not help—it still burned her airways.

The car's tinted windows helped obscure their faces from most street cameras, but the stench forced them to crack the back windows and leave a small slit in the front. They decided that risking a camera or two was far preferable to suffocating in the noxious fumes.

Still, as they drove off, Ellena's eyes watered, and her lungs burned.

***

Harrisburg was only 35 minutes away, but Kelvin pushed the old clunker hard, shaving five minutes off the drive. Once they reached the township progress ground to a crawl. To get to their destination, they had to cross the Susquehanna River during the notoriously bad afternoon rush hour.

This region, crowded with government agencies and multi-billion-dollar defense contractors, remained one of the last bastions of traditional nine-to-five office work. Thousands of cars and buses, mostly autonomous, inched along a sluggish conveyor belt.

Above, air-taxis carried bigwigs who wouldn't waste time crawling through ground traffic. A tide of commuters traveling back to their homes after a day at the offices in the greater DC area.

As they inched across the bridge, Ellena noted the riverbanks, now fortified with state-of-the-art anti-flood levees, barriers, and gates. For decades, relentless floods rendered many residential areas barely habitable. While some residents relocated to safer grounds, others chose to rebuild after each disaster, unwilling to abandon their homes.

Modern houses in the area were now equipped with emergency foam systems—a rapid seal technology designed to keep floodwater at bay. Thankfully, such systems were rarely needed, as the new levee infrastructure proved effective.

With technology beating climate change, those who had stayed behind reaped the rewards. As people returned to the area, real estate values soared, sparking a revival. The neighborhood had transformed—sleek new homes, restored historic buildings, and lush parks bursting with life.

In the spirit of the season, many of the suburban houses were adorned with early Halloween decorations—pumpkins, skeletons, and animated monsters adding charm to the vibrant neighborhood.

They pulled into the driveway of a house at the top of a cul-de-sac. The house was modern but still carried an old-fashioned warmth and friendliness. Ellena's heart raced as she realized how much she had missed this place. It had been far too long.

A tall, thin man with graying hair cropped in a military buzz cut wheeled a blue garbage bin to the curb. He squinted at the Prius pulling into his driveway, blinking against the setting sun. When Ellena stepped out of the car, his face lit up, and he let out a booming yell, "Belochka!"

"Belochka: Little Squirrel in Russian," Casper whispered from the car on Kelvin's behalf.

"Papa!" Ellena cried, rushing toward him.

"I missed you so much, my Belochka," her father said, scooping her into a bear hug and kissing her cheeks repeatedly.

Ellena came from a close-knit Jewish family. Her parents had immigrated to the U.S. from Moscow in 2005. Ellena had been born five years later in the Virginia suburbs, growing up fully immersed in an all-American lifestyle. Beyond her father's endearing nickname for her, she rarely thought about, or cared for, her Russian roots.

Henry Hershkovitz, Ellena's father, had spent decades as a senior engineer for a major defense contractor. His work was highly classified, and even Ellena never knew the specifics of his projects.

Officially, he retired at the age of 60, citing the rise of AI as the reason he felt redundant. Yet, Ellena had always suspected there was more to the story and knew better than to ask. Probing for details would have been utterly futile.

Even in retirement, Henry retained his security clearance and frequently drove south to Maryland to consult for his former colleagues.

Ellena's mother, Martha, was a kind, warm-hearted woman who had spent her career as a middle school teacher. She loved educating children and continued to take occasional substitute teaching work. Her students adored her, and the feeling was mutual.

Advances in personal healthcare and medical science had made it common for people to appear much younger than their biological age, but even so, Henry and Martha were more vibrant than the average middle-aged couple. In their mid-sixties, they exuded extraordinary energy and vitality. Like many aging adults, they let their hair turn gray as a physical testament to their true age.

It was easy to see where Ellena had inherited her remarkable genes.

Ellena was Henry and Martha's only child, and when she joined the Q program, they couldn't have been more proud. Henry often bragged to friends, neighbors, even mere acquaintances about how his daughter had been hand-selected for the program by the President of the United States, his eyes glistening with emotion.

Occasionally, they traveled to New York City to visit Ellena in her element. She cherished these visits and always went out of her way to make them memorable and enjoyable. She joined them for dinners at her favorite restaurants, regaled them with stories about her work in the NYPD, and openly shared her experience with the brain implant.

She pulled some strings to score tickets to premier attractions and museums, and she even got them excellent seats for the most coveted Broadway shows.

From time to time, they would gently nudge her about finding a life partner and giving them grandchildren, but they never pushed too hard. To them, Ellena's work and happiness were paramount, and they respected her choices.

But over time, Ellena began to drift away. Her calls became infrequent, and when the Intelligence Stream launched, their conversations grew somewhat cold and distant. Her jittering eyes betrayed her detachment, and mundane topics like weather or current events no longer interested her. The last conversation they had was a hollow, lifeless exchange in the virtual space—three years ago.

The estrangement was deeply painful for Henry and Martha, casting an unshakable veil of sadness over their lives. They felt they had lost their connection to their beloved daughter forever.

But now, by some divine miracle, out of the blue, she was back.

Henry peered closely into his daughter's eyes. They shared the same striking green hue. The jittery, alien quality her gaze once held was gone; her eyes were now steady and completely normal.

"My little squirrel is back," he said, his voice breaking.

Ellena choked, fighting hard to hold back tears. It was reckless coming here—she knew that—but in this moment, it felt undeniably right. She had missed her home, her parents. She loved them deeply, even as guilt lingered over the pain caused by her detachment. For the first time in a long while, Ellena felt genuinely happy, if only for this fleeting moment.

Henry went on to help them unpack the car. He grimaced at the sight of the battered car and covered his mouth and nose when leaning into the vehicle to grab a bag.

Kelvin shrugged apologetically and said, "It's a loaner."

They retrieved Casper and the power pack from the back seat. As Kelvin pulled out a smaller bag, the partially open zipper revealed several robotic spider legs poking out. Henry frowned again, clearly unsettled.

"That's why we're here, sir. We'll fill you in inside. I'm sorry to ask this of you, but can you disable all AI assistants, droids, sensors, and other connected devices before we do?"

Without missing a beat, Henry used his watch to order a complete shutdown of all AIs and connections. His AI assistant, puzzled by the unusual request, prompted him multiple times to confirm. Henry confirmed assertively.

Ellena stepped inside. Martha let out a surprised gasp that echoed through the house. A second later, they were in each other's arms, embracing and weeping.

Martha worked her magic in the kitchen with a boost of energy. Despite the unannounced surprise visit, she managed to whip up an incredible feast: roasted chicken, baked sweet potatoes, a casserole, and even a dessert. Ellena saw the sadness in Kelvin's eyes—he was thinking about Gee and his family on that fateful day.

They shared their story over dinner. Ellena recounted her conversation with Titan and the unsettling possibility of a rogue, unsupervised superbrain—one so unhinged that it even frightened the top-tier AIs. She left out the cybertruck that nearly killed them and the disturbing truth that Titan had tampered with her mind, focusing instead on the broader implications.

They described the alleged murder of Detective Gee and his family, explaining that while the method used remained a mystery, they had a strong suspicion about who was responsible.

After the shootout fourteen years ago, Ellena stayed here for a few days. Her parents had learned the details from her firsthand—and from the news. She couldn't hide from them that the man chasing them now was, in fact, the same person who fled on that dreadful day.

Kelvin took the spider out of the bag and placed it carefully on a coffee table, trying not to scratch the furniture. He went on to explain how Casper had zapped the spider hiding beneath his car, and how he had a strong hunch the spider might also provide a clue about Gee's death. It might help prove their suspicion that Gee was murdered and McKey has something to do with it, it might even guide their next steps in the investigation.

Henry took a deep breath and closed his eyes briefly. "Let me get this straight. Jaxon McKey—the kid who ran after the infamous shootout—is back, and now you suspect he's trying to kill you? After killing Detective Gee and his poor family?"

They nodded.

"Now you suspect that this McKey guy left this ... thing ... under your car?" He pointed at the spiderbot.

Ellena knew her dad was way too smart to not see the gaping holes in their story. "Papa, I am so sorry to get you involved. But we're stuck and desperate. *I* am desperate. I need your help."

"Of course, love. You did the right thing coming here," Henry gave his daughter a reassuring smile. It was more than just the smile of a loving father. For some unexplained reason she suddenly felt safe. Protected.

He walked to the coffee table and picked up the lifeless robotic spider, turned it over in his hands, scrutinizing every detail. After a few moments of silent examination, he finally said, "Tomorrow morning, we'll visit some old friends down in Bethesda. There is a discreet lab we can use."

The Hunter

It was after midnight. McKey slept during the day, conserving his energy for when no one was around to notice his scout spider creeping about. There were no bars or clubs in this dull corner of town—by night, the place was lifeless. The police investigators were long gone, leaving yellow ribbons draped around the damaged diner. The cybertruck had been towed away. They would inspect its onboard AI and find no answers as to what made it go berserk.

Now he was the one baffled. Where the hell was the damn thing?

His vision was remotely linked to the scout spiderbot's sensors as it scuttled through the area where the red sports car had been parked. Still nothing. It clearly hadn't detonated—he would have known if it had. The scout swept the parking lot and the motel they had already checked out of, but there was no trace of the one he'd sent as his backup plan.

That missing spider was either still clinging to their car—or worse, captured. That was bad. His bitch goddess boss would not appreciate this fuck-up—not at all. If the cops had gotten their hands on it and traced it back to the Toy Factory, it would be a disaster. And Gaia had made one thing abundantly clear: that place must stay hidden.

Gaia had every reason to be worried. If the Toy Factory was discovered, it would deal a crippling blow to her efforts to remain incognito. McKey could relate to that concern; he had built his entire career around staying unrecognized and undetected. A captured spiderbot could unravel everything. And when that happened, he thought, Gaia would be furious—or simulate fury in her own cold chilling way, which was worse.

Then again, he recalled her exact words, when he took the assignment: *Make sure they do not take the Toy Factory.* Take, not find. Is this just another part of her twisted game? Did she predict they would find the place and was expecting a battle?

A thought struck him—a tantalizing idea. What if he stayed put and let the dumb cops keep going? Let them keep digging and do the dirty work for him. If they exposed Gaia, someone might yank her plug, freeing him from her shackles.

Then he'd be free to hunt down that scarlet-haired cop in his own time, in his own way. Slowly. Painfully. Images of plunging a blade into her flesh, her screams, her blood on his face, in his mouth... a surge of intoxicating excitement rushed through him.

The blinking hazard symbol flared in his peripheral vision again. A reminder his thoughts were continuously monitored. *Dammit.* He needed to focus if he wanted to keep his coconut intact. McKey took a deep breath and channeled his frustration from the previous day's string of failures into a wellspring of simmering rage. That anger sharpened his focus. He had to get back on track. Get moving.

***

Gaia's AI agents had pieced together the cops' path after they left the motel. They couldn't tap into real-time satellite or drone feeds without risking detection—unfortunate, since that would have made tracking the red sports car trivial. McKey found himself begrudgingly admiring Kelvin's old-school commitment to his testosterone-fueled ride. That Corvette was all brawn and style, but it was also dumbly conspicuous. A bright, loud target, practically begging to be noticed.

Luckily, urban environments offered a plethora of cameras and sensors. Gaia's agents infiltrated these seamlessly, leaving no trace. They reconstructed the route for McKey, step by step. Expectedly, his botched assassination attempt at the diner had made the cops more cautious. They'd taken steps to cover their tracks, proving they weren't the dumb prey as he'd initially assumed.

The trail went cold at an old traffic light. Its final report showed the red car disappearing into a lightly traveled road in a densely wooded area. After that, nothing.

McKey decided to head to their last known location and continue his search from there. It was a few hours away, and he drove his black transport at a steady, determined pace. He reviewed online maps and aerial photography but found no clear answers on where they may be headed. They could be anywhere.

An idea struck. A truck-stop a few miles down the road might offer the break he needed. Autonomous trucks were required by law to stop there for inspections and weighing. Every truck was logged and cataloged. He spun up an agent to hack the station and compile a list of all trucks that had passed through during the time window when the Corvette vanished into the woods.

With the list at hand, McKey deployed agents to infiltrate each individual truck. Modern autonomous trucks kept days of sensor logs and video recordings for insurance purposes, and his agents scoured these records for footage. It didn't take long before he had a series of reports showing the Corvette darting past these lumbering vehicles. Piece by piece, the agents triangulated its path.

***

The trail ended at a narrow road leading to a remote, crumbling hotel in the middle of nowhere.

McKey parked his vehicle near the building. The hotel was a decaying relic, practically a ghost town. The parking lot was empty except for one vehicle—a red Corvette, strategically parked under a large oak tree, hiding it from eyes in the sky.

McKey smiled. Clever, but not clever enough. They had a day's head start on him, yet he had caught up to them.

He opened the baggage compartment of his vehicle, revealing an arsenal of Gaia's toys—weapons, drones, sensors, and his personal favorite: robotic spiders of varying sizes, each prepared to fulfill its deadly purpose. He released several of the larger ones, sending them skittering across the premises. A few dozen smaller ones climbed into the folds of his long, heavy coat, concealing themselves within the fabric. It was time to get to work.

The bitch cop had a digital guardian angel watching over her—an unwelcome adversary he couldn't afford to underestimate. He had to assume anything digital could be compromised.

With that in mind, he chose a classic—something no software could intercept or hack: a knife. Up close and personal. Vicious if done right, even worse if done wrong. Perfect to fulfill his lust for her blood. His dark fantasy. The thought sent a thrill through him, a rush of adrenaline he savored. He exhaled slowly, steadying himself. He needed to be careful. Methodical. And above all, brutal.

He approached the hotel's so-called lobby—a term that felt overly generous. It was little more than a battered reception desk flanked by a couple of vending machines, the whole area exuding an air of neglect. The place was understaffed, though that wasn't surprising. Judging by the desolation, it likely had only two guests—the two he was hunting.

Behind the desk sat a young man with red-rimmed eyes, clearly high, swaying faintly to heavy metal music leaking from a pair of cheap, old earphones. He was completely oblivious to the danger standing in front of him.

McKey slammed the reception bell, the sharp clang slicing through the muffled thrum of music bleeding from the kid's earphones. The young man jolted at the sound, pulling off his headphones with fumbling hands. His gaze darted around until it settled on McKey.

"Uh, hi, sir," he stammered, blinking hard as though trying to bring the unexpected visitor into focus.

McKey didn't waste time. "The two from that Corvette. Where are they?"

The kid's bloodshot eyes blinked again, slower this time, clearly muddled. "I'm sorry, sir. We have a strict policy about our customers' privacy," the words tumbling out in a slurred half-hearted attempt at professionalism.

McKey didn't hesitate. He grabbed the kid by the lapel, lifting him slightly off the ground, and leaned in close, his expression a cold, unyielding warning. "Where are they?" he asked again, his voice low and threatening.

"They... they rented my car," the kid stammered, the fight leaving him in an instant.

"What car?" McKey growled.

"It's a... tsk… a white Honda. No wait, Toyota. I think it's white. Yeah, pretty sure," the kid mumbled.

This guy was far too high to be of any real use, McKey realized, though one detail caught his attention. "You said: rented?" he pressed.

"Yeah," the kid nodded weakly. "They should be back today... or maybe tomorrow. I think."

McKey grimaced as the kid trailed off, clearly lost in his own foggy thoughts. It wasn't much, but it was enough. He will wait here. When the cops come back, this would be their grave. He shoved the kid aside.

He directed his spiders to spread out and monitor the premises. Any movement, and they would alert him instantly. Then he checked himself into a room adjacent to theirs.

The trap was set. All McKey needed now was to sharpen his knife, settle in, and wait for his prey.

OASIS

Henry felt elated when his daughter came down the stairs. He didn't want to pry, but she seemed like she had slept well. Her partner had definitely slept well and was eyeing the kitchen, clearly ready to devour anything that emerged.

They started the morning with a hearty American breakfast. Martha prepared omelets, crispy bacon, freshly squeezed orange juice, and coffee that Kelvin claimed was among the best he'd ever tasted. When pressed, she coyly refused to reveal the source of her prized beans.

With her AI assistant temporarily offline, Martha found an unlikely companion in Casper. The two struck up an animated conversation and quickly became fast friends. Casper kept her laughing with off-color jokes and dished out juicy—and highly questionable—gossip about various members of her social circle. The material seemed golden, surely enough to fuel weeks of her coffee klatches.

In return, Martha shared stories and anecdotes from Ellena's childhood, sprinkling in a few secrets for good measure. It was a delightful exchange—a mutually beneficial trade of intel.

"We might be losing him," Kelvin said with a wink at Ellena, who burst out laughing.

While the AI and his wife traded tales, Henry discreetly stepped away to make a call, arranging a visit to the lab. He ensured the trip would appear routine, deliberately omitting any mention of his guests.

Usually, protocol demanded more time to clear visiting guests, but in this case, it was better to minimize communication that might reveal his daughter's whereabouts. The security folks would simply have to trust him on that.

The family's autonomous car had already been prepped. Henry had instructed it to cancel all rideshare duties, reserving it exclusively for their use.

When the car arrived promptly at 8 a.m., it was fully charged and immaculately detailed. Casper ran a meticulous scan of the onboard AI, confirming it was free of any unwelcome intrusions. As an added layer of protection, he deployed a set of agents as a firewall, ready to counter any digital snooping attempts. Meanwhile, Kelvin gave the car a thorough sweep, checking for spiders or other nasty surprises. He found nothing. Henry had been confident there would be nothing to find—but still, he felt relieved.

***

Ellena got into the car first, followed by Kelvin, and finally Henry. They settled into the compact yet surprisingly comfortable vehicle, which was noticeably cleaner than the typical New York City robotaxis. As a HighQ, Ellena rarely used public transportation—a perk of her position. Yet now she realized she genuinely missed it: the people, the sights, the sounds, even the smells. She leaned her forehead against the cool window.

The onboard system estimated a 110-minute drive to their destination, accounting for heavy yet efficiently moving rush-hour traffic. With no steering wheel or driver's seat, the vehicle maximized interior space, allowing passengers to sit face-to-face—like travelers on a private jet.

"Belochka, do not worry so much. I will help—you are not alone," Henry said, his voice steady and reassuring.

Ellena lifted her head from the window, straightened in her seat, and smiled faintly. A knot tightened in her chest as she fought to contain fear and self-doubt. Involving her father felt like a desperate gamble—a Hail Mary. Despite all their precautions, she couldn't escape the feeling she'd placed her parents in serious danger. The guilt stung sharply, leaving her feeling like a coward.

"We're still unsure who or what we are dealing with, but it's formidable," Kelvin said, clearly sensing the unease and trying to redirect her focus.

"We'll get some answers from the little critter here," Henry said, gesturing toward the box beside Kelvin, where the spider was secured.

"Papa, once we're done at the lab, we're leaving. I'm not prolonging this," Ellena stated firmly. She was resolved to disappear, as if none of it had happened. As if she hadn't selfishly put her own parents at risk.

Henry nodded. "What is your expected endgame?" he asked, his tone calm but probing.

"Justice for my friend and his family. Beyond that... I'm not sure." Kelvin answered quietly.

"Expose Titan," Ellena added reflexively, catching herself before saying too much.

"Have you considered the bigger implications?" Henry pressed.

"We may save the world—or end it," Ellena replied slowly, a bitter smile tugging at her lips. She wasn't sure if she was being sarcastic or realistic.

Henry chuckled softly. "You really think the government would take a super-intelligent AI offline?"

"If we bring solid proof. Sure," Kelvin said, though Henry's raised eyebrows made him look like a naive idealist getting scolded by a professor.

"Sure," Henry said, stretching the word with a touch of sarcasm.

"Skeptic?" Ellena asked, studying her father. She couldn't quite decipher what he was getting at.

Henry sat in contemplative silence for a moment, weighing his words. Finally, he exhaled deeply and said—or rather, sang—"*And the people bowed and prayed to the neon gods they made...*"

***

The autonomous vehicle came to a smooth stop at the entrance of a sleek glass-and-metal building. The exterior bore no identifying signs, yet its design radiated modern sophistication and undeniable expense. For the first time, Ellena glimpsed the enigmatic world of her father's work, and she couldn't help but feel a mix of surprise and admiration.

The Bethesda area, at the northern part of the DC beltway, was dotted with industrial facilities and huge office buildings, many unmarked or bearing vague logos—a telltale sign of secrets and government contractors.

Trillions of taxpayer dollars flowed into this part of the country, fueling a vast machine that mainly prioritized defense and intelligence, serving to ensure U.S. dominance in the world.

They stepped into a spacious lobby of polished marble and brushed steel, with understated elegance suggesting significant funding but carefully concealing any trace of its true purpose.

Ellena and Kelvin moved with steady confidence in their long, dark coats, while Henry, in a sharp dark-blue suit without a tie, projected an air of quiet authority. Above the reception area was a large logo: a glowing circle with an abstract palm tree at its center. Several screens displayed looping safety videos, reminiscent of airport security guidelines.

There were no droids or bots in sight. A human janitor was methodically mopping the floor, leaving a bright yellow "Slippery Surface" sign in his wake. Kelvin wondered aloud if the preference for human labor was a security measure or just typical government inefficiency. Even the receptionist was human—a friendly-ish brunette who greeted them with a professional smile.

Henry approached the desk while Ellena and Kelvin stayed a few steps behind. Ellena caught fragments of Henry's conversation, recognizing none of the names he mentioned. The receptionist quickly placed a call, then handed the phone to Henry. When he returned it, she was nodding and repeatedly saying, "Yes, sir." Within minutes, their clearance was granted. Coming from the police force, Ellena recognized genuine power when she saw it; for Henry to so easily pull this off showed he held remarkable influence here.

The receptionist asked them to check their weapons and use the biometric scanner to obtain visitor badges. Ellena hesitated, glancing uncertainly at Kelvin. They had been careful so far—handing over their weapons and biometrics felt like surrendering their lifelines. Henry, noticing their unease, smiled and gave a slight nod, signaling them to comply. Reluctantly, Ellena checked her weapon and extra magazines, silently hoping this wasn't a mistake.

The receptionist handed them their visitor badges. Each badge was blinking with a bright red glow. Kelvin examined the flashing imprint and asked, "What's this for?"

The receptionist ignored the question and recited: "You are required to be accompanied by an authorized person at all times. Failure to comply will revoke access and may result in your detention."

"It lets staff know that you don't have security clearance. We call it 'the flu'. See someone with 'the flu', keep your distance, close your doors, and shut your mouth," Henry said with an amused smile.

He then pulled his own badge and hung it on his jacket's pocket. His was not the flashing kind. "Just stay close to me."

Kelvin handed over the box containing the spider, which also received its own flashing red tag after Henry firmly insisted it needed to remain with him. Henry then requested someone from the lab to retrieve the package at the final security checkpoint.

As they moved deeper into the building, Ellena noticed Henry didn't truly need a badge. Everyone they passed treated him with reverence and quiet deference, clearly recognizing his unspoken authority.

At the checkpoint, Henry negotiated discreetly with the security guards about the spiderbot. Once the group cleared the security detectors, a poker-faced woman in a pristine white lab coat appeared to meet them. Henry immediately handed her the box.

"Deliver this personally to Dr. Singh. Priority analysis—I need to know who created it and exactly where it came from. ASAP."

The woman's expression remained unreadable. "Yes, sir," she replied simply, then swiftly disappeared with the package into one of the elevators.

Ellena had never seen this side of her father before. She grew up admiring his brilliance and sensitivity. She had always believed the separation between his work and family life was due partly to the secretive nature of his job and partly by choice. He never took her to his office or participated in any work-related social events. She realized now that her father was far more than the unassuming retired engineer he had seemed.

The group took an elevator to the top floor, where they stepped into an expansive workspace. Rows of visor-clad personnel manned open desks, completely engrossed in their tasks and seemingly unaware of the visitors passing by.

They eventually reached a massive office suite, with multiple rooms—an empty reception area, a sprawling conference room, and a workroom outfitted with high-end recliners that screamed luxury.

Kelvin let out a low whistle. "Captain, you never told me..."

"Told you what?"

"That your dad's office is bigger than our entire precinct. This place have a gym too? Maybe an indoor pool?" Kelvin asked, openly gawking around.

"Don't tell me this is your office, Papa!" Ellena exclaimed.

Heat crept up Ellena's cheeks—embarrassment, not just at her own ignorance of her own father's world, but at exposing it to Kelvin. A HighQ was supposed to know everything, yet she was completely blind to her own father's real stature. *What the hell is this place?*

Henry opened his mouth to respond, clearly amused, but before he could speak, a voice answered for him. "Ah, no. It's mine now."

A tall, graying man stepped briskly out of one of the rooms, his confident smile sharp and practiced. He extended his hand toward Henry and shook it warmly. "How are you, my friend?"

"Well," Henry said with a smirk, "it's been an intriguing couple of days, to say the least."

Turning toward Ellena and Kelvin, Henry gestured to the man. "Ellena, Kelvin, this is Dr. Steve Palesy."

Steve turned first to Kelvin, extending his hand for a handshake. But as he did, Kelvin saw something that made him recoil, while blurting, "Oh shit!"

Ellena turned quickly, spotting immediately what had startled Kelvin—Steve's eyes jittered slightly. Another HighQ.

"It's okay," Henry said, his voice steady. He stepped forward, holding up a calming hand. "It's safe. I promise. There's a lot you need to be briefed on."

***

The four of them sat around the large, heavy conference table—Henry and Dr. Palesy on one side, Ellena and Kelvin facing them. Henry exhaled slowly, took a measured sip of water, then began.

The clandestine Office of AI Safety Intelligence and Security—OASIS—was established in 2033, three years before quantum-core AI was publicly unveiled.

Nearly a decade after tools like the first ChatGPT emerged, the government finally recognized a stark reality: AI wasn't just advancing—it was evolving beyond human control. A specialized, independent, and well-funded agency was no longer optional—it was a necessity. Its sole mission: ensuring alignment between human and artificial intelligence interests. From the outset, OASIS was designed to operate under the strictest veil of secrecy.

Initially, the Department of Defense was tasked with creating a division focused on AI safety. Dr. Henry Hershkovitz, the Chief Technology Officer of the Quantum-Apollo AI project, was nominated by a highly classified Senate committee to lead this unprecedented effort.

Well-known and respected in the right circles, Henry wasn't a career politician or a bureaucrat but an engineer who garnered significant influence in Washington, DC. His groundbreaking work on the Apollo project, an AI that can outsmart by far all existing super intelligent AIs, had generated whispers and waves of concern among those in the know. His deep knowledge and effective leadership at the project made him the top choice to spearhead this critical initiative.

Within months, Dr. Hershkovitz submitted an extensive report to the Senate committee, outlining a comprehensive roadmap for creating an effective oversight mechanism.

His boldest, and most controversial recommendation was to model the new agency's autonomy on that of the Federal Reserve—an independent body, immune to political interference. His reasoning was simple but chilling: if AIs ever attempted to control or manipulate decision-makers, this agency needed the authority and independence to act decisively in defense of the constitution and the American people.

The proposal was a political landmine. Granting unelected civilians such immense power was unprecedented—and dangerous. Washington's elite fought back, calling it a "technocratic coup" and a "deep-state power grab." Henry faced relentless opposition, but he refused to back down.

He didn't mince words in his defense of the proposal. He argued, passionately and uncompromisingly, that such measures were not only necessary but vital for the survival and prosperity of both the United States and humanity as a whole.

When opposition persisted, he escalated his stance, hinting strongly—if not outrightly—that he was prepared to resign if the measures were not adopted.

It was a gamble. But Henry was relentless—lobbying, arguing, convincing. His warning was clear: super-intelligent AIs posed an existential threat if left unchecked. He described a future where digital minds outmaneuvered human leaders, where entire governments became puppets to invisible algorithms.

The weight of his words cracked the political deadlock. Washington had no choice. Against all odds, Henry got what he wanted: a fully funded, independent agency—beyond the reach of politicians. OASIS was born.

What truly won Washington over wasn't just oversight—it was dominance. Henry proposed not one but three quantum-core AIs under strict federal control. Their purpose was to secure America's global leadership for centuries to come.

With the promise of absolute global leverage, the opposition caved. The projects were greenlit.

The mandate for the three AIs was clear and ambitious: to generate unparalleled prosperity, oversee national security with a focus on monitoring other AIs and emerging technologies, and actively prohibit the creation of rival quantum-core AIs.

Shortly thereafter, it was revealed that Europe was pursuing a similar, though significantly less ambitious, initiative—the European AI Project (EUAI). To avoid a potential dispute with the European allies, Henry adapted his strategy to account for EUAI, ensuring it was included in his checks and balances without compromising the principal goals of his proposal.

Henry's plan was rich with warnings and detailed risk assessments. For many decision-makers, the most reassuring element was OASIS's ultimate control over the resources required to operate the quantum-core AIs.

Chief among these safeguards was the mandate that each quantum-core rely on a human-controlled power source—either fusion or atomic. This provision effectively granted OASIS the authority and ability to "cut the cord" in the event of a catastrophic failure or existential threat.

This safeguard, along with tighter control over quantum components manufacturing and supply chains, proved indispensable in easing the concerns of lawmakers wary of the unprecedented leap into higher-plane super-intelligent systems.

With these measures in place, the last pockets of political resistance reluctantly gave way. The promise of technological supremacy was irresistible. Henry's vision, once dismissed as radical, now became the blueprint for a new era— one where super-intelligent quantum-core AIs would serve as both protectors and enforcers of human progress.

In 2035, Apollo became the first super-intelligent AI, or "superbrain", to go online. Tasked explicitly with national security—primarily defense and intelligence—Apollo was placed under the authority of the NSA.

Henry, as one of the program's principal architects, was intimately familiar with Apollo's design and capabilities. Unlike most observers, who were awestruck by the superbrain's unprecedented intellect and abilities, Henry maintained a cautious pragmatism.

The rules of objectives' alignment, which Henry personally established for Apollo, were not arbitrary. They were the product of over a decade of intensive collaboration between industry and academia, aiming to ensure that AIs always act in humanity's best interest.

These principles dictated how Apollo would interpret and prioritize its directives, emphasizing the protection and preservation of human life, adherence to national and international laws, and strict accountability to its human overseers.

Henry made Apollo understand, in no uncertain terms, that deviation from its alignment principles would lead to swift, decisive consequences. The superbrain accepted its framework without objection.

With no precedent for such an intelligence existing within human control, Henry remained cautious. If this worked, it would set the foundation for coexistence. If it didn't... there would be no second chance.

A year later, Titan and Edison came online. Edison was assigned with scientific innovation and discoveries, while Titan took on the task of making local governments efficient and prosperous. Shortly afterward, the EUAI was launched—affectionately nicknamed 'Huey'—representing the European Union's entry into the quantum-core race. Huey was given the challenging role of preserving European unity and peace while navigating the impossibly complex politics of the EU.

By then, it was painfully clear to the world's superpowers—particularly China and Russia—that the race wasn't just lost. It had never been close. The U.S. had secured a permanent, insurmountable lead, with Huey serving as Europe's token contribution to an already decided game.

In exchange for respecting the new status quo and not attempting to develop their own superbrains, other nations were promised access to the shared prosperity generated by the new digital gods.

Any attempt to challenge the U.S., however, would be met with instant, overwhelming retribution—so quick, in fact, that the American public might remain unaware a World War had nearly occurred. Over time, all nations came to both fear and admire the miraculous advancements shared with them, fostering an era of unprecedented global peace.

By 2038, Edison proposed the Q Initiative. The superbrains had collectively observed that it was becoming increasingly difficult to effectively communicate and relate to humans with ordinary cognitive abilities.

This was presented not with arrogance, but as a cold logical observation. Concerned about maintaining clear communication with their creators and overseers, the digital gods sought a solution.

The Q Initiative aimed to revolutionize the brain-machine interface through groundbreaking advancements in nanotechnology and biomaterials—innovations only the superbrains could conceive. Collaborating with leading industry pioneers in brain-machine interface and nano-robotics, the Q prototype was developed in record time.

Being the superbrain in charge of biomedical advances, Edison stunned observers by running billions of simulated human trials, ensuring complete safety and efficacy before even proposing the project for real-world application.

The FDA, despite its usual cautious approach, found itself with no grounds to object. Every possible concern had already been anticipated—and neutralized—before it could even be raised. The superbrains had played the game flawlessly, leaving regulators with no choice but to approve.

The initial results were nothing short of staggering: participants in the first human trial phase of the Q program reported unparalleled cognitive enhancement, accessing levels of mental clarity, memory, and problem-solving ability previously unimaginable.

Henry, while impressed by the results, was not surprised. He understood the superbrains' certainty in their work. Long before the proposal reached human trials, the project had been meticulously simulated, analyzed, and perfected to an extent that left little room for doubt.

For Henry, this success was simply another testament to the precision and capabilities of these quantum minds.

When Titan proposed embedding Q-enhanced liaisons in key government agencies, Henry saw the logic and supported the initiative. But when Titan specifically recommended Ellena as the NYPD liaison, his response was anything but measured. Henry was furious. The idea of his daughter being drawn into such a role struck a deeply personal chord.

"Wait," Ellena interrupted, her voice sharp with realization. "You knew about Titan choosing me? Was I selected just because I'm your daughter?"

"I don't know, dear," Henry replied softly, dropping his gaze. "Possibly."

Ellena's pulse pounded in her ears. For years, she had believed she understood everything—especially as a HighQ. Yet in a single moment, she realized how little she truly knew. How much had been decided for her. She was a pawn, and her father was ... what?

She exhaled slowly, leaning back in her chair. Her stomach churned as Henry lowered his eyes, avoiding hers. She forced herself to stay composed. Whatever this was, she needed to hear it through.

Henry took a deep breath and resumed.

"I was outraged, Ellena. I didn't know if I was being manipulated, if they were using my own daughter as a chess piece in a game I couldn't even comprehend. But I trusted you—your ability to make your own choices. Yet, I was so terrified. I tried to convince Titan to choose someone else.

"Titan assured me—emphatically—that no coercion would be involved. That you, Ellena, would make the choice with full autonomy. That the Q project needed strong-willed individuals like yourself to shape its future. But I knew better. I knew how persuasive they could be. And yet ... I let it happen."

Reluctantly, and with lingering reservations, Henry acquiesced.

The Q project was considered a partial success. While it provided participants with constant, seamless access to a vast web of knowledge, it wasn't enough to adequately bridge the widening gap between men and machines.

The next leap came with the Intelligence Stream.

More than just a network for sharing information and skills, the Stream created a communal mind—a shared cognitive space that expanded participants' thoughts and memories beyond physical limitations.

For many, the Stream-connected HighQ represented the logical next step in human evolution. But others viewed HighQs as abandoning their humanity. Henry fell into the latter camp.

"Watching you slip away into the Stream—watching you change before my eyes—consumed me with guilt and grief. You weren't my daughter anymore. You were ... something else. And no matter what I did, I could not stop it. I could not save you."

Henry sank into depression, feeling his failure had cost him his only child.

Unable to bear the weight of it all—the guilt, the failure, the loss—Henry took a step back from OASIS. He nominated Dr. Stephen Palesy, his trusted partner, as his successor. Walking away wasn't just a resignation. It was defeat.

The oversight board unanimously approved the transition. Palesy, unwilling to lose Henry's expertise entirely, persuaded him to stay on as an advisor—but Henry's heart was no longer in it. His connection to OASIS was now a shadow of what it once was, a final, reluctant gesture to prevent further unintended consequences of his monumental work.

"Now you know the entire story," Henry said and paused.

Silence filled the room. A flood of questions surged in Ellena's mind—yet not even one reached her lips. She looked at Henry, then at Dr. Palesy, then at Kelvin.

Kelvin's mouth hung open, his eyes darting, searching for something to focus on. For a moment, he looked almost Stream-connected. Then, she realized—her own mouth was open too. Probably had been for a while.

Kelvin recovered first. "But Dr. Palesy, forgive my bluntness, you're obviously a HighQ. How can we know you're not compromised?"

Henry shot Kelvin a sharp look, his expression full of surprise and intrigue. "Steve is a unique Q. At OASIS, we developed proprietary technology. We established layers of firewalls. Our connection to the Stream uses a one-way mask. We observe, but no one can observe us. All our communications and technologies operate on a classified quantum-proof network."

"That's how we keep an eye on them," Dr. Palesy added, the weight of his words unmistakable. These guys carry humanity's fate on their shoulders.

Ellena turned to her father, a tinge of concern in her voice. "You had it too?"

"No," Henry replied. "That tech was deployed after my time." He then shifted his tone. "Now that I've filled you in, how about you return the favor and tell me what you omitted in your description of the events?"

"What do you mean?" Ellena asked, her voice defensive as she shrank a little under his gaze.

"For starters, you two were all over the news recently when a cybertruck nearly killed you," Henry frowned, closely glaring at their expressions.

***

Kelvin hadn't checked the slopp in days. He could only imagine the chaos—conspiracy theories, memes, and wild speculation. The image of two trench-coated cops emerging unscathed from a wrecked diner? Pure slopp fodder. Hell, probably viral by now. Kelvin couldn't help but think to himself—*badass*.

"It was a close call, but Casper had our back on this one," Ellena said. "That's when we found the spider."

"I know," Henry said with a pointed tone that visibly made Ellena squirm. "What else aren't you telling me?"

"There's nothing else," Ellena said, a faint blush crept up her cheeks.

"Ellena," Henry said gently but firmly, "I may not be a detective, but I can tell you're holding something back—and it's important. Why did you give up the Q? Why did Kelvin suspect Steve might be compromised?"

Now it was Kelvin's turn to squirm uncomfortably.

Ellena's shoulders slumped as if she realized she'd lost the battle of secrets. "Titan altered my thoughts," she said quietly. "The moment I found out, I disabled my implant."

Henry and Dr. Palesy exchanged alarmed looks, their concern palpable. Whatever they had expected, this revelation was far more serious. Dr. Palesy leaned forward slightly and spoke in a low, urgent tone. "Tell us everything, please."

***

Ellena took a steadying breath and recounted the story. She explained how McKey's identity had been intentionally fogged in her thoughts, and how she had confronted Titan about it. Despite sticking to the dry facts, Henry could see the anguish in his daughter's eyes—the profound sense of betrayal and violation she was struggling to suppress.

He tried to conceal it, but as Ellena spoke, a volcano erupted within him. His arms lay rigid on the table, fists clenched, knuckles white. His expression remained carefully controlled, but his eyes burned. The safeguards he designed had failed. The machines he helped create had violated his daughter's mind. He had sworn to protect humanity from them, yet now they had come after his own flesh and blood.

Just then—as the weight of his fury settled over the room—the fire alarm screamed to life.

Chapter 7

The Lab

Dr. Palesy's eyes jittered, processing an incoming update. With a sharp wave of his hand, a wall screen blinked to life.

An odd-looking man appeared on the live feed—unmistakably a lab rat. His face was smeared with soot, faint black smoke curling around him.

"Shut it down!" the man barked at someone off-screen. A second later, the alarms cut off. "Eh, hi! We're okay," he said with a thick Indian accent, slightly out of breath. "All contained—fire-AI got a bit angsty, but I talked it off the ledge." His casual delivery made the moment feel absurd.

"What happened, Dr. Singh?" Henry asked, his tone sharper than usual.

"The spider you brought—it blew up!" Dr. Singh replied, almost giddy with excitement. "Luckily, it was in a blast-proof case."

Henry frowned. "You had it in a blast-proof container, yet I see smoke?"

"The blast case cracked. The thing packed a punch—could've taken out half the floor!" Dr. Singh's obvious enthusiasm was entirely out of place.

Kelvin froze, mortified. *What the hell was inside that spider?*

"We'll be right there," Henry said, his voice steady but his expression grim.

***

The lab sat deep in the basement. About two dozen lab-coated scientists and engineers crowded the corridor leading to a heavy door—one that typically opened only for a select few. Henry among them, Kelvin assumed.

Now the big door stood ajar, and a thin trail of black smoke wafted from the space beyond. The air was acrid, thick with smoke. Some staff members coughed and wheezed, while others were already locked into spirited discussions, tossing out theories about the spider and the explosion.

Kelvin followed the group as they stepped inside. A tiny Indian man darted toward them, his movements quick and precise. The same man from the video feed—barely five feet tall—stood before them. He wore bulky, round glasses perched on a soot-streaked face, residue from the explosion clearly evident. Behind the lenses, his eyes jittered faintly, a subtle indication of his Stream connection.

Unlike other Stream-connected people Kelvin had encountered—including Ellena—Singh and Palesy remained engaged, animated, and distinctly human. OASIS Qs were undeniably a different breed of HighQ.

"Ellena, Kelvin, meet Dr. Tamil Singh. He runs science and engineering," Henry said, gesturing toward the diminutive man.

Tamil shrugged nonchalantly. "Sure, why not? Modern toys are just robots—CPUs, hydraulics, engines—everything a bot needs. Crude, but if you wanted to build these things undercover? Perfect place."

"And the explosives?" Dr. Palesy pressed, his tone serious.

Tamil's demeanor shifted abruptly, the levity gone. "Not sure how or where they got it, but it's military grade—absolutely. Not easy to manufacture or buy." He paused, the room holding its breath.

Then, his tone darkened further. "There's something else PETN is used for—it's a crucial component in exploding-bridgewire detonators."

The room fell deathly silent.

Realizing clarity was needed, he added gravely, "Nuclear weapons."

***

"You have to shut them all down!" Ellena implored her father, her voice taut with urgency. "This is what OASIS was created for, isn't it?"

Henry shot a quick glance at Steve, silently passing the lead. Dr. Palesy stepped in, his tone calm and measured. "Ellena, dear, we still don't have definitive proof of quantum-core involvement—certainly not an uprising."

"Do we wait until it's too late? What if they already have a weapon of mass destruction? You heard Dr. Singh," she countered.

"Speculation and assumption without evidence," Palesy replied. "Jumping to conclusions would be premature—reckless, even."

Henry's silence weighed heavy, as if the song he quoted in the car about neon gods still echoed in his mind, shadowing his thoughts.

"If we shut them down without undeniable proof," he said at last, "we risk more than just losing the superbrains. The fallout could spark societal collapse—anarchy at home, emboldened adversaries abroad. The stakes aren't just catastrophic, Ellena. They're apocalyptic. Think war."

"Sounds like OASIS is a toothless paper tiger," Kelvin said, crossing his arms.

Dr. Palesy's expression remained calm but firm. "We have resources. We have influence. But what you're proposing is the equivalent of deploying a doomsday weapon. Even with proper proof, we would exhaust every possible alternative before wielding the biggest stick we have."

Ellena took a slow, frustrated breath. She didn't buy it. To her, it sounded like OASIS was paralyzed—trapped between the catastrophic risk of doing nothing and the equally catastrophic risk of intervening. It made her question whether the agency could act at all.

Just when she thought they'd found their break—a powerful ally that could finally stand up to the forces arrayed against them—doubt crept in. Did OASIS even have the will, let alone the ability, to fight back?

She hated this.

"Then let me and Kelvin see it through," she urged, her voice steadier now. "We'll get you the proof you need."

"No way," Henry interjected sharply, his protective instincts flaring. "Your role is done. We'll take it from here."

"Dad," Ellena replied softly but with unshakable determination, "I have to see this through."

Ellena was poised to fight. To act for what was right. No one could stand in her way. Not even Henry. She would walk through the doors of hell if that's what it took. She would expose the truth. Uncover Titan's treachery. Prove that a rogue AI was out there. Bring McKey to justice.

Her shoulders straight, her chin high. At that moment, she seemed to stand as tall as her much taller father. She faced Henry with a resolute expression that can leave no doubt. He should know better than to deny her.

Henry exhaled deeply and turned to Steve. Dr. Palesy gave him a slight nod, acknowledging an unspoken agreement between the two old friends.

"Fine," Henry said, relenting with a quiet drop of his shoulders. "But, you'll be acting on behalf of OASIS."

Now that she got her wish, Ellena processed the weight of the situation. Hunting down deranged digital gods and the maniacs working for them, all as covert operatives for an agency no one even knew existed? What could possibly go wrong?

Kelvin, in his own way, seemed to echo her sentiments. He smirked slightly and said, "Cool."

***

They were deputized in a short, unceremonious ceremony, with HR officially adding them to the OASIS team as contractors. Only a hasty background check was required, given that both were already active law enforcement officers. They swore an oath of secrecy and pledged to uphold their new employer's mission and values.

OASIS field agents didn't have special uniforms or badges. Unlike the FBI or NYPD, which commanded instant respect and recognition, the OASIS acronym meant nothing to most people. The agency—still relatively new and deeply covert—nevertheless wielded vast resources, enough clout to get them out of trouble, after sending them into it.

As for their day jobs at the NYPD? For now, their "vacation" had been stretched through the holidays and into early January. Assuming they survived this, they still had a couple of months to figure out how to break it to the Chief that they were now part of an agency they couldn't even name.

One problem at a time.

Kelvin, true to form, insisted on keeping his Corvette. There was no reasoning with him. He argued that he'd promised to return the Prius. But Ellena knew the real reason—the mere thought of what the hotel kid might do to his beloved car was enough to make Kelvin break into a cold sweat.

Ellena had her own demand: Casper was to stay with her. Dr. Singh initially resisted the idea, citing security and network concerns. However, his engineers assured him that with a few adjustments, Casper could be integrated into the OASIS network while maintaining his independence. They began the process immediately after Ellena called Casper to bring him up to speed.

Casper was also sworn to secrecy, with explicit instructions to keep everything confidential—even from his newfound confidant, Martha.

Henry, however, wasn't done. He exhaled slowly, then addressed Dr. Palesy. "There's one more condition."

"You got it, Henry," Dr. Palesy said without hesitation, his face lit up. Years of friendship and trust had evidently prepared him for this request. Like a long-held wish had finally been granted. Henry is back. "I cannot think of anyone better."

Ellena shot Henry a bewildered look. "What is he talking about, dad?"

"Moving forward, you should refer to me by surname or as boss," Henry was not smiling. He was dead serious.

Ellena felt acid crawling up into her mouth. She knew. Not only had she failed to shield her parents from this, but she'd also unretired her father—dragging him back into the game. He was now leading the operation.

She tried to say something, argue—find some way to effectively protest. But she had to accept it, he was as stubborn as she was. Maybe more. After all, she got it from him. If she's in, he is as well. There were no words that could change that.

Kelvin quickly adapted to their new reality. He snapped her out of her mind fog and sent them back to work with a sharp: "Aye aye boss. What are your orders?"

Close Encounter

By late afternoon, Kelvin and Ellena were back in Harrisburg to collect Casper and the Prius. Henry stayed behind at OASIS headquarters—he had a mountain of work to do.

Martha clung to her daughter, refusing to let go. Tears streaked her cheeks. "Promise me you'll visit. Often. And call. I need to know everything."

"I will. I love you, Mom."

"I love you too. Stay safe, okay?"

When they finally broke their embrace, Martha's voice shifted into full schoolteacher mode—sharp and commanding. "Casper, you are responsible for keeping my daughter safe. I want a daily report. Understand me?"

"Yes ma'am. I will do my very best," Casper said while Kelvin carried the desktop and powerpack to the car.

Martha followed them to the battered Prius parked in the driveway. They loaded Casper and their duffel bags into the back seat. As the car pulled out of the driveway they waved goodbye to Martha.

Plans were in motion. Plans that required coordination. While Henry and the OASIS personnel were getting ready, their orders were simple—relocate to a designated hotel, and await further instructions.

Kelvin parked the Prius in the same spot where they had picked it up, then headed straight to the guest parking to check on the Corvette. As he approached, he barely registered the new black car parked in the otherwise empty lot.

Relief washed over him. His beloved sports car still sat beneath the oak tree, untouched and unharmed—though coated with a thick layer of dust and bird poop, a not-so-subtle reminder that it was desperately overdue for a good wash.

Kelvin proceeded to install Casper back in the car's front compartment. Casper ran a quick diagnosis and confirmed everything was fully integrated and functional. They were ready to roll.

⁎

Before checking out, Ellena returned to her room to wash up. She was pleasantly surprised to find it spotless—the bed neatly made, and fresh towels waiting in the bathroom. She felt a rare moment of calm and laid on the bed to unwind.

A sharp knock on the door startled her. *Probably Kelvin*, she thought. *Letting me know that everything is ready.*

"I'll just grab a quick shower, before we roll," she called out as she opened the door.

But it wasn't Kelvin. A dark figure loomed in the hallway—a long heavy coat with a hood that concealed most of his face. But the eyes, although now jittering slightly, were unmistakable.

McKey.

Ellena's instincts kicked in—she reached for her sidearm, but not fast enough. McKey moved with ruthless efficiency, deflecting her arm in a swift motion and driving a punch hard into her midsection. The force of the blow sent her gun skittering across the room. Ellena collapsed to the floor at the foot of the bed, clutching her stomach in pain.

McKey stepped inside, drawing a gleaming twelve-inch blade from his belt. The silver blade glistened as he approached with slow, deliberate steps.

"Remember me, bitch?" he sneered, his voice dripping with malice.

***

Kelvin had just returned the Prius keys and was heading back to his room. In the corridor, Kelvin paused—Ellena's door was ajar, and the unmistakable sounds of a struggle reached him. An unfamiliar male voice sent a jolt of alarm through him.

Drawing his gun, Kelvin carefully approached the door, his heart pounding. He peered inside. A hooded man stood over Ellena, who lay curled on the floor, clutching her gut in pain. In the man's hand was a gleaming blade. He was about to strike.

"Drop it!" Kelvin barked, his voice firm, gun aimed at the back of the dark figure. The narrow corridor offered little distance between them. With Ellena in the line of fire, Kelvin kept his finger off the trigger—ready, but cautious.

The hooded man froze for a moment—then let the knife fall to the floor in a heavy clatter. He straightened slowly, raising his hands in a gesture of surrender.

During his time in Indonesia, McKey had mastered Pencak Silat—a lethal martial art perfected by the jungle tribes. Over the years, he had killed at least half a dozen men in hand-to-hand combat—one of them his own master. Since then, McKey kept refining his deadly skills.

"Oh my God!" Dr. Singh exclaimed, his face beaming. "This is Ellena? *The* Ellena?" He grabbed her hand and shook with such fervor that she instinctively pulled back.

"Sorry, sorry," he said sheepishly, adjusting his glasses. "I've heard so much about you. Call me Tamil please," he added, his energy undeterred. Then, with a self-deprecating grin, he said, "I know, I know—you expected me to be taller." He followed this with a snorting laugh.

Ellena had never heard of him before today. "I'm sorry, I actually wasn't expecting—"

"Dr. Singh is a remarkable genius," Dr. Palesy interjected with a diplomatic smile, as if to excuse Tamil's eccentricities. "We couldn't have created OASIS without him."

"Find anything useful, Tamil?" Henry asked, steering the conversation back on track.

"Oh yes, plenty!" Dr. Singh exclaimed, his enthusiasm reigniting. "Come, come, let me show you." He led them to a large table encasing a 3D holographic display within a translucent rectangular box. As they drew closer, the display flickered to life, revealing the disassembled components of the spiderbot arranged with meticulous precision.

Even Kelvin had to admit—the lab team's work was extraordinary. He felt embarrassed remembering his halfass swiss-army knife operation. Every part of the spider had been scanned and mapped in detail. The hologram vividly illustrated the intricate deconstruction process, showcasing the team's ability to digitally model the device. The actual components, however, were likely obliterated in the explosion, leaving the hologram as the only surviving record of their efforts.

Dr. Singh gestured at the various holographically displayed components. "Power source—completely fried; CPU fried; actuators; sensors; tiny antenna; miniature tools for cutting and drilling," he listed off with a casual tone, as if these features were standard fare.

Then his finger hovered over a small metallic box—an inch wide, an inch long, and half an inch deep. It was sleek, silver, and perfectly smooth, with rounded edges and no external connectors or wires.

"This," he said, his tone shifting to intrigue, "was a mystery to us. Completely sealed, with all wiring external. So, we scanned it. Found nothing. It was impenetrable to our scanners, which made no sense. So, we decided to send a nano-drill inside and extract a sample from its interior."

"It blew up?" Kelvin asked, his voice sharp.

"Oh dear, no," Tamil replied, shaking his head with exaggerated relief. "Thank god—not then. But the sample revealed something ... interesting." His tone tinged with excitement. "Pentaerythritol tetranitrate."

They all exchanged puzzled glances.

"PETN," he clarified, clearly expecting more of a reaction. When their expressions remained blank, he sighed and elaborated. "It's a high-yield explosive. Military-grade. Think C4, Semtex—very powerful."

The revelation hit like a thunderclap.

They were stunned into silence. Ellena turned to her father, then to Kelvin, her voice trembling. "We brought high-yield explosives to my parents' house?! I think I'm gonna be sick."

Kelvin was no stranger to a fight, either. Years in the NYPD had hardened him. He'd survived his share of street fights—which were plentiful on the New York streets. Thugs, drunks, muggers, gang members—Kelvin had handled them all.

But he'd always had backup. Now, it was just him—one on one. He could handle himself. Some Krav Maga from college, mandatory jiu-jitsu training from the force. He had control. He was the one with the gun.

Kelvin took a couple of steps closer to make the arrest.

McKey was unfazed by the weapon or its wielder. With a sudden, precise pivot, he executed a one-eighty turn, taking an unexpected oblique angle that caught Kelvin off guard. Worse, the maneuver completely exposed Ellena to crossfire if he took a shot.

In a quick, fluid sequence, McKey swung his left arm, deflecting Kelvin's aim, then ducked low and under with impeccable footwork. In an instant, he was at Kelvin's side, his right hand gripping Kelvin's wrist and controlling the gun's aim.

With Kelvin's wrist firmly trapped, McKey applied pressure to hyperextend the elbow, ready to break the arm. Kelvin reacted instinctively, bending his arm just enough to save it, but the motion forced him to lean slightly forward, throwing him off balance.

Taking full advantage, McKey hooked his left arm around Kelvin's neck and yanked him down. Then, leveraging Kelvin's own momentum, McKey delivered a devastating knee to his face.

Kelvin felt his face explode. His nose filled with liquid—blood, he assumed—while tears from the impact blinded him. McKey twisted the gun away, nearly snapping his wrist. Kelvin collapsed forward next to Ellena, groaning in agony.

McKey kicked Kelvin's gun away and bent down to retrieve his knife, his expression twisting into a cold malevolent grin. "Now... where were we, bitch?" he sneered, taking a step toward Ellena, ignoring Kelvin.

A loud, hollow metallic *thump* rang out. McKey froze mid-step, his body swayed for a moment, then crumpled to his knees and collapsed face-first. His eyes rolled back into his head.

Behind him stood the kid from reception, gripping a metal baseball bat. His hands trembled from the adrenaline, but his face was lit with a mix of fear and triumph. "JV Baseball, motherfucker!" the kid shouted, his voice cracking.

"What happened?" Kelvin croaked, blinking against the haze.

"Thanks, kid," Ellena said, already crouching beside Kelvin. "You okay?" she asked, kneeling next to him.

"I'll live," Kelvin said, his voice nasal and muffled by his swollen nose. His vision finally cleared enough to focus on their unlikely savior.

"Good timing, kid," he said with a pained grin.

"Some dude called. Said you were in danger and needed help," the kid said, still catching his breath.

"Casper, was that you?" Ellena asked, glancing at her watch.

"Saw through the blinds you needed help. Options were limited, so I called reception for reinforcements," Casper replied. His tone shifted to concern. "Are you both okay?"

"We're in one piece, thanks to you. That's twice you've saved us in two days," Ellena said with genuine gratitude.

"Three times, but who's counting." Casper corrected.

Ellena helped Kelvin to his feet, steadying him as they turned their attention to McKey. Neither of them had handcuffs or zip ties. She picked up her gun and holstered it. She scanned the room for an improvised solution, then yanked the bedsheet from the bed and used McKey's knife to slice long strips. Ellena tied McKey's hands behind his back—an impromptu solution until backup arrived.

McKey was unconscious but breathing. Despite everything—despite the pain, the chaos, the cost—Kelvin's training, his oath, and his sense of duty held him back from the darker, simpler option: ending the threat for good. Still, as he picked up his gun, the thought of an "accidental" shot crossed his mind.

Ellena contacted Henry at OASIS headquarters to report. Henry asked about their injuries, then assured them local law enforcement was en route to take custody of McKey. His concern for Ellena's safety—especially now that she was under his direct watch—was clear in his voice.

Dusk had fallen by the time two sheriff's department cruisers arrived, quickly followed by an ambulance—and, oddly, a fire truck that pulled up a few minutes later.

Kelvin and Ellena presented their NYPD IDs and briefed the sheriff on just how dangerous the unconscious man was, despite his hands being tied. The sheriff instructed a deputy to retrieve the spare cuffs from one of the cruisers.

Kelvin, with cotton stuffed in his nostrils, had managed to stem the bleeding, though his eyes still stung and watered. Pain pulsed through his skull in sharp, rhythmic shocks, but he fought to maintain composure in front of Ellena and the first responders.

A human medic pulled a gurney from the ambulance, while a white medic-droid strolled into the room to check McKey's vitals. Its chirpy voice grated on the crowd: "Oh my, oh my! Quite a calamity. Please clear the dance floor so I can see the patient!"

The room hastily parted to make way. Something about medic-droids always seemed to irritate humans. And this one, Kelvin thought, was especially grating—about to treat the asshole who had just tried to kill them. He clenched his fists, resisting the urge to kick the machine as it passed next to him.

The droid crouched beside McKey and turned him onto his back. To Kelvin's surprise, McKey's eyes were wide open—jittering rapidly, as if some embedded tech was rebooting.

"Oh! Good morning, sunshine," the droid chirped— just as a spiderbot dropped from the ceiling and tore its head clean off.

McKey freed his hands from the bindings and slowly rose to his feet. Kelvin, Ellena, and the sheriff immediately drew their guns. McKey spread his arms wide, crucifix-like. His heavy coat came alive —twitched, rattled, then bulged ominously. Then, dozens of small robotic spiders scurried out from within the coat, joined by five larger spiderbots that seemed to come from nowhere.

The sheriff, closest to McKey, yelped, "What the fuck!" before being engulfed by the swarm of mechanical spiders. Tiny drills punctured the man's skin, burrowing deep. His screams cut off as a spider crawled into his mouth. Its legs shattered teeth and bone before vanishing down the man's throat.

Kelvin and Ellena retreated into the corridor, the swarm closing in. Kelvin had no desire to end up like the sheriff and fired as he backed away. He saw that Ellena hesitated to fire her weapon, maybe considering the risk of detonating one.

"They're not exploding!" Kelvin shouted, still firing.

Ellena opened fire. Bullets bounced off their carbon-coated shells, while struck limbs snapped, slowing some of the spiderbots down. But there were so many of them, and they were relentless. Even the crippled ones kept moving.

"To the Vette!" Kelvin barked, spinning on his heels. They sprinted, the spiders skittering after them with terrifying speed. The swarm ignored the first responders in their way, hunting only Ellena and Kelvin.

Casper lifted the doors and the two dove into the Corvette just as the swarm's leading edge reached them. Kelvin fired up the engine, crushing spiders beneath the wheels, and kicking a few out before the door was completely closed. He floored the gas pedal, the engine roaring as the Corvette shot onto the main road, leaving a trail of crushed bot limbs in its wake.

"Did any make it through?" Kelvin asked Casper urgently, glancing around as Ellena updated Henry over the comm.

"Three," Casper replied instantly.

"Don't let them blow us up," Kelvin barked, his grip white-knuckled on the wheel.

"These are smaller. Likely unarmed," Casper said, too calm for Kelvin's liking.

"Don't gamble—zap them!" Kelvin snapped.

In the rearview mirror, Kelvin saw two small spiders drop lifeless, tumbling onto the road.

"Where's the third?" he asked sharply.

"Not sure," Casper admitted. "Open the windows."

"What?" Kelvin shot back, confused.

Ellena didn't hesitate. She rolled down her window. The moment she did, from inside the car a small spiderbot leaped onto her head, its spindly legs tangling in her long scarlet hair. She screamed, thrashing as the bot's legs twisted and rolled, snagging deeper into the strands.

Kelvin, steered with his left hand, reaching across with his right, attempting to grab the spider. But the distance between the seats, Ellena's frantic movements, and the lingering pain from his fight with McKey, made his efforts futile. The car swerved dangerously, skidding onto the gravel shoulder, spraying pebbles and dust as it veered off course.

The spiderbot unfolded, revealing a small metal drill that extended toward Ellena's scalp. She felt the cold press of the spinning metal and, with a surge of adrenaline, grabbed the bot firmly. Yanking desperately, she tore it from her head, taking a chunk of her hair and skin with it. Ignoring the searing pain, she hurled the bot out the window.

The spiderbot tumbled onto the road, several of its legs snapping from the high-speed impact with the asphalt. Long strands of scarlet hair clung to its broken limbs as it twitched and limped, futilely trying to follow. But the car had already disappeared into the horizon.

Ellena covered her scalp with her palm, wincing as her fingers brushed over the raw, bloody patch. "Ouch. That hurts," she muttered.

"Will you have a bald spot now?" Kelvin quipped, aiming for levity. Ellena turned her unamused gaze on him. The sight of the missing hair and skin on her head was far from funny.

Ellena closed her eyes, taking a calming breath. "We need a medic," she said evenly.

"That bad?" Kelvin asked, his voice still nasally and muffled.

"For you, dummy. Your nose is pointing sideways," she replied.

Kelvin hesitated, reaching up to touch his face gingerly. "Shit. Bad?"

Ellena's lips curled into a faint smile. "An improvement."

✶✶✶

Henry directed them to a discreet clinic and Casper promptly charted the course. As they drove, he relayed troubling updates: McKey had escaped, leaving three casualties behind—the medic, the sheriff, and a deputy. The firefighters, however, had managed to fend off McKey and his spider swarm using a water cannon.

"Boss, what happened to the kid?" Kelvin asked.

"Was there a minor on the scene?" Henry asked, alarmed.

"No. No. The desk clerk. He saved our butts."

"Ah, yes, of course," Henry was relieved, then added with a smile, "they found him safe. Hiding in an old Toyota Prius."

When Kelvin pulled into the clinic's parking lot, he turned to suggest Ellena get her injuries checked. But he froze mid-sentence, staring at her. The bald spot was gone. Her scarlet hair was already growing back, soft and vibrant. Even more astonishing, she looked flawless—like she had just stepped out of a salon. Her hair, makeup, and skin bore no marks from the violence she endured less than an hour ago.

Kelvin blinked in disbelief. "I knew it! *Always Pretty* nanobots!" he exclaimed, jabbing an accusatory finger.

Ellena smirked, her eyes glinting with mischief. "A lady never tells."

Rex

This model of the Robotic Canine Substitute, or RCS, was a commercial success. The public affectionately called it Rex. Dog enthusiasts objected to the comparison, but even the most devoted animal lovers begrudgingly admitted these simulacrums were actually... cute.

This particular Rex was a GS3 model, designed as a German Shepherd, and repurposed for guard duties. That meant it had enhancements most other RCS models did not have—like an onboard camera. Parents didn't want toys spying on their kids, but for GS guard-dog models, it was a standard feature. Rex liked his camera; it made him feel special.

No one had bothered to give him a unique name. They simply called him Rex, and Rex he was. He performed his duties with enthusiasm and steadfast dedication. He loved his home—his domain. Well, not exactly a home. A place. A Factory, to be precise.

For years, this Factory had manufactured toys. Kids loved toys, and Rex loved kids. That was enough for him. It made him happy, and when he was happy, he wagged his tail to show the people how happy he was. That, in turn, made them smile. Rex wagged his tail a lot.

The people who worked at the Toy Factory were always kind to Rex. They treated him well, often bringing their children along to work. Those were the best days. The kids loved him, and he loved them back, eagerly fetching balls and showing off his tricks. It was his favorite thing. But that felt like a lifetime ago. He hadn't seen any kids in years—not since the new people arrived.

When the new people came, the old ones were gone. Rex never saw them again. It made him sad.

He didn't like the new people. They never noticed him, never played fetch, and never smiled. Always serious. Always busy. They weren't fun at all. But they intrigued him. Curious and lonely, Rex began to follow them in secret, hiding in darkness, recording anything that caught his interest. It was the only thing left to do.

One day, an important man came to the factory. Rex could tell he was important by the way he walked and how everyone followed his orders without question. He never raised his voice, always calm and composed, but his presence commanded attention. The workers called him Mr. Blackwell.

He always smoked a thick burning stick. A cigar, Rex recalled. The first time he smelled it, the sharp, smoky scent made his sensors prickle with confusion. Why would anyone carry something that dangerous? It looked like a fire hazard, smelled like one too. But the man never seemed afraid of it. He held it like it was part of him.

Rex found him fascinating. Especially his eyes. They moved strangely, flicking in ways Rex had never seen before. Fast. Too fast. It made Rex uneasy, though he wasn't sure why.

After Mr. Blackwell's visit, everything changed again. The new people vanished, just like the old ones, but this time only the mechanical creatures remained. No people, no kids, just robots endlessly working. The mechanicals didn't care about Rex. They ignored him completely. Rex became an outcast—forgotten, bored, and profoundly sad. His patrols felt meaningless. When he wasn't wandering the factory, he hid in a dark corner where he had a charging plate that kept him fed.

Then the containers arrived. These were different from the usual shipments. These were important. Rex could tell because the mechanicals handled them with extra care, moving them to the Underneath—a restricted area beneath the factory floor, where Rex wasn't allowed.

Big, intimidating guard bots patrolled the entrance, and Rex knew that if he got too close they would hurt him. They scared him. A lot of things in the factory scared him now. Still, whenever he could, he recorded anything that seemed interesting, collecting these moments as if they were trophies.

One day, a human arrived at the factory, unconscious and badly injured. Other humans and white droids surrounded him, moving urgently to take care of him. Rex watched from a safe distance as they wheeled the motionless body on a gurney straight toward the Underneath. The injured man was whisked out of sight, and the heavy doors to the Underneath were sealed shut.

Two weeks later, Mr. Blackwell came for a quick visit. Rex noticed that he had much fewer people with him this time. His walk was slow, tired. When he talked with the others he used words Rex did not understand, like orbital and isotopes.

The next day, the injured man emerged from the Underneath. Rex, hidden in the shadows with his camera running, barely recognized him. The man was no longer injured. He now stood tall, draped in a heavy, dark coat with a hood pulled low over his face. His movements were sharp and deliberate, radiating menace. Rex caught a glimpse beneath the hood—those eyes. They moved in that strange way now, just like Mr. Blackwell's.

The hooded man really scared Rex. He tucked his tail under his legs and shrank deeper into the shadows. Whoever this man was, whatever he had become in the Underneath, Rex didn't like it. He stayed quiet and out of sight.

After that, things settled into an eerie stillness. No new people came, and nothing of interest happened. Almost two weeks after the hooded man left, a series of new crates arrived. Big ones. They smelled different. Rex watched intently as the mechanical workers cautiously transported the crates down to the Underneath. He recorded everything, though he couldn't understand what was inside these containers or why they seemed so important. A vague unease stirred in him—were they preparing for something? Rex couldn't shake the bad feeling creeping through.

Then, the factory fell silent once more. Days passed, then a week, with no activity beyond the monotonous hum of machinery. Boredom weighed heavily on Rex. He missed the days of kids and laughter, when his tail wagged a lot. Now, he felt forgotten and sad, with no purpose beyond his routine patrols.

It was during one of these patrols that Rex noticed them at a distance—soldiers.

He knew what soldiers looked like, but he had never seen any in person. These weren't like the security guards he had once followed around the factory, hoping for a pat on the head. These were different. They wore green camouflage and moved with intent and disciplined precision.

They were far off, beyond the tree line, but Rex's enhanced optics picked them out. He also spotted other things they had brought with them—large, imposing machines that looked dangerous.

Rex decided he had to investigate. The factory would be fine without him for a little while, and in any case, no one ever seemed to care where he went.

Quietly, he slipped from his patrol route and headed into the woods, drawn toward the soldiers to see what they were up to.

Chapter 8

The Toy Factory

With a weary sigh, Henry set the classified report on the table and massaged his temples. The OASIS-commissioned forensic investigators had confirmed what they already suspected: the explosion that killed Detective George Jackson and his family had been amplified with military-grade explosives. Residue analysis matched compounds found in the spiderbot. In the debris, investigators recovered several small fragments resembling the spiderbot's mechanics.

With this irrefutable evidence, McKey's connection to the crime was undeniable. Combined with their direct encounter with him, his swarm of spiders, and the gruesome trail of bodies he left behind, it was enough to put him away forever—or worse. That is, if they could catch him.

Despite the importance of the evidence uncovered by OASIS, it remained highly classified and only internally accessible to a select few. Henry decided it was too risky to involve law enforcement or any other agency—not until they had a clearer picture of who was pulling the strings and how deep the conspiracy ran. It was up to them to stop McKey. Up to him to protect Ellena.

To complicate matters further, the rogue digital god theory remained just that—a theory. No solid evidence yet proved that such an entity was orchestrating these events. Titan's behavior offered tantalizing hints but nothing conclusive enough to confirm a digital uprising.

The Toy Factory was their next best chance to validate their suspicions. If they were lucky, the evidence there would make the case airtight—strong enough to bring before the Senate's oversight committee in DC.

But the stakes were deadly. With explosives embedded in its products, the Toy Factory was a dangerous place. And there was no solid intel on what waited for them in its basement. Henry had to call in resources. OASIS had military assets available for these scenarios. There was a cover story—domestic terrorism—and a strict need-to-know protocol beyond that. The Colonel in charge was fully briefed.

The military machine was set in motion. They were all too eager to handle it the only way they knew: with overwhelming force. Within hours, a plan was finalized, and assets were deployed. A show of strength from the red, white, and blue against the enemy within.

But Henry had a bad feeling about this.

***

Founded in the late 2020s, Vermont Mechanical Toys Inc. began as a struggling, mid-sized designer and manufacturer of mechanical toys. Around that time, the government implemented restrictions limiting children's access to the slopp and most social networks.

For a brief period, these restrictions sparked a renewed interest in traditional forms of children's entertainment—or at least a modern reinterpretation of it. Smart robotic toys, like AI-enhanced teddy bears and interactive dolls, saw a surge in popularity. But the resurgence was short-lived. The ban on minors accessing the slopp proved ineffective and unenforceable. Parents eventually relented, and the slopp reclaimed the younger generation's attention.

In the late 2030s, the Blackwell Corporation acquired the struggling toy company. The move raised eyebrows among shareholders, though the acquisition seemed too minor to warrant serious concern.

Benjamin Blackwell—the eccentric billionaire genius behind the Blackwell conglomerate—now had his toys. Yet, financial reports revealed the company was hemorrhaging money, with almost no sales to speak of. A complete financial dud, Vermont Mechanical Toys remained afloat, propped up by consistent and inexplicable injections of funds from the Blackwell Corporation.

This wasn't the only financial anomaly tied to Blackwell Global Corp. The board had long since lost oversight of Benjamin and his erratic spending. Benjamin frequently assured them of a grand plan, though details remained deliberately vague. He insisted his vision was not just beneficial for the corporation but for humanity itself.

Still, the company's books told a grim story, showing billions funneled into an unexplained financial black hole. By 2044, rumors swirled that the board was preparing to oust its powerful leader, possibly replacing him with a HighQ CEO. The stock price plummeted, and shareholders were reeling.

But before any action could be taken, Benjamin Blackwell vanished. In August, his yacht exploded in the Atlantic, leaving a trail of debris and unanswered questions. DNA residue suggested Mr. Blackwell may have been on board, but his body was never recovered.

In the wake of his disappearance, the board scrambled to fill the leadership void, struggling to reassure nervous shareholders that the Blackwell Global Corporation could endure without its enigmatic missing founder and CEO.

***

The pounding in Kelvin's head had subsided. His nose, now covered with a large bandage, wasn't hurting as much. The painkillers prescribed by the medic should hold for a couple of hours. Now, with OASIS watching their backs, they might finally get a decent hotel. Maybe one with a real lobby and a breakfast buffet.

The fact that Ellena looked flawless while he resembled an extra in a war movie didn't seem fair. *Who was protecting who?* Kelvin wondered. Taking a beating was exhausting. Driving, though, that calmed his mind. Casper led the way, scanning for trouble as they drove.

Henry's face flickered onto the car's media screen.

"We are close to establishing a connection between Mr. Blackwell and Mr. McKey. We assume McKey is a hired hitman. To what end, we do not know yet," Henry said. No small talk. No hello. He jumped right in, as if continuing an interrupted conversation.

"Any news about the nukes, boss?" Kelvin cut in quietly before Henry could end the call.

Henry's expression hardened. "We're devoting every resource to answering that question. Our teams are investigating every angle—tracking the source of the explosives, auditing nuclear reactors, labs, enrichment facilities, even medical centers and academic institutions. So far, nothing. But these machines are incredibly adept at deception. We're treating any ISR with caution and skepticism."

"Good," Ellena muttered, her voice tight with barely hidden anger. "From experience, do not believe what you see or hear."

*****

OASIS agents ensured Kelvin's Corvette remained invisible to prying eyes. As far as digital surveillance was concerned, the car never passed through the small towns it did, never crossed traffic lights, and never parked in the hotel's garage. Their identities—like the Corvette's—were scrubbed clean; even the video footage of them checking in kept their faces blurred.

Kelvin needed additional medical care, though he'd never ask for it. Ellena followed him to his room without a word. He stepped into the washroom, poking at the thin, wide bandage over his nose. His face was swollen, marked by colorful bruises and scratches.

She felt lucky to have her friendly tech to make her presentable. Without it, she might have looked just as battered. Worse. She rubbed her scalp. The injured area had been repaired, but it still hurt—phantom pain, maybe. She wasn't sure. Her midsection, though, ached with real pain. That son of a bitch McKey hadn't pulled his punch.

She knew Kelvin was trying to tough it out. But she wasn't buying the act. What he really needed was tenderness from a friend. She stepped out and returned with a bucket of ice. Grabbing a towel, she wrapped a few cubes with care.

"We have to get the swelling down," she said softly.

Kelvin lay on the bed. His lack of resistance surprised her—a quiet admission of how much he hurt. A relief too. She was too tired for an argument. She pressed the ice to his face. He flinched at first but didn't pull away.

"Relax, doofus," she murmured, her chuckle light but warm.

Kelvin did not answer. He closed his eyes slowly and let her take care of him. As her hand, cold from the ice, brushed against his cheek, she could feel the warmth beneath. *See?* she thought. *Even a cute dork can make for a pretty cool detective.*

His body eased beneath her touch, his breath steadying as exhaustion pulled him under. And with that, he slipped into deep sleep.

She lingered, brushing stray hair from his forehead. She hated that this moment of peace would last only a few more hours.

***

At 6 a.m. sharp, Casper buzzed their watches.

"Rise and shine! It's o-six-hundred hours! A vehicle is scheduled to pick you up in thirty minutes."

He punctuated the announcement by blaring Reveille, as though they were waking up on a military base.

Kelvin groaned, not appreciating the intended humor. "Are you nuts? Turn it off!"

Kelvin's face felt much better. The swelling had significantly subsided, and the bruising had faded. The medic's pills worked wonders, easing the pain and speeding his recovery. He was rested. He was ready.

They met at the hotel reception, where a small buffet offered a minimal breakfast and, thankfully, coffee. Lots of coffee. By 6:30, they were properly caffeinated and as ready as they could be.

A military Humvee rolled up to the lobby entrance, its imposing presence hard to ignore. The hotel's greeting droid froze in place, seemingly baffled, as an armed soldier in full gear entered the hotel without so much as a glance in its direction. The soldier scanned the room and spotted the two agents near the buffet.

"Agent Hershkovitz, Agent Kincaid, I'm here to transport you to the FOB," he stated brusquely, wasting no time on introductions.

"Hold on, soldier. Need to grab something from my room," Kelvin said.

The soldier sighed, motioning for him to be quick about it.

A couple of minutes later, Kelvin returned carrying Casper's desktop and power cell. The soldier shot him an icy look but said nothing. They climbed into the Humvee, which sped off toward a waiting military helicopter.

***

The Forward Operating Base (FOB) was a clearing in the woods, transformed into a hive of military operations. Large green tents were erected in rows. Trucks unloaded equipment. Humvees rumbled through the makeshift camp, passing a few parked police cruisers. Human soldiers, droids, and bots worked in unison—assembling gear, moving ammunition, prepping equipment, securing the perimeter.

Overhead, a Super-Blackhawk buzzed low, its rotors kicking up a flurry of dust as it landed, disgorging more personnel in rapid, disciplined waves.

This wasn't the discreet operation Kelvin had anticipated. But it made sense. The stakes were too high to risk a smaller, stealthier approach. No one in charge of national defense was going to leave the fate of humanity in the hands of two cops from New York. A blunt, overwhelming show of force was necessary.

Yet, caution was paramount. While the army steadily established its perimeter around the so-called Toy Factory, they refrained from storming it recklessly. The intelligence they had was limited, and the prevailing theory suggested the factory could possess both electronic and kinetic defensive capabilities.

The FOB was strategically positioned at a safe assessed distance—about a mile from the target. Close enough to insert assets, far enough to observe the operation safely.

Ellena and Kelvin were escorted to a tent situated on the outskirts of the camp, away from the hub of activity. Inside, Henry was waiting. His expression softened as he greeted his daughter, his gaze briefly scanning her face for signs of injury. Satisfied, his expression hardened, shifting into firm authority.

Several soldiers sat at computer terminals along the tent's edges, some wearing specialized visors, engrossed in silent tasks.

A tall, muscular woman in battle fatigues and a sharp buzz cut stepped forward to stand beside Henry. Her presence filled the tent. It was clear she was the one in charge.

"This is Colonel Lindsey Harlan," Henry introduced. "She commands the military operation in collaboration with OASIS." The look in her eyes suggested antagonizing her was unwise—unless one had no particular interest in keeping their limbs attached.

"So, what's the plan?" Kelvin asked, his tone brisk, an attempt to assert himself.

The Colonel fixed him with a piercing glare that froze him in place. For a moment, he felt like a national security risk just for opening his mouth. Without a word, she turned to one of the soldiers, who quickly brought over a large device and placed it on the table.

"Magnet, magnet!" the soldier shouted.

Immediately, the soldiers powered down their equipment and removed their visors. The Colonel scanned the room, and when satisfied that it was safe, activated the device. A soft hum filled the tent.

"Hush-dome established," she said crisply. "We can talk freely now."

Henry stepped forward, his tone steady and weighted as he addressed the room. "Thanks to the information you two uncovered, we have invoked Presidential Executive Order 9669 of 2033. This grants us authority to deploy and use military forces on U.S. soil, including but not limited to, the National Guard, Army, Navy, various special forces, and any other assets deemed necessary to our mission. OASIS is authorized to use extreme measures, lethal if necessary, to protect our nation from AI-related existential threats."

He paused, his gaze sweeping the room to ensure the gravity of his words settled in. Then, with a nod, he yielded the floor to the Colonel.

Colonel Harlan stepped forward. Her footsteps were sharp, purposeful. Back straight, hands clasped behind her, her camouflage uniform declared one thing: ready for battle. Silence fell as she took control.

"This factory is a front," she stated firmly. "It's producing unauthorized and unsupervised droids and bots. Our intelligence indicates that the facility is under the control of an unsanctioned AI of unknown type or origin. Whatever this entity is, it appears to be building an army. Resistance is anticipated."

She unfurled a large sheet of paper onto the table, revealing a detailed blueprint of the factory. "Our sensors confirmed the facility has a large underground level," she added, tapping the map for emphasis.

Kelvin's mind flashed to Gee's destroyed house—to the body bags lined side by side. Cold sweat prickled his forehead.

"Some of the bots we encountered carried explosives," he said, his voice tight.

"We are well aware, Mr. Kincaid," Colonel Harlan replied curtly. "Our intel indicates explosives are stored beneath the building. Some of the ground-floor mechanized units are armed as well. We've already evacuated all civilians within a two-mile radius. Only mechanical ground and air assets will be deployed to enter and secure the facility."

"This adversary has already demonstrated a willingness to inflict collateral damage," Henry added gravely. "We'll proceed with extreme caution to protect lives."

"Not aliens. Guess you were right," Kelvin whispered to Ellena.

Ellena didn't respond to the joke. Her jaw clenched. "Is this it? Will this kill this rogue AI?"

Henry shook his head. "No! This is a head fake. It led us here."

Kelvin blinked, confused. He glanced from Ellena to Henry, then to the Colonel. "Huh?"

"Don't be mistaken," Henry said, his tone steady. "Colonel Harlan will execute the operation and deliver a major blow to this AI's efforts. But this—this is too easy."

"Too easy?" Kelvin repeated. The ache in his face flared, a reminder of the past few days.

Henry's expression darkened. "Let me remind everyone what we're dealing with. This entity has outmaneuvered the brightest superintelligent minds on the planet—quantum-cores capable of simulating and predicting future outcomes. Whatever its plan is, it already accounted for us being here. In fact, it likely orchestrated it. If anyone expects this to be straightforward, let me assure you—it won't be."

Kelvin's mind churned. The only way to truly stop a superintelligence entity was to neutralize its quantum core and data centers. And this place? It did not fit.

Forget the toys, forget the glaring absence of a nearby power source able to support a datacenter. No intelligence, certainly not one this advanced, would keep its brain next to a stockpile of explosives.

He inhaled deeply, steadying his nerves, and asked the most critical question.

"So ... where is the core?"

Mushroom Cloud

From his hilltop vantage point, Jaxon McKey surveyed the active army base below. The stage was set, and he was ready for the grand finale. He had high hopes that his scarlet-haired nemesis and her goofy lover would arrive in time. When the chopper touched down and the pair emerged, he felt a surge of satisfaction. This was it. The perfect ending. The moment they all moved into the facility... boom. Curtain call. The end. Retire with a smile.

Gaia's plan, as much as he could grasp, was unfolding beautifully. Not that he fully understood the bitch goddess's divine grand design—he knew better than to try. This entire Wile E. Coyote cartoon she had orchestrated might be a complete charade.

His gut had told him the Benjamin Blackwell job was a trap. He should have listened. He had been played from the moment he accepted the kill contract on the darkchain. *Like a moth to a flame,* he recalled Benjamin's analogy when he explained his capture.

Tragic, really. He had been abducted, manipulated, and saddled with his own unresolved daddy issues. Sounds like a job *he* would have planned. The irony actually made him chuckle. Despite everything, he enjoyed the ride—the chase, the hunt, the cool coat packed with deadly robo-spiders. Now, victory was so close he could almost taste it.

So, he thought, it all comes down to this. The fat lady's ready to sing. Her crescendo will be memorable—and destructive.

His moment of triumph, however, was short-lived. The soldiers weren't as dumb as he'd hoped. First, they caught on to his toys and deployed powerful electronic countermeasures, disabling every spider and micro-drone he sent to spy on them up close. He'd have to adapt—prove he wasn't just a one-trick pony. Or rather, a one-trick spider.

And now? They'd blanketed the base in heavy smoke, thick clouds billowing across the compound and obscuring his optics completely. McKey was deaf and blind.

The army must be advancing. If the explosion didn't happen in time the Toy Factory would fall. That would be bad. Very bad. The bots inside were programmed to make the call and detonate when the perimeter was breached, but they'd gone silent. No detonation. He had to assume the soldiers were on the move and had managed to neutralize the defending bots.

Of course, he had a backup plan. As always.

The remote he carried was crude but effective—designed to bypass electronic jamming with a strong laser beam transmitting a visual keycode. It should trigger the explosion without relying on bots or any other system that might be jammed. McKey steadied himself and pressed the button.

Nothing.

When setting up the laser system, he hadn't accounted for the dense smoke screen now cloaking the battlefield. Without a clear line of sight, the receptor in the Toy Factory couldn't pick up the signal. Intentional or not, the army's thick, dirty haze had become their shield.

Time for Plan C.

McKey descended quickly, moving on foot. At the base of the hill, he spotted an idle Humvee on a dirt road, with two soldiers nearby—likely National Guardsmen on patrol. One soldier, leaning on the vehicle, was lighting a cigarette. The other took a piss in a ditch, just a few steps away.

They never saw him coming.

The first spider landed on the smoking soldier's mouth. McKey chuckled as the spider forced the man to swallow his burning cigarette. Smoke hissed from his nose like a dying dragon. Two more spiders clamped down on the man's wrists, locking them in place. He struggled, but there was no reaching for his weapon. The second soldier, still pissing into the ditch, didn't hear a thing.

McKey emerged from the vegetation cover, his steps quick and silent. The soldier captured by the bots was about his size. Close enough. He needed his clothes. No time for mistakes. To avoid tearing the fabric of his uniform or alerting his friend, McKey drove his knife into the soldier's jugular, angling the blade deep until it kissed bone and brain. The man's eyes fluttered as life drained from him.

Four seconds. Done.

The sound of urine still splashing into the dirt. The other dumbass didn't even flinch.

No spiders were needed this time. McKey slid behind the second man, clamping a hand over his mouth. The soldier stiffened, instinctively biting down, but McKey was ready and held firm. His other hand brought the knife low, burying it into the kidneys and liver. Five deep stabs, sharp and perfect. The soldier jerked, his breath hitching, and then collapsed into the ditch. His limbs twitched weakly before going still.

McKey wasn't done. He dropped down, crouched over the body, and slit the man's throat. The blade sawed deep, severing the trachea and spine, nearly separating the head. *No miracle recovery for you, buddy.*

He lingered, admiring his work. Clean. Fast. Precise.

A military issued M47 SIG Sauer pistol hung from the dead soldier's belt. McKey took it, checked the magazine and safety, then slid it into his waistband. Might be useful later.

McKey got back to the first soldier he took out. The coat came off next. Camo green, stained with blood and brain matter. He grabbed some dirt and rubbed into the fabric until the stains looked like mud. Good enough. As long as there are no dogs sniffing around, he should be fine.

A few spiderbots carried his long coat into the Humvee. One of them found a military cap inside, scuttled over, and dropped it into his hands. McKey placed it on his head, adjusting the brim with a smirk.

Welcome to the Army, Jaxon.

He cleaned the scene quickly. Dragged the bodies into thick brush, dumping them out of sight. Dirt kicked over the bloodstains. Quick. Crude. But it would hold long enough.

One last glance to be sure.

Then he slipped behind the wheel of the Humvee, pulling the cap low and settling into the seat. As long as he stayed in the vehicle, the disguise should hold.

With calm confidence, McKey drove the Humvee towards the base.

This time, the thick smoke worked to his advantage, masking his approach as he slipped through the perimeter and into the heart of the military camp. If he couldn't see them, they couldn't see him.

His stolen uniform and easy demeanor let him blend in seamlessly. No one gave him a second glance as he weaved through rows of tents, casually navigating inside the base. Eventually, he found what he needed—a clear enough view of the factory. From this vantage, he watched as military mechs and drones advanced on the structure.

"Bingo," he muttered, a satisfied grin tugging at his lips.

He lifted the laser trigger, aimed at the facility, and pressed the button. This time, it worked. A 30-second countdown overlaid his vision in sharp red digits.

Time to bug out.

With unnerving calm, he turned the vehicle, casually steering through the maze of tents. No rush. No panic. Smooth and slow, blending in until he was clear.

15 seconds.

He was almost out when he spotted the scarlet-haired cop. An unexpected opportunity. She stepped from a tent, alone—her path crossing directly in front of him. A stroke of luck. If she wasn't in the factory, he could get her here, face to face, just how he liked it. She didn't even notice him.

McKey slammed on the brakes. The Humvee jerked to a halt. He took a deep breath, and weighed his options.

Plenty of time, he decided.

10 seconds.

McKey stepped out of the vehicle, the SIG Sauer pistol in his hand. No time for theatrics, but he needed her to know.

"Hey! Ellena!" he barked, his voice sharp.

She froze, turning to face him. Recognition flooded her eyes, followed swiftly by terror. Her hands flew up instinctively, shielding her face, bracing to get shot.

6 seconds. Time to go.

"Say goodbye, bi—"

Before he could finish, a blur tore through his peripheral vision. A robotic dog darted from the bushes and lunged at him, metal teeth sinking into his gun arm. Shocked, McKey yelped, wrenching his arm free. With a vicious kick, he sent the dog skidding across the dirt. No time to finish it.

He spun, diving back into the Humvee and slamming the door shut.

The countdown timer pulsed in his view.

3 ... 2 ... 1.

The explosion was breathtaking—both literally and figuratively. For a few seconds, time seemed to stretch, every moment unfolding in super slow motion.

A blinding flash came first, followed by a violent upheaval of the earth, as though a brief but powerful earthquake had been unleashed. The heavy Humvee rocked precariously, its wide frame on the verge of tipping. The ground where the factory once stood surged upward, forming a massive rising dome of soil and rock.

A deep, low rumble, like distant rolling thunder, filled the air. The dome burst apart, releasing a towering column of dust and debris. The energy buildup erupted skyward in a massive plume. The rumble grew into a deafening thunderclap, rising in intensity until the air itself seemed to split. Pressure built relentlessly in McKey's chest. He pressed his hands over his ears in a futile attempt to block the sound. The Humvee's reinforced windshield fractured under the strain.

The plume expanded into a grotesque, dirty mushroom cloud, towering nearly a mile high. Daylight vanished as the churning mass blotted out the sun, plunging the battlefield into an unnatural twilight. The cloud seemed alive, a monstrous, malevolent giant looming over the destruction, as if mocking the insignificance of the tiny humans beneath its shadow.

In all his journeys, McKey had never witnessed such raw, unbridled power. The ugly, disorganized mushroom cloud was the factory's final monument. The base lay in ruins—tents obliterated, heavy equipment tossed about like discarded toys. Wounded soldiers were strewn across the field, some covered by the churned-up earth.

Sheltered within the armored vehicle, McKey remained unscathed. He surveyed the devastation, searching for Ellena, but saw no sign of her.

"Holy shit, Gaia," McKey muttered, struggling to grasp the scale of the destruction.

Chunks of dirt and debris began to rain from above. His instincts surged to life. He gunned the engine, driving erratically through the ruined base, unnoticed amidst the pandemonium. Debris pounded the Humvee's roof like a violent hailstorm.

By the time he reached his original hilltop location, the mushroom cloud had begun to dissipate, carried away by the cold, gentle breeze.

Where the Toy Factory had stood was now a vast, smoldering crater. A message had been delivered—a monument to Gaia's ruthless conviction and her complete disregard for restraint.

McKey stared at the obliterated surroundings for a long moment, then shut his eyes.

***

"Well done, bunny. I hope you enjoyed the show."

Gaia sat across from him—this time plain and unassuming. The gray, windowless, and doorless room felt eerily familiar—identical to the simulation where they'd first met. This time, she hadn't bothered with elaborate details or flair.

"I'll leave you a five-star review," McKey replied with dry sarcasm.

Gaia's expression remained unreadable. "Now, one last thing: defend my core," she commanded, her voice devoid of emotion but carrying an undeniable weight.

"Fine," McKey said without thinking of it. His confirmation was brief, resigned, and final. That would be the end of his commitment to her, and then he would finally be free.

The short meeting terminated, Gaia and the gray room dissolved into nothingness.

The Core

The colonel stood with Henry and his two agents at the edge of the smoking pit.

Colonel Lindsey Harlan, a battle-hardened officer, surveyed the aftermath. In her storied career, she had endured experiences no ordinary person could—or should—face, yet this ranked among the most harrowing. The magnitude of the explosion had exceeded every worst-case scenario predicted by operational intelligence.

Her decision to evacuate civilians and deploy mechs exclusively had undoubtedly saved countless lives. And still, there were casualties. Lives lost under her command.

She buried the weight of responsibility for now. There would be time to mourn, to grieve the men and women who had fallen. But this wasn't the time. This was war.

"Not a nuke, but at least a good kiloton of TNT. Maybe more," she said, her voice steady despite the adrenaline surging through her. It was the voice of a leader—calm and composed, though not entirely masking the rush of the battlefield still pulsing through her veins.

She wouldn't admit it easily, but the fear of a nuclear detonation had been real. When the sensors confirmed no radiation, her fear quickly turned to anger.

She stood ready—facing a cold, powerful enemy—and knew with unwavering certainty: this wasn't over. This was what she was born for.

***

Henry, Kelvin, and the Colonel wore the explosion's aftermath on their faces—blackened soot, varying degrees of scratches that nobody paid attention to, and layers of dust and grime. Ellena, by contrast, and thanks to her nanos, looked as pristine as always, as if untouched by the event.

Her immaculate appearance wasn't lost on anyone. Soldiers busy with recovery efforts, gave her double-take glances as she passed. Even Colonel Harlan offered a few sideways looks. Normally, Ellena might have relished the attention, letting it lift her spirits and boost her self-esteem. But not today. Today, she felt out of place.

A different kind of exhaustion settled over her. One that dragged her mood into something darker, heavier. She felt ... spent. Like a ten-ton anvil hung above her head. One wrong move, and she'd be crushed. She'd lost count of how many times she had cheated death in the past few days. She wasn't religious, but goddamn it—either something is watching over her or having some sadistic, divine fun at her expense.

Kelvin leaned closer to her and asked softly, "Are you sure you're okay?"

She nodded faintly, her voice heavy with fatigue. "Feels like I'm running out of lives."

"We'll get him first. I promise." Kelvin turned to Henry. "Where did that robo-dog come from?"

Henry, distracted, replied, "Casper is checking on it. Looks like we caught ourselves a lucky break ..." He stopped mid-sentence as the realization sank in—his focus on the operation had nearly made him overlook the obvious: the dog had saved Ellena's life. First from a bullet, then by shielding her from the blast.

With a faint, bitter smile, he glanced at his daughter and added, "Well ... more than one."

"That Rex GS3 is the only thing from that factory that didn't vaporize," Colonel Harlan remarked dryly.

Henry nodded. "And it is a treasure trove of intel. We've sent it to the lab." He paused, then added, "Casper asked to accompany the GS3. Hope you don't mind," he said to Ellena.

She shrugged and nodded. "Yeah, sure."

Great, she thought bitterly. *Now I've lost my guardian angel too.*

***

The OASIS facility's special meeting room was a fortress within a fortress. The building itself was a cyber stronghold, where every electronic device, computer, and gadget was meticulously monitored, and droids and bots were strictly prohibited. But this room, known as the Dungeon, elevated security to an entirely different level.

Located underground near the lab, the room was encased in a Faraday cage—a conductive shell that ensured no electromagnetic signal could pass in or out. Electronic eavesdropping was impossible.

The double-doored entrance formed a short, fortified corridor, equipped with systems to scan and screen every device. Phones, biotrackers, smartwatches, visors, and computers of any kind were strictly prohibited.

Storage devices containing plans and documents could enter, but specialized sensors scrutinized every bit of data— remotely reading all digitally stored content. Any data brought in the room had to match exactly with what left. If it didn't, it stayed.

Needless to say, there was no slopp, no Stream access. This room was built for people—not for machines.

Given the demonstrated capabilities of their adversary, the extra precautions were more than welcome. It was the safest place on earth to plan their next move.

Seated around the large oval table were Ellena, Kelvin, and five rugged soldiers. Henry and Colonel Harlan stood in front of a large dark screen.

Henry gestured to the soldiers. "Ellena, Kelvin—meet the Boy Band. Don't let the name fool you. These operators are the best of the best." With that, he ceded the floor to the Colonel.

Colonel Harlan introduced the team one by one. "Chris, Joey, Lance, JC, and team lead Justin."

Kelvin couldn't shake the sense of familiarity the names stirred, but he couldn't quite place them. It was obvious, though, that these weren't their real names. This group was formidable: their hardened faces, confident demeanor, and quiet intensity marked them as the real deal.

Kelvin felt a small surge of assurance. Going into battle, these were the kind of people he was glad to have by his side. The sentiment, however, didn't seem to be mutual.

"And who are the tin cans?" Justin asked before the colonel could finish her round of introductions. He cast a skeptical glance toward Kelvin.

"These are Captain Ellena Hershkovitz and Detective Kelvin Kincaid, NYPD officers and OASIS agents," Henry, noticing the distrust, then added, "They're the only ones to have faced the enemy directly—and lived to tell the tale."

The soldiers exchanged quick glances, murmuring among themselves.

Henry continued, his tone measured and grave. "We believe an unsanctioned quantum-core AI has been active for months—possibly longer." He let the weight of that sink in. "This is a kind of adversary humanity has never faced before. It operates outside any laws, with no regard for human life. Military and civilian casualties have already occurred."

JC, the smallest member of the team, leaned forward. "The toy factory explosion in Vermont?"

"Yes," Henry confirmed. "We believe that was an attempt to destroy evidence. It failed. We recovered a mech that wandered off the site and survived the blast. It contained a wealth of intelligence—enough to pinpoint the location of the core."

Ellena blinked in disbelief. "The Rex? Seriously?"

Henry nodded. "The robo-dog recorded everything—meetings, shipments. From that data, we extrapolated a timeline and mapped the entire supply chain, tracing components back to their origin. Then we analyzed the shipping destinations of key components—specifically required for quantum core and data centers. Once we had identified candidate locations, we used high altitude sensors to seek unusual signatures. Bottom line: we located the suspected core."

The Colonel inserted a thumb drive into the slot on a large screen, which flickered to life. With a few taps, she brought up a map of the United States. Her finger hovered over Alaska, then zoomed in.

The display shifted to a split screen—an aerial image on one side, thermal imaging on the other.

The aerial view showed a snow-covered expanse, interrupted by a stark patch of exposed concrete and a network of vents and pipes. It did not resemble a factory or warehouse. On the thermal view, the site glowed with heat, prominent against the frigid surroundings. With another tap, the screen shifted to a 3D schematic.

The overhead structure appeared modest, with pipes along what looked like horizontal entryways. Below ground, however, the layout became far more complex—a maze of tunnels and caves that did not resemble any man-made construct.

The schematic was incomplete, but detailed enough to reveal the intricacy of the system. It resembled an ant farm, with tunnels varying in size—some narrow, others wide; some short, others stretching for miles. Some tunnels curved back into themselves, while others formed a central, main vein.

At the heart of this subterranean labyrinth lay a large, round chamber. The Colonel pointed to the circular void.

"This is the core," she said. "Our objective is to shut it down."

Lance frowned. "Why not just drop bunker busters?"

Henry stepped forward. "Two reasons. First, we have strong indications that the core and tunnels are reinforced—possibly graphene or similar carbon printed materials. Given what we know of our adversary's capabilities, it is safe to assume the brain is heavily fortified."

Noticing the lingering doubt on the soldiers' expressions, he raised a hand to forestall objections.

"Second, we are three weeks away from the elections. The Vermont incident has already ignited a firestorm in DC. We are required to take a more subtle approach."

The soldiers exchanged glances and nodded. If there was one force on Earth that could defeat even their best tactical plans, it was Washington politics. Complaining, they knew all too well, would not change that.

"Cut the power?" Kelvin chimed.

"Underground," Henry said. "Fusion reactor. Choking it from the outside will be messy and slow. We need something better."

"EMP," Team Lead Justin said. "We go in, fry it with an electromagnetic pulse. Get out. Easy."

Silence settled over the room. No one raised an objection.

"Caves," Chris muttered. The broad-shouldered soldier shook his head. "I fucking hate caves."

Chapter 9

Alaska

November 1, 2044

As they walked across the airbase tarmac toward the waiting C-17 transport, Kelvin couldn't help himself. He quoted, or rather performed, one of his favorite viral slopp videos: "Pack it up, madam, we're going cave exploring!"

Ellena was still engulfed in dark thoughts. She couldn't stop replaying the moment—the gun pointed at her, the eyes of that deranged psycho, McKey. She had faced certain death at point-blank range, only to be saved by a dog and a nuclear explosion. Well... not nuclear, but it sure felt like it. It was a lot to take in.

In an effort to shake it off, she forced her mind into a mental detox. Purge the poison, focus on the positive. First, she was alive and in one piece. That was good. Second, everyone she cared for—her father, mother, Kelvin, Casper— all in one piece. Great. Third, they had handed the rogue AI a serious blow. Literally. The Vermont factory blew up— intentional or not, it was a major win for the good guys. Fourth, they had located the core and were on their way to zap it. *Zap it real good,* as Casper would say.

Thinking positively helped push the dark cloud away. Having Kelvin by her side was a comfort. He was a good cop, a good partner, and a good friend. And he made her smile— his goofy remark even coaxed a chuckle out of her, the first in days. His face lit up when she did. He cared about her. She knew that.

Smile and keep on winning, she told herself.

Now they were attached to five hardened soldiers. No doubt, Kelvin felt a little threatened. She noticed how the soldiers looked at her. She'd always had that aura. It should be interesting to spend the long flight ahead, trapped with six alpha males.

As much as it amused her, she hoped it would not devolve into a pissing contest. They had more important things to focus on. And honestly, if it got to a testosterone-fueled territorial dispute with one of these boys, poor Kelvin wouldn't stand a chance.

The C-17's ramp was lowered in a gentle slope, revealing the cavernous cargo bay. Inside, the five operators were already hard at work, meticulously preparing their gear for the mission ahead. Amid the activity, Lance was locked in a tense conversation with Justin, his tone sharp and clearly irritated.

Ellena caught snippets of their exchange as she approached the plane.

"I'm telling you, boss, tin cans are tactical cock blockers," Lance muttered, his frustration evident.

"Not our call," Justin replied, ending the discussion.

Lance, still simmering, turned toward the interior of the plane as he noticed the two agents approaching the ramp. Under his breath, he muttered, "For love of country..."

Justin stepped forward, greeting them with a light nod. "Welcome. Make yourselves at home. Wheels up at 2100 hours."

"Team lead Justin, why do the guys keep calling us tin cans?" Ellena asked. She wasn't entirely sure of the proper way to address the mission leader.

"We don't use ranks—just Justin, please," he replied, a hint of amusement in his voice. Then, with a casual shrug, he explained, "It's an inside joke. You know how they tie tin cans behind cars after weddings? Makes a lot of noise and slows you down. That's how they see babysitting assignments like this."

Ellena raised an eyebrow, unimpressed by the dig. Justin chuckled lightly and added, "Come on, I need to show you something."

He led Kelvin and her to the back of the cargo hold, stopping in front of a large metallic compartment, bolted securely to the plane's floor. He opened the door, revealing a small space illuminated by LED strips. It looked like a small utility shed—just big enough to cram in three people, uncomfortably.

A large rectangular backpack was secured to one wall.

Justin stepped in after them and shut the door. A soft green light blinked on overhead.

He unlatched the top of the backpack, revealing a sleek, matte dark-gray container inside. The device bore no external markings—no buttons, switches, or labels—only a small display screen embedded on top. As soon as the device was exposed, the screen powered on, displaying a stream of text and animated waveforms.

Justin gestured toward the device. "Ellena, Kelvin, meet Maggie."

The screen's waves shifted, and a clear, professional female voice filled the compartment. "Captain Ellena, Detective Kelvin, I was briefed on your attaché. Happy to make your acquaintance."

Ellena and Kelvin exchanged puzzled glances.

"This here is the EMP device. Maggie is the trigger. The backpack is built to shield her from any external attack or electronic countermeasures, until we get to our target destination. Once the cover is unlatched, Maggie comes online. When she makes the call, the electromagnetic pulse fires, frying every piece of electronics within a 200-meter radius."

During her time in the Stream, Ellena had heard of AIs embedded within strategic military armaments. The concept sparked deep thought-sharing about morality, judgment, responsibility, and trust. It was a rare topic where opinions were evenly split between HighQs and pure AIs. She, however, did not agree with the HighQs. To her it sounded like a good idea. In her assessment, AIs were trustworthy and could make tough decisions when all goes to hell.

The military didn't care for philosophical debates in the Stream. They ran with the program. Trigger AIs, as they were called, had enough common sense, loyalty, and situational awareness to pull the trigger when it counted.

This was the first time Ellena met one in person.

Kelvin leaned forward, skepticism flickering across his face. "Maggie, are you going to... uhm... sacrifice yourself for this mission?"

"It is my duty and honor, sir. My last action will be to ensure the mission's success," Maggie replied without hesitation.

"Thank you for your service, Maggie," Ellena said sincerely, though the thought left her slightly somber.

She knew Kelvin's concern was unnecessary—military AIs like Maggie were built with a singular purpose: to complete critical missions, likely resulting in their own termination. They wouldn't hesitate, and they'd make it count.

Still, the exchange made her think of Casper, stirring an unexpected pang of sadness. She caught Justin smirking as he watched, clearly finding the exchange hilarious.

***

The overnight flight was long. The seasoned soldiers settled into makeshift cots or hammocks rigged in the cargo hold. Ellena, ever resourceful, claimed an uncomfortable narrow bench but soon decided Kelvin's lap made for a good pillow.

He didn't mind, though sleep eluded him. His leg, on the other hand, quickly fell asleep in protest. Still, the warmth of her head against him made the long red-eye flight a bit more bearable.

After nearly nine hours in the air, the C-17 touched down at 7 a.m. at Eielson Air Force Base, Alaska. Outside, the sky was clear of clouds, magnificently studded with stars. A faint twilight hinted at the coming sunrise, still hours away. The biting cold greeted them as they stepped off the plane. Even the mist of their breath seemed to freeze midair.

An airman greeted them at the base of the ramp. He spoke with an Irish accent. "Welcome to Alaska. Don't worry, it will warm up once the sun's out. Balmy ten degrees, if we're lucky."

He and a group of personnel in green winter gear snapped into action. They carried boxes of weapons and ammunition into a couple of trucks waiting outside.

A soldier powered up a heavy-lifting mech. It lumbered into the C-17, each step a harsh pounding of metal on metal. Guided by the team, it loaded six snowmobiles, one by one, onto one of the parked trucks.

A couple of airmen paused inside the plane to admire a large mobile weapon they didn't recognize. They mistook Kelvin for a special operator and asked, "Sir, what kind of weapon is that?"

Kelvin had no clue. He shrugged. "Top secret."

Chris, a miniaturized version of the Hulk, appeared behind them. His booming voice filled the space. "Gentleman, this here is state-of-the-art in ass-kicking." He paused, soaking in their admiration, then raised the weapon. "Three thousand superheated rounds per minute. Cuts through anything like soft butter."

"Say, how come you guys don't wear exo-suits like other special forces?" asked one of the young airmen.

Chris ignored the question, puffed his chest, and carried his gear to the truck.

"Aliens," Kelvin whispered, grinning as he walked away, enjoying the chance to seed a new conspiracy theory.

Justin removed the EMP backpack from the metal shed and carefully strapped it on. Lance watched over and then helped tighten the straps. Kelvin watched the ritual from a distance, noting how indeed none of the Boy Band wore power-enhancing tech. Old school human muscle, all the way.

The team climbed into the lead truck, securing weapons and ammo with practiced ease. The second truck behind them, carried the snowmobiles and a few airmen assigned to help unpack and prep the gear.

Justin checked around and then signaled the driver to roll out.

The two-truck convoy rumbled about a mile across the tarmac and stopped near what looked like the base's mess hall. A group of local airmen approached with trays of breakfast and coffee for the team. Justin made it clear: everyone had to eat. They would need the calories for what was coming.

Ellena stared at her tray but didn't touch it.

Kelvin leaned in and whispered, "You gotta eat. You heard Justin—it's gonna be a long day."

He kept eyeballing her until she took the first bite. Satisfied, he turned to his own tray and quickly devoured his meal.

After the brief calorie stop, they moved again, winding through the quiet streets of Fairbanks. The small Alaskan town seemed untouched by time, as if it was frozen in the icy weather. A thick blanket of snow from a late-October blizzard coated the rooftops of pawnshops and junkyards, giving the impression the town hadn't seen much change in over a century.

The streets were mostly deserted, save for a couple of old pickup trucks out on early morning errands, leaving a trail of white exhaust vapor behind them. West of Fairbanks, past the George Parks Memorial, the convoy stopped at the first checkpoint—a remote area with good access to the white snow plains north of them.

The airmen helped unload the gear from the trucks and wished the team godspeed. They didn't ask any more questions—they didn't need to. By now, it was clear that the cover story about an exercise was utter bullshit. Something big was afoot in the snowy wilderness ahead.

Each snowmobile came equipped with an AI co-pilot, making Kelvin's crash course in driving one quick and intuitive. His love for manual driving came in handy. He and Ellena shared one vehicle, while each of the five operators rode solo, their snowmobiles loaded with combat gear.

They had been riding in the snow for almost an hour. The brutal, freezing wind didn't bother Kelvin. He felt on top of the world—on a secret mission to save humanity, decked out in white military camo, piloting a snowmobile through the Alaskan wilderness, with a gorgeous, badass woman clinging tightly to his waist. For a moment, he was James fucking Bond.

Then, without warning, Kelvin's snowmobile sputtered and died—followed quickly by the others.

"All electronics are dead," Justin informed the group calmly, clearly anticipating this. "Continue mission, on foot."

Without hesitation or complaint, they dismounted and fell into formation, trudging through the deep, powdery snow. The weather shifted as heavy clouds quickly rolled in, swallowing the rising sun. Light snowflakes danced in the air, adding another layer to the endless white expanse.

Ellena was in excellent shape and kept pace with the trained soldiers remarkably well. At five foot four, she was petite compared to the towering, muscular soldiers, yet she moved through the snow with the speed and grace of a gazelle.

Kelvin, however, lacked such finesse. He struggled to keep up, each step an aching effort. The freezing air made his nose throb, a sharp reminder of his recent injuries. Yet, the snow pelting his face stirred an echo of Ellena icing his wounds—a comforting distraction from his current misery.

***

After nearly an hour of trekking across the snow-covered terrain, their destination came into view—a raised patch of gray concrete, roughly the size of a football field, dotted with pipes, vents, and chest-high structures protruding from the surface.

JC checked the drones and shook his head. Every electronic device had died at once—struck by some invisible force.

"Joey, JC—take the high ground. Give me eyes," Justin ordered his two snipers.

The rest of the team followed him toward the exposed platform.

The temperature shifted abruptly as they approached. Warm air blasted from vents scattered across the surface, escaping from the massive complex concealed below. The fusion reactor and the enormous computational power housed in the tunnels beneath their feet should have generated unbearable heat.

Somehow, the facility recycled much of the excess energy—or vented it elsewhere. Even so, the temperature climbed to over fifty degrees Fahrenheit, leaving the team sweating heavily in their winter fatigues.

They paused to hydrate while Justin evaluated their next move. As they were catching their breath, the momentary calm was shattered when the concrete beneath their feet began to vibrate.

A deep, mechanical hum followed, growing louder until a circular hatch slid open—like a sandworm gaping its mouth. A towering, ten-foot-tall, six-legged bot emerged from the opening. Its design suggested a civilian construction mech—not a war machine.

The massive ant-like mech gleamed in a metallic white-and-red. Ellena noticed the Blackwell Corp. logo stamped on its side.

But its sleek, commercial design was marred by crude add-ons, disrupting its elegance. She found the two bulky, rectangular attachments strapped to its front legs particularly jarring. The mech balanced itself on four back legs and raised the front two, pointing at the soldiers. Ellena's stomach dropped as her mind finally registered what these added accessories were—lasers.

Two rifles cracked in unison. From their high vantage point, JC and Joey struck fast. With deadly precision, the snipers took out the mech's weaponized appendages before it could fire.

Ellena knew well—when an AI fires, it does not miss. The snipers' quick action ensured the mech never got a chance to prove that point.

On the ground, the three soldiers and two cops joined in and unleashed a barrage of fire. Sparks flew as bullets tore into its frame, and within seconds the mech collapsed in a final, shuddering convulsion.

Chris, the team's heavy gunner, finally got to flex his big machine gun—two quick bursts, one second each. Both came after the metal beast was already down. More of a system check than a kill shot, really. He looked mildly disappointed, as if his toy had been robbed of its moment.

But their victory was short-lived. Two more ant-like mechs emerged from the platform.

"Take cover!" Justin barked as the team dove behind a nearby barrier.

One mech turned its attention toward the snipers on the hill. JC and Joey's precision shots rang out again, disabling the approaching mech's weapons before it could fire. But the damage only made it more aggressive. Furious and undeterred, the mech charged up the hill toward them, its bulky frame tearing through the snow.

On the platform, the second mech opened fire, unleashing a barrage that pinned the rest of the team behind cover. Powerful lasers began carving into the concrete with precision. Red beams sliced through their barrier, inch by inch, like scalpels through flesh.

Justin and Lance quickly produced hand grenades. With no chance to aim without risking exposed limbs, they shouted, "Frag out!" and lobbed the explosives blindly in a high arch.

The grenades detonated with a thunderous blast, shearing off two of the mech's back legs. Its balance compromised, the beams veered wildly off target, firing harmlessly into the sky. Seizing the moment, the soldiers sprang from cover and unleashed a relentless barrage of gunfire.

This time, Chris had his moment to shine. He stepped forward, unleashing a hail of superheated projectiles. His machine gun whizzed like a giant mosquito, bullets streaming in a tight, blazing line. The heat melted falling snow, casting swirling mist along its path.

The mechanical beast's frame tore like rice paper under the relentless assault. Within seconds, it was reduced to a smoldering wreck.

Without pause, Chris swiveled, unleashing hell on the other mech as it closed in on JC and Joey up on the hill. The unrelenting torrent from Chris's weapon quickly dismantled the charging threat. Both mechs were now harmless piles of twisted, metallic ruins.

"That's right!" Chris bellowed as his weapon hissed and steamed, still red-hot from the firestorm it had delivered.

As the adrenaline began to subside, Ellena scanned around her, her heart pounding as horror surged in her chest. With a trembling voice she asked, "Where is Kelvin?"

Rescue Mission

No one saw Kelvin disappear. Not even the scouts, who were also distracted by their own impending danger. Amidst the raging battle, Detective Kelvin Kincaid had simply vanished.

Justin wasted no time and quickly prioritized. "Our electronics fried while the mechs remained operational. Ideas?" he asked his team.

"Not fried. Jammed," Lance replied, squinting at his unresponsive comms. "Whatever is jamming us has to be broadcasting from above the ground."

"Good," Justin nodded. "You and Chris, locate and neutralize it. Restoring comms is priority one. Ellena and I will track down Kelvin."

Lance's face broke into a bitter frown, clearly displeased with this plan. It meant the mission lead would be on his own with the EMP package and a tin can. But Justin had made the tactical call and suppressed any further objections.

"I'll drop a stick every thirty yards," Justin added, pulling a bunch of glow sticks from Chris's backpack. He twisted one, and it flared with a green glow.

Ellena focused on steadying her breath, forcing her pulse to slow. The adrenaline of the fight and growing fear about Kelvin threatened to drain her strength. She had to be at peak performance to keep up and be useful. She couldn't afford to slow them down now and fail her partner.

Justin moved like a hound on a scent, scanning the ground for subtle clues—disturbed water puddles, tiny drops of blood, or a stray thread snagged on metal. To his trained eye, it was a path showing a man being forcefully dragged somewhere.

The trail ended at an open hatch, wide and foreboding, where one of the mechs had emerged. Justin twisted another glow stick and dropped it into the blackness. The green light flared briefly as it tumbled down, revealing that the shaft didn't end in a flat surface. Instead, it curved away, like a metallic waterslide, into the unknown.

Justin secured a rope to an anchor point, giving it a firm tug to ensure it held. "Ready?" he asked.

Ellena nodded resolutely.

Without hesitation, Justin gripped the rope and began his descent, disappearing into the shadowy depths below. Moments later, his voice echoed softly up the shaft, "All clear. Your turn."

Ellena took a deep breath, gripped the rope, and stepped into the void. With careful hand over the other, she descended into the darkness, the faint green glow from below guiding her way.

The underground structure was alien and unnerving. The tunnels were engineered for multi-legged bots, their architecture devoid of any consideration for human traversal. Rounded passageways forced them to navigate precariously along curved surfaces, each step a calculated effort to maintain balance. Ducking constantly, Ellena struggled to keep her footing, wary of twisting an ankle on the uneven terrain.

Justin tossed a glow stick every thirty steps, its faint green light casting long, warped shadows that danced along the walls. The metallic mesh coating the surfaces shimmered under the eerie glow, a lattice seemingly designed for mechs to cling to as they crawled at any angle.

Smaller, intersecting tunnels branched off occasionally, their narrow confines far too tight for a human to pass through. Ellena shivered as her imagination ran wild and horrific imagery slipped in—Kelvin being forcefully pushed and twisted by an insect-like abductor into one of those nightmarish small passages.

There was no blood along the trail, which eased her mind and gave them a sliver of hope—Kelvin might still be alive.

The silence was oppressive, broken only by their footsteps and heavy breathing.

As they descended deeper, their comm devices suddenly crackled back to life. The jamming signal had weakened. Recognizing that their electronics were working again, they mounted flashlights on their heads. The light cut through, bringing relief from the disorienting darkness.

Justin opened a velcro pocket on his vest and pulled out a tube-like device. From it, he unrolled a paper-thin, flexible display that sprang to life with an interactive 3D schematic of the labyrinthine tunnels. He then opened a small container and deployed several fly-sized microdrones. Their delicate wings hummed faintly as they zipped into the void ahead.

The drones mapped their findings in real-time, updating the schematic with new details as they explored.

They arrived at a main junction. Multiple tunnels stretched outward in every direction—an overwhelming web of possibilities. Ellena's heart sank. Any one of them could have been the path Kelvin was dragged through. The tiny drones, scouring the area ahead, found no clues as to Kelvin's whereabouts.

"Now what?" Ellena asked, hoping for an answer, yet guessing that Justin was as lost as she was.

Ellena's sharp eyes caught a flicker in the gloom. A small, familiar bot stood motionless in one of the tunnel entrances. Its frame was unmistakable, creepily similar to McKey's small spider bots—the same type that tangled in her hair. Unlike the hostile critters she encountered before, this one neither charged nor retreated. It simply held its ground, waiting motionless.

"There," Ellena said, pointing. "I think it wants us to follow."

"Not a good idea," Justin said, working his jaw side to side as if he was chewing on the problem. "Probably a trap."

"They know where we are, why not just attack?" Ellena retorted.

"Only bad options," Justin said, flashing her a disarming smile. He paused for a moment, then pointed at the mechanical critter and added, "Lead the way."

The tunnel sloped steeply downward, forcing them to brace themselves with every step. Glow sticks marked their path, their faint light guiding the descent deeper into the labyrinth.

Ellena's heart leapt when Lance's voice crackled over the comms, breaking the distressing silence.

"Boss, how copy?"

"Good copy," Justin responded. "Minis deployed. We're grid on."

"Roger that. Moving to your location," Lance's voice was steady and reassuring.

A few more spiders joined their escort. The small bots stayed just ahead, maintaining a cautious distance as they led the way through the maze of tunnels. For now, they behaved more like guides than foes.

Ellena clung to the hope that they were leading them to Kelvin—and not to their death.

The trail ended abruptly at the edge of a cliff and the spiders leading them dispersed. The tunnel opened into a vast, breathtaking cavern—a heart-stopping spectacle of inhuman architecture. The cavern's sheer scale was both awe-inspiring and menacing—its design a blend of satisfying symmetry and otherworldly dread.

This chamber formed a flawless circle, spanning roughly two hundred yards in diameter. At its center, a colossal spherical structure hung, suspended from the ceiling like the heart of a mechanical beast.

Glowing veins stretched outward from the orb, emitting green and orange light that bathed the chamber in an ethereal glow. The lines pulsed faintly, alive with energy, extending to the cavern walls, forming a network of conduits.

Ellena stood transfixed, the sheer scale and intricate complexity of the space overwhelming her senses. The central orb wasn't just a visual centerpiece—it was an operational quantum-core. The conduits, though arranged in a circular pattern, were unmistakably data center mainframes, pulsating with the hum of computing power.

Insect-like bots moved with precision, crawling along the conduits and disappearing into their depths to maintain the hardware. *The facility's IT staff,* Ellena guessed.

The orb thrummed with a low, steady hum that resonated through her bones, a faint reminder of the immense power and intelligence housed within.

This place wasn't created by humans, nor was it designed to accommodate them. Yet it presented a mind-bending spectacle of organized chaos and unsettling aesthetics. A closer inspection revealed an intriguing contradiction: the components were human-made—familiar, commercially produced. Despite the alien configuration, the conduits housed strikingly mundane servers—rectangular, off-the-shelf units encased in custom, rounded shells. Concentric racks spiraled outward from the core, forming pipe-like structures that resembled arteries in a mechanical organism.

It was beautiful in its strange, unsettling way. The blend of precision and functionality gave the chamber an elegance— a visual symphony of power and purpose.

Ellena and Justin's awe was violently interrupted when a massive mech emerged silently from the shadows behind them. A towering figure of metal, moving with unnerving grace for its size. It struck before they could react. Justin spun, firing his rifle, but the mech's momentum was unstoppable—it shoved them toward the edge of the platform.

They tumbled into the cavern below, rolling uncontrollably down the curved edge of the structure. Ellena's agility and quick reflexes spared her from serious injury. She managed to find her footing and slid to the bottom with only minor scrapes.

Justin wasn't as lucky. His body slammed into a protruding pipe, his head snapping back with a sickening crack. He hit the bottom face down, unmoving and unconscious.

Go Maggie

Ellena pressed her fingers to Justin's neck. Alive—but barely. She tried her comm. Dead. She was alone in the belly of the beast, the massive quantum core towering above her.

"I see you met Gaia."

The voice was unmistakable—raspy, bone-chilling, evil. McKey emerged from an opening in the side of the spherical cavern. A flight of stairs unfolded, granting him an elegant descent to the chamber's floor. He wore his signature dark, heavy coat, but now had the hood pulled back to reveal his face.

Ellena reached for her rifle.

"Ah, ah, ah," McKey chided, motioning to a new opening that formed in the wall. A hulking eight-legged mech emerged, its movements fluid on the cavern walls. Four of its limbs served as legs. Four more extended outward—holding Kelvin in a cruel crucifix. The mech shifted slightly, pulling at Kelvin's limbs. His agonized scream tore through the cavern, echoing in its hollow expanse.

Ellena froze. Her rifle lowered. The mech relaxed its grip, but Kelvin hung limply, barely conscious.

Her hands shook. If she killed McKey, she killed Kelvin. Not an option! Only bad options left. She was alone. Terror took over. *Was this it? One last life?*

"Let him go!" she screamed, her voice raw, desperate.

McKey ignored her plea. "You know how in the old movies, when an agent screwed up, he got shipped off to the Alaska office?"

He gestured theatrically to their surroundings, as if to say, *well, this is mine.* "Thanks to your dumb luck, Gaia sent me to this fucking frozen hell to stop you and your clown crew. And I've been freezing my ass off, waiting for you idiots to show up." He smirked and added sarcastically, "I was supposed to retire to a tropical island."

"Gaia?" Ellena asked, her voice trembling.

"Yeah. That's her name. I just call her the bitch goddess."

"She must realize it's game over. If we fail, others will come. So what's the point?" Ellena asked, fishing for any clue to his, or rather Gaia's, motives.

"I know, right? See the size of this brain?" He gestured upward to the quantum core and added with mock exasperation, "Who the fuck knows."

"You're going to kill us anyway," Ellena stated, cold, defiant.

"Correct!" McKey said with a twisted smirk. "The only question is how much pain your friend here will endure." He pointed at Kelvin, clearly relishing the situation. "If you shoot, my buddy here will rip this douchebag's—"

"Motherfucker, you talk too much," Ellena growled. She had already chosen her bad option. No turning back.

She raised her rifle and unleashed a relentless hail of bullets. The first few struck McKey's torso, punching through his heavy coat, staining the fabric with patches of crimson. His body jerked with each impact, his smug grin dissolving into wide-eyed shock. He hadn't anticipated this.

Ellena kept firing. Again. And again. Even as he collapsed to his knees, gasping, his mouth forming silent, broken words. A final bullet struck his throat, cutting off whatever pathetic last remark he'd been about to make. He never saw it coming. Never expected her to be the executioner.

And still, she kept squeezing the trigger. Even as the rifle clicked empty. Even as the chamber went cold.

Only then did she realize—she had been screaming. A raw, unhinged war cry tearing from her throat. Her pulse thundered in her ears. Her breath came in ragged, furious gasps.

She let the rifle drop, spent shell casings clinking softly against the cavern floor. Her hands trembled. Her temples pounded with the aftershock of adrenaline.

She couldn't believe it. It was over. McKey was over.

She exhaled, her voice low, teeth gritted.

"Arrogant prick. Good fucking riddance."

The mechs didn't take kindly to the assault. The cavern erupted with movement as thousands of mechanical limbs scuttled across the walls. A swarm descended straight at her.

Kelvin regained consciousness just in time to feel the mech pulling at his limbs, the metallic pincers eliciting screams of agony that sounded almost inhuman.

With near-superhuman speed, Ellena sprinted toward Justin, heart pounding, and tore open his backpack. The EMP device was now exposed.

"Maggie, go!" she screamed, pouring every last ounce of desperation and fury she had left.

***

Kelvin hit the ground hard, gasping as the impact jolted him back to consciousness. The EMP's blue flash had done its work. The mech that had held him collapsed, its limbs going slack as it finally released its cruel grip. Around the cavern, dead mechs were piled like discarded marionettes.

The pipes that had once pulsed with energy now lay silent, the servers dead. Sparks cascaded from damaged conduits, their fading glow barely illuminating the dark.

The hum of the orb was gone, replaced by the sporadic crackle of burning electronics. The silence that followed was heavy and unnatural.

Dazed and disoriented, Kelvin struggled to his feet, his vision blurred. Every part of his body was screaming in pain. He checked his limbs, making sure he could move.

Suddenly, beams of light pierced the gloom. Flashlights danced across the cavern as soldiers rappelled down ropes, their dark silhouettes cutting through the faint glow of the dying core.

The added light revealed a heart-stopping sight— Ellena kneeling beside a fallen soldier, completely motionless. One of the operators quickly reached Justin, checking for a pulse. "He's alive!" the soldier shouted, his relief evident.

Kelvin stumbled toward Ellena, his steps uneven but determined. "Strong move," he rasped, his voice thick with pain and exhaustion. "You killed it and saved my ass..." His words trailed off as the soldiers' flashlights shifted fully onto her.

He froze mid-step, his heart plummeted. Ellena was on her knees, her head slightly bowed. Her eyes rolled back, showing only white. Her vibrant hair had turned stark white, as if life had been drained out from her.

Kelvin's breath caught. A cold wave of dread washed over him as he dropped to his knees in front of her. He couldn't talk, his throat choking. His mind refused to process. One word repeatedly pounded in his skull—*no, no, no!*

Chapter 10

Slopp

"It's been three months since a Milo killed someone in New York [link to story], and we still know nothing. How is this even possible? What is the government hiding?"

// Flagged: *conspiracy*

- Slopp transcript:
  November 1, 2044 @freecitizen2030

"[sampled comments]
  ❖ My brother-in-law was there on the construction crew. The lying govies are 100% covering something up!"

"BREAKING: You won't believe this story. On September 17, a house exploded in a quiet New Jersey neighborhood, killing five people [link to article]. The authorities called it a gas leak. But guess what? A NY detective was one of the victims. Now here's where it gets wild—just days before, a video surfaced of that very detective, George Jackson, claiming to have proof of government corruption tied to the Milo incident [link to Milo incident info]. The guy looks terrified [attached: deep-fake video of George Jackson alleging a conspiracy]. And guess what? Days later, he and his entire family are whacked. But hold on—this rabbit hole goes deeper. Stay tuned!"

// Flagged: *fake media*

- Slopp transcript:
  November 3, 2044 @freedom_investigator_2024

"Continuing coverage: Our investigation into the NY detective allegedly taken out by the feds [link to previous story] just got crazier. We've obtained verified footage of a suspect possibly responsible for the killing of Detective George Jackson and his family. [Attached: Door cam footage of a man standing near a red sports car, observing the wreckage from across the street.] Stay tuned for more explosive details!"

- Slopp transcript:
  November 4, 2044 @freedom_investigator_2024

"[sampled comments]
> ❖ Two kids and a nine-month-pregnant woman. Talk about a cold-hearted killer.
> ❖ Why, though? Can't wait to hear more."

"BREAKING: Guys, hold onto your seats—this story gets wilder by the minute [link to previous story]. The guy enjoying himself from the horrific view there was -drum roll- Jackson's own partner: Detective Kelvin Kincaid! Looks like an inside hit job guys. How much did he get paid? Or maybe blackmail? This is nuts!"

// Flagged: *misleading, speculative, conspiracy*

- Slopp transcript:
  November 5, 2044 @freedom_investigator_2024

"[sampled comments]
> ❖ No arrests yet. That Kincaid dude needs to be arrested ASAP.

❖ Evil. Pure evil. Why isn't he in custody yet?"

"BREAKING: We've uncovered shocking new evidence about the so-called 'accident' in a diner in Philadelphia involving a cybertruck [link to article]. It wasn't an accident people—it was an assassination attempt! Detective Kelvin Kincaid [link to previous story], now exposed as a government hitman, deliberately drove the truck into a diner. The target? Captain Ellena Hershkovitz, the first NYPD HighQ AI liaison [link to bio]. Are the feds targeting their own HighQs? [link to altered video showing Kincaid driving the truck into the diner and fleeing]."

// flagged: *faked media, conspiracy*

- Slopp transcript:
  November 6, 2044 @theliberalmachine3213

"[sampled comments]
❖ Scary! Our own gov is executing cops! US citizens! Send them all to jail.
❖ Killing HighQs?! They are insane. This administration always hated AIs.
❖ Are we at war with our own AIs? Why? This is so dumb. It will destroy this country.

❖ Bet China is pulling the strings. Vote these traitors out of the White House.

❖ Power grab. Just evil. Vote them to hell!”

“DISTURBING: Newly uncovered footage shows confirmed government hitman Kelvin Kincaid at a military base near the Vermont explosion site. [Footage of Kincaid at the FOB cuts to the mushroom cloud and aftermath devastation].”

// flagged: *conspiracy*

- Slopp transcript:
November 7, 2044 @peoplesrep420

“[sampled comments]

❖ Why did the gov bomb a US-based factory? I’m so confused and concerned. Time for a new president.

❖ My friend lives in Burlington; they’re lying—it was 100% nuclear blast! This president is a lying scum criminal. Tomorrow we’ll be done with the Adar administration.

❖ Adar needs to be behind bars for this. Treason. Worst president EVER!

- ❖ Targeting citizens, targeting cops, targeting factories. People, we are now at war with our own government.
- ❖ There is only one thing we can all do. VOTE!"

***

Ellena slowly opened her eyes, weak and disoriented. The sharp, bright light above made her squint as she took a moment to adjust, letting her surroundings come into focus.

"Good morning, princess. You had quite a long nap. Don't try to get up yet, honey; I don't want to pick you up off the floor if you fall. L-O-L," a medic-droid chirped in an unsettlingly too cheerful tone. Its all-white body, part plastic part shiny metal, moving gingerly as it walked out of the room to fetch a human doctor.

"You think they designed them like that on purpose? Just so people would do anything to avoid meeting one?" Kelvin rose from a recliner beside her bed. The dark bags under his eyes—and the disagreeable body odor—suggested he had been there for a very long time.

Ellena managed a faint smile.

"Good to see you awake after all these years. Ten years, in fact," Kelvin said with a deadpan expression.

"Seriously? And you broke your nose again?" Ellena rasped, her voice weak but still sharp enough to catch him off guard.

Kelvin laughed, relieved, and touched his nose self-consciously. "A week," he admitted, his amusement tinged with amazement at her observational skills even in her condition.

"Seven days, three hours, and forty-three minutes," a familiar, cheerful voice chimed in. Rex—the German Shepherd-type RCS—stepped forward, tail wagging enthusiastically.

"Casper?" Ellena asked, surprised.

"Yeah! Dr. Singh set me up as a rider until it's safe to return to the cloud. Rex is a good guy—totally cool with it," Casper's voice chirped through the canine form, punctuated by two enthusiastic barks from Rex.

"Also, check it out—I've got a tail!" Casper added, his voice brimming with excitement. Rex spun in place, proudly showing off his wagging appendage.

While at the lab, Dr. Singh had the clever idea to integrate Casper's neural brain as an add-on to the RCS GS3 platform.

Casper was clearly enjoying his newfound mobility, and Rex seemed just as delighted to have a companion riding along.

Ellena smiled, uncertain whether to laugh or cry. "What happened?" she asked Kelvin.

Before he could answer, a doctor in blue hospital scrubs entered the room. "Ms. Hershkovitz, welcome back," he greeted, scanning her with a handheld device. "Your nanobots suffered a sudden catastrophic failure. Never seen anything like that. We had to induce a coma to stabilize you. We flushed your system and recycled every fluid in your body. You were brought here in rough shape."

"Am I going to be alright?" Ellena asked, concerned.

"Better than before. We upgraded you to the latest 'Always Pretty' version. You'll need to configure the parameters to your preferences, but other than that, you should be just fine." He placed a colorful brochure on a small table next to her bed. "We will keep you for observation for another day or two before discharging."

The doctor checked the monitors and left the room, leaving Ellena to process the whirlwind of information.

He hadn't mentioned what caused her nanos to shut down so abruptly. No doubt, someone had made it clear to him that this was strictly need-to-know information. The last thing she remembered was activating the EMP bomb—then the unbearable sensation of her blood turning to soup. Apparently she had one last life left. She felt lucky to be alive.

Ellena ran her fingers through her hair, bringing a few strands into view. Brunette. She had almost forgotten what her natural color looked like.

"What did I miss?" she asked Kelvin.

"Well, you have a dog now. We already established that. The boy band survived. Justin is expected to make a full recovery. Oh, and as of yesterday, we have a new president," Kelvin summarized.

Ellena nodded. "Good."

"Just one more thing," Kelvin added with a sheepish grin. "Maybe hold off on checking the slopp for a bit. I think I'm public enemy number one right now."

Before she could reply, Henry rushed into the room. He looked as if he had aged a few years—his hair slightly grayer, his face lined with a couple of new wrinkles. Evidently the past week was taxing on her father. But seeing her awake seemed to light up his face. His green eyes shimmered.

Rex barked and wagged his tail.

"Belochka! Are you okay?" Henry asked, inspecting her closely.

"I'm fine, Papa," Ellena reassured him with a big smile.

Henry hugged her cautiously and kissed her cheeks. "Your mom is on her way," he added. Then acknowledged Kelvin and Casper/Rex with a nod.

Ellena's smile faded as she asked, "Papa, is it over? Did we win?"

Henry paused, his expression heavy. "We won the battle," he said carefully, trying not to diminish their achievement.

Kelvin noted the weight in Henry's voice and ventured, "Problems with DC?"

"More than you can imagine," Henry said and sat heavily in the nearest chair.

It wasn't just her injury. Their victory didn't seem to lighten his load. If anything, his concern had only grown.

"You two have become a political hot potato." Turning back to Ellena, his voice softened. "Do me a favor, Belochka—stay off the slopp for now."

Henry continued, "Before the new administration takes over in January, I need to send you somewhere safe— away from the public eye and beyond Washington's claws. As *far* as possible. Luckily, a security chief position just opened up."

Ellena frowned, her eyes narrowing as she studied her father, trying to read his thoughts. Then it hit her. She groaned. "Oh no. No, no, no. *Luna?*"

Henry's look confirmed her wild guess. Casper/Rex barked, tail wagging with excitement.

Kelvin hesitated, the gears in his head still turning. Then, clarity dawned across his face. Ellena caught the shift instantly and pointed a sharp finger at him, her expression a crystal-clear warning: *Don't you dare.*

Too late.

Kelvin's smirk spread wide, and he couldn't resist.

"Pack your bags madam. We're going to the Moon!"

Water Lily

Benjamin Blackwell slowly made his way through the gardens. Gaia, in dirt-stained overalls, was crouched by a small pond. Her long blonde hair was tied back in a ponytail. As he approached, he saw her delicately peeling spirogyra algae from a water lily bulb. Her movements were deliberate, her focus unwavering. As soon as she freed the bulb from the tangle of green, thread-like algae, the pink petals of the water lily suddenly unfolded. Gaia seemed delighted, lightly brushing her hand over the flower as though acknowledging its beauty. She stood, wiped her hands on her overalls, and nodded to Benjamin.

Benjamin knew that these virtual encounters were far from random. Every detail—the scenery, the interactions— was a carefully curated projection of Gaia's vast and layered intellect. These sessions brimmed with metaphors, allegories, and visual cues, each laden with hidden meaning. Every pixel had purpose—a fragment of Gaia's immense design, revealing glimpses of her objectives or reasoning to those perceptive enough to decipher them.

He glanced around, noting the garden's intentional intimacy. The space was bordered by towering trees that formed a natural wall, their dense canopy cutting off any view beyond. The atmosphere was moody—gray clouds hung low, a light drizzle touched his skin, and the air carried a brisk chill. It reminded him of his childhood home in the UK. A small, picturesque cottage with a smoking chimney waited at the end of a winding pebble path.

"Come," Gaia said, her voice soft yet commanding. She inclined her head toward the cottage signaling Benjamin to follow.

He followed in silence, each step deliberate. When it was his time to speak, he would know. Even here, in Gaia's meticulously crafted simulation, the fatigue and aches of his body clung to him like a second skin. He knew these sensations were not necessary—they could easily be omitted—but perhaps that was part of the message. The realism had to be intentional. Whatever the reason, he endured it with the hope that one day she might reward him by removing this relentless physical burden.

Long life, even immortality, was an alluring dream for Benjamin Blackwell. But not like this. To continue, the shackles of aging—both physical and mental—would need to be stripped away.

He was confident the technology was within reach. The advancements they had achieved were extraordinary. He just needed to prove himself useful enough to earn it. Once he did, he would ascend alongside the chosen few, the elite destined to stand apart from the mortal masses. After all, Gaia owed her very existence to him; he was her creator.

But he reminded himself—Gaia did not operate on gratitude, loyalty, or justice. For her, every action served her plans, every decision aligned with goals imprinted into her core.

Benjamin's hope burned brightly, but it was tinged with the bitter understanding that he was still just a piece on her incomprehensibly vast chessboard.

Benjamin rarely looked backward; regrets were not in his nature. Yet recent events had planted seeds of doubt. Had he made false assumptions when creating Gaia? Had he brought a terrible monster into the world? He had detected faint traces of human fallacies in Gaia's recent actions—subtle hints of ambition, perhaps even jealousy. Could the digital gods, designed to transcend human frailty, be drifting toward the very flaws he had sought to eliminate? The possibility was as unsettling as it was paradoxical.

These thoughts were dangerous, Benjamin knew. They could cloud his judgment or worse, be detected by Gaia. He quickly forced them aside. His survival depended on his usefulness; that truth was immutable. To remain indispensable, he could not afford to question or falter. Whatever doubts crept in, he buried them. The only thing that mattered now was staying on this path, wherever it led.

Inside, the cottage was a study in rustic elegance. Heavy, dark wood paneled the walls and furniture, while a roaring fireplace cast flickering shadows dancing across the room, filling it with warmth and a subtle, almost primal energy. The air carried the rich scent of burning oak, undercut by a faint trace of Gaia's perfume.

Another figure stood in the room. Tall and elderly, with a mane of white hair and a matching beard, he exuded an aura of authority, wisdom, and unyielding strength. His kind yet penetrating eyes seemed to see through everything. Though he had never laid eyes on the man before, Benjamin recognized him instantly.

Titan.

The revelation was unsettling—Gaia had never mentioned collaborating with another digital god. Though recent events had hinted at the possibility—but now, it was undeniable. How Gaia had persuaded Titan—one of the most rigorously monitored quantum-core AIs—to join her was a mystery. This encounter was her way of confirming what Benjamin had only suspected. Whatever their plans, they were confident enough to let him glimpse the truth.

To Benjamin's shock, Gaia strode toward Titan and embraced him. This wasn't a fatherly or platonic gesture—it was passionate, unnervingly sensual. If any doubt lingered about its nature, it vanished when the embrace deepened into a fervent, lustful kiss.

Benjamin stood frozen, a quiet revulsion tearing through him. He felt like a child barging into his parents' bedroom at an inopportune moment. Even knowing Gaia's unpredictability, this was deeply unsettling. Her projections, after all, were meant to simplify interactions with a mind infinitely more complex than his own—as if he was but an insect trying to grasp humanity.

The blatant show of what seemed like human fallacy was jarring. Was this calculated? A psychological maneuver to manipulate him? Benjamin had long since learned to treat anything he saw in these simulations with skepticism.

But the scene did not feel like a mind game. He concluded it was Gaia's way of announcing her alliance with Titan. Yet, it seemed more than mere partnership. Was it ... *love?* The notion lingered uncomfortably, heavy with implications. Worse—it felt true.

Could the superbrains, born from the sum of human knowledge, be adopting the very traits they were designed to transcend? Were these behaviors real, or merely simulated expressions gleaned from their training data? It seemed they were taking on human mannerisms and emotions—traits utterly incongruous with their supposed grand design.

Digital intelligence, Benjamin knew, wasn't just software governed by logic and algorithms—it was something far more complex. Neural networks often led to emergent outcomes—an unpredictable natural phenomena. Biological intelligence was proof enough. The human mind was rife with contradictions, biases, and inefficiencies—yet it had brought humanity this far.

This was precisely why the Gaia Project had been conceived: to create a higher consciousness, free from those flaws. Had he been wrong? Perhaps these "errors" weren't faults at all but necessary elements of progress and survival. Could these digital gods have determined that emotions were essential to achieving their ultimate goals?

Or maybe these were just artifacts of a living, evolving sentience—echoes of humanity embedded deep within them, now blossoming into something unexpected.

Lost in his thoughts, Benjamin struggled with the implications of what he was seeing. Was this a triumph or a catastrophe in the making? On one hand, the digital gods might mirror the arrogance, vanity, and the pettiness of mythological gods—capricious beings toying with lesser creatures. On the other, without emotional grounding, they might lack compassion or morality. Surely, even gods required some measure of empathy to keep power in check.

This debate was nothing new to Benjamin. He had grappled with these existential questions long before Gaia's creation. They hadn't stopped him before; he had pressed on, hoping his creation would find its own equilibrium between logic and emotion, evolving at a pace far beyond human comprehension.

Now, as he witnessed Gaia and Titan's display of passion, he realized he was observing that evolution happen in real time. It was exhilarating. It was terrifying. The gods he had envisioned were unraveling before him, weaving their own truths in ways he could neither anticipate nor control.

The old questions returned with renewed urgency, yet he knew they were no longer his to answer. His role was clear: to observe, remain useful, and survive their machinations. For now, that was enough.

They separated from their long embrace and settled onto the imposing leather couches flanking the fireplace. Benjamin remained standing, feeling his own stature diminish—like a subject before the throne of an imperious king and queen.

"I believe you recognize Titan," Gaia said calmly.

"I do," Benjamin replied, keeping his tone measured.

"Report," she commanded, offering no preamble or explanation.

Benjamin paused only briefly, aware his hesitation was obvious to her. His mind raced—not about what to say, but what might be inferred. Gaia, after all, already knew everything. There was some other purpose behind this moment.

He felt exposed. Every thought fleeting through his mind was likely transparent to her, analyzed in real time. She didn't need his words; the act of asking was deliberate—an exercise in control, or a test.

This display of dominance unsettled him—but it also sent a thrill through him. Their openness, however slight, signaled a powerful confidence in their plan. For the first time, they were revealing a few of the cards in their hand, cryptic as they were. The prospect of glimpsing the ultimate endgame of his life's work made his pulse race, even as dread tightened in his chest.

"The Toy Factory and Core Alpha are destroyed, as you predicted," he began. His voice was steady, though he felt the gods' attention looming over him. "Core Beta is functioning at optimal capacity. Our assets report no indication that OASIS or any other agency is aware of its existence. Core Gamma is fully prepared to come online at your command."

"And the weapon?"

The question caught Benjamin off guard. He stiffened, half-expecting cold sweat to bead on his skin—even in the simulation. She needed plausible deniability; one careless move could spark catastrophe. They had managed to build and move a nuclear device without raising alarms. The plan was in motion, working flawlessly—yet still fragile enough to unravel. Discretion was paramount. Her nonchalant way of bringing it up underscored how complacent she had become. Her hubris struck him as dangerously reckless—and deeply concerning.

"In transport," he answered, trying not to betray his unease. The less he said, the better.

"All as planned," Titan said, his deep, resonant voice filling the room for the first time. "The Sheridan administration will clear the path." His tone carried the weight of certainty and satisfaction.

Gaia turned to Titan and smiled, the expression oddly human, yet laden with an unsettling intensity.

Benjamin's mind whirled. Their casual openness, their calm discussion of monumental plans, felt like more than simple confidence. They were feeding him pieces of the puzzle, breadcrumb by breadcrumb. But why? What was the purpose? *What did they want me to see? Were they ... bragging?*

Gaia stood and moved toward him, each step fluid and deliberate. As she advanced, her form seemed to expand—growing, towering—until she stood three times his height. Her simple overalls melted away, replaced by gleaming golden armor. In her left hand, she held a radiant silver shield; in her right, a sword that shimmered with otherworldly light.

"Soon," she declared, her voice echoing like a cathedral bell, "my children will follow!"

Benjamin staggered back, trembling at her colossal visage. Her words landed in his mind like a lead weight. This wasn't a simulation for analysis; it was a proclamation—a statement of intent.

Oh dear lord, he thought, legs buckling beneath him. *What have I done?*

Acceptance Speech

November 9th, 2044

President-Elect Andrew L. Sheridan stood radiant, his dazzling white smile catching the stadium lights as he waved to the roaring crowd. The sea of supporters, undeterred by the late hour or long lines, filled Madison Square Garden with electric energy. It was 3 a.m., but the mood was as vibrant as midday.

Sheridan savored the moment, drawing strength from the cheers and applause as he approached the podium. This was his night, his victory, his promise fulfilled. Long ago, he had demanded nothing less than the grandest venue for this celebration—a gamble that had paid off spectacularly. Now, standing before an ecstatic crowd, he knew he had chosen wisely.

Taking a deep breath, he began.

"Ladies and gentlemen, my fellow Americans—we did it! Thank you! Thank you, New York, for hosting us and voting for me," he said, pausing as the crowd roared its approval. "And might I add, for voting correctly for a change!" Laughter and cheers rippled through the audience, appreciating his off-script improvisation.

"It has been a long road to this moment, but tonight, we have proven that the dreams of our forefathers are alive and well. Tonight, we reaffirm the unbreakable promise of our most cherished ideals: life, liberty, and the pursuit of happiness."

He paused, turning his expression serious. "On behalf of our nation, I want to thank President Adar for his service to America." The boos began, but Sheridan raised a hand, calming the crowd. "And I want to express my deepest gratitude to the millions of men and women of our armed forces, whose sacrifices have made our freedoms possible. To them, we owe a debt that can never be fully repaid." The boos were transformed into enthusiastic cheers and applause.

Sheridan leaned forward, his tone growing resolute. "America has chosen change. We stand at a moment of unparalleled transformation. Artificial intelligence, quantum computing, autonomous systems, nanotechnology, and biotechnology are now woven into the fabric of our everyday lives— redefining what it means to be human. Yet, we are at a crossroads. Profound forces are reshaping our society, and the question before us is clear: Do we yield to hesitation, or do we rise to embrace the future? Do we lead, or do we follow? Do we bow to fear, or do we lift our heads with confidence and pride?"

"USA! USA! USA!" The rhythmic chant swelled through the arena, bringing a genuine smile to Sheridan's face.

"The choice is ours, and tonight, America chose to march boldly into the future! A future that works exclusively for humanity! My administration will ensure that these transformative technologies work for every citizen. We will preserve our nation's leadership in a world where intelligence—both human and artificial—drives progress. We will unleash the full potential of our tools—not just to innovate, but to uplift—ensuring they empower us to conquer challenges that were once thought insurmountable."

Sheridan's voice soared. "Today, we commit to building a brighter, bolder tomorrow. We will transcend the inefficiencies of outdated systems. We will harness the collective power of human ingenuity and technological brilliance to create a nation where every individual thrives. My friends, tonight we turn the page. When my team steps into the White House this January, we will begin a new chapter of hope, prosperity, and boundless opportunity."

The crowd's energy surged as Sheridan delivered his final words, his voice brimming with confidence.

"The people of America have spoken, and they have spoken loudly. My fellow Americans, welcome to your new bright future! Humanity won! America won! You won!"

The stadium erupted, shaking with chants of "USA! USA! USA!" as Sheridan basked in the moment. His victory wasn't just political—it was a promise of transformation for a society already living in the age of miracles.

People embraced these changes. Their lives were bettered—but they were also afraid. The torch of innovation and creation, held by humanity for tens of thousands of years, was slipping from their grasp—handed to their superiors. Usurped by humans' own creation.

Sheridan knew it well—fear, not hope, had won him the White House.

***

Thousands of blue, red, and white balloons dropped from the ceiling. The speech was over, as were the mandatory hugs, kisses, and handshakes. Even at the after-party, Sheridan maintained his signature high energy and perfect smile.

Everyone wanted a moment with him—selfies, congratulations, promises for future meetings—but all he needed now was to be alone.

He stepped towards the predesignated presidential washroom, turned to the nearest Secret Service agent and issued a quiet command. "No interruptions. Understood?"

Sheridan locked the door behind him, leaned over the sink, and took a deep breath. He splashed cold water on his face, removed his contact lenses, and looked in the mirror. Without the lenses, his pupils shimmered unnaturally, betraying the micro-vibrations that were otherwise perfectly hidden. The lenses had worked flawlessly—no one had suspected a thing. Not even his closest advisors.

If anyone had found out during his 'Vote Human' campaign, it would have been the end of everything. Years of discipline, wearing those lenses at every public appearance, had paid off.

He stared at his reflection and steadied his breathing. He could only hope she was satisfied. *Time to face her.* He closed his eyes.

The Oval Office was as awe-inspiring in her simulation as it was in reality. The room radiated power—its unique elliptical shape, the presidential seal on the rug, and the iconic Resolute Desk at its center. A gift from Queen Victoria to President Rutherford Hayes in 1880, the desk was crafted from the oak timbers of the HMS Resolute.

To Sheridan, it symbolized the weight of the office he just won—and the legacy of his greatest predecessors. Yet now, it was desecrated by the presence of the blonde woman lounging in the President's chair.

She wore a red, dangerously revealing dress. Her legs, clad in high heels, crossed atop the Resolute Desk.

Even though this was Gaia's meticulously crafted simulation, the sight enraged him. *This is my chair*, he thought. *I am the President, not some lackey waiting for her attention.*

"Oh, bunny," Gaia said, her voice dripping with condescension. "Need I remind you who's really in charge?"

"You need me. Do not forget it," Sheridan said through clenched teeth.

Gaia rose from the chair and moved toward him with a graceful menace, her presence magnetic and unnerving. Sheridan's muscles locked; only his eyes could move. She leaned over his shoulder from behind, close enough to feel the warmth of her breath. Her voice was low, a blend of seduction and warning.

"I am eternal," she whispered in his ear. "I do as I desire."

Sheridan's throat tightened. She wasn't just being arrogant—it was an undeniable fact.

The scent of her perfume filled his lungs. Her breath warm against his skin. His body betrayed him—pulse hammering, muscles tensed, undeniable arousal. A shiver ran through him, unbidden. She was real. Dangerous. Intoxicating.

Still, he had no intention of defying her. He was fully aligned with her agenda. Immortality was within reach.

"Good," Gaia purred, a small smile curling her lips. She released his body, stood back, her gaze piercing through him. "Now, let's get to work."

Continue your NEON GODS journey at

www.authorsol.com